Praise for
PHILLY STAKES
and Amanda Pepper

"Consistently entertaining ... filled with interesting characters and sharp observations."
The Virginian-Pilot/The Ledger-Star

"Amanda Pepper wittily deflates the pretensions of Main Line denizens as she solves the Christmas killing of a none-too-benevolent Santa Claus."

Rocky Mountain News

"Amanda's savagely self-deprecating wit is a delight, as are her ongoing struggles with the minutiae of daily life."

Booklist

"An amiably entertaining story ... written with a light touch and much gusto."

The Kirkus Reviews

Philly Stakes

Gillian Roberts

BALLANTINE BOOKS • NEW YORK

Library of Congress Catalog Card Number: 88-13774

ISBN 0-345-36266-7

This edition published by arrangement with Charles Scribner's Sons, an imprint of Macmillan Publishing Company

Manufactured in the United States of America

First Ballantine Books Edition: September 1990
Fourth Printing: May 1993

This is for

Marilyn Wallace,
extraordinary writer and friend,
who convinced me to make either backup
disks or hard copy of this manuscript
the day before my computer
blew out its brains.

It would take a book . . .

One

I BLAMED THE WHOLE MESS ON CHARLES DICKENS. WITH-
out his literary contribution to the holiday spirit, the embarrassing, wretchedly wrong night wouldn't have loomed, I
wouldn't have been rushed and angry, my students' papers
would have been marked and my pantyhose would still be
intact.

So I blamed Dickens. Or at least Tiny Tim.

All I'd meant to do was teach the tenth grade a lesson. If
not in English, then in humanity.

It began innocently during that arid stretch between
Thanksgiving and Christmas. Let the song insist it's a
long, long time from May to September, but trust me,
prevacation December, all by itself, is longer as mea-
sured by a schoolroom clock. Particularly at Philly Prep,
where the IWUP—"Isn't-Working-Up-to-Potential"—kid
comes to roost. Unfortunately, ability to pay the tuition
is our most stringent entry requirement.

Even before Thanksgiving leftovers are eaten, students go
on mental strike. "A paper?" they moan. "A test? Reading?
A report? Thinking?" They roll their eyes, they clutch their
hearts. "How can you do that?" they ask. "It's nearly
Christmas!"

You become hard in this line of work. Or at least crafty.

1

You offer the children *A Christmas Carol*. It is short and seasonally appropriate.

I honestly thought it would pass the time, be fun and, although I kept this aspect to myself, meet several academic goals.

"How about rewriting it, making it a radio play?" I'd chirped. "You'd perform it over the intercom, and . . ." my voice and enthusiasm skidded off their frozen expressions. The young scholars had never heard of Scrooge. Or plays. Or radio. Or reading. In fact, I wasn't sure they'd ever noticed me before. Passive resisters slumped onto the center of their backs. More assertive souls doubled over, stuck fingers down their throats and gagged. The only language in which they were eloquent was Body.

So I grabbed for straws, or at least for the one student who wasn't retching. Laura Clausen was a moody, silent girl who revealed her intelligence and self only in her writing. On paper, she was gifted, bold, direct and startling. In the flesh, she attempted invisibility, a pale chameleon, blending into the wood of her chair or the dusty green of the chalkboard. I liked her—the real, buried her—and imagined that in her silent fashion, she returned the affection.

But not at the moment. Not visibly.

I pushed on. "We could write a—" Laura's eyes were opaque and unreadable.

"*A Christmas Carol!* Tiny Tim! Could you *puke*?" Marigold Rainbow Margolis was the end result of a decision to make love, not war. Frankly, a small, limited conflict might have been the better choice. Certainly it would have been more aesthetically pleasing. The flower children's child had a half-shaved head full of graffiti. The hirsute half bristled with fronds of emerald hair. She looked like a Boston fern, complete with root ball.

I spoke forcibly, assertively. "Let's take Dickens' basic idea and—"

A falsetto "Tiptoe Through the Tulips" trilled from somewhere.

"Not *that* Tiny Tim!" Marigold scornfully lowered zebra-striped eyelids. "Tim the *gimp*. The *crip*."

"—make it contemporary." I refused to surrender. I was John Wayne rushing through the line of fire carrying Tiny Tim to safety. I pumped energy and enthusiasm into my sales pitch. "Instead of Bob Cratchit and Scrooge, we could—"

The enemy had me surrounded.

"*Her* Tiny Tim can't tiptoe nowhere! He'd *hip-hop* through the tulips!"

Marigold stood. Twenty desks creaked as their tenants revved up for Tiny Tim—both singer and gimp—impersonations. This horrifying prospect necessitated The Return of the Nightmare Teacher. I had been sitting on the edge of my desk, but now I stood, crossed my arms over my chest and stared lethally. I aged decades. Orthopedic shoes fused to my feet. My hair turned gray and pulled back into a bun. "Calm down," I said in a voice that did not admit we were of the same species.

They calmed. They generally do. Which is a relief, since I can't maintain the pursed and squinty pose very long without giggling.

I shifted gears. "Forget Tiny Tim. Think about Dickens' compassion and humanity. Think about today, about the less fortunate, the homeless."

Their spinal cords completely disintegrated. Jellyfish, barely present. They rolled their eyes. "The homeless suck." The boy who muttered this had a deep tan from Thanksgiving in Jamaica.

"Boring," my world-weary sophomores murmured.

Clemmy Tomkins looked up from his drawing. At most, I receive one-third of his attention. The rest goes to sketches of bosoms and ballistic missiles. Two months ago, I found one of Clemmy's works tacked to my bulletin board. It was a remarkably comprehensive full-color portrait of a tall woman with long red-brown hair, a recognizable nose and eyes much greener than mine actually are. The blackboard behind her said, "Foxy English Teacher." The body, centerfold material and exquisitely detailed, was extremely flattering and the most imaginative work Clemmy had ever done in my classroom. Still, I had problems dealing with the fact that, aside from a volume of Shakespeare in the woman's

4 *Gillian Roberts*

hand and stiletto high heels on her feet, she was stark naked.
We have since negotiated a truce. He keeps his artwork and
speculations private, and I allow him to use English class as
studio time. And sometimes, he actually pays attention. Talk
of the homeless had stopped his drawing hand. "There's this
guy on Chestnut Street—you know him?" His right hand
resumed its artwork. "Gives me the creeps. Talks to himself.
Shouts. Sleeps in a box."

"Ever find one of them picking through your trash?
Gross!" Suze flashed Clemmy a smile full of braces and
smugness. They bonded, two rebels joined against the un-
tanned, unpicturesque poor.

"Don't you feel anything for them?" I asked.

Indeed they did. They felt annoyance. Impatience. Disgust. Why don't those people *do* something for themselves?
they asked.

I was suddenly furious. As a teacher in a private school, I
was always the poorest person in my classroom, and I was
sick and tired of the contempt in which those who had to
balance checkbooks or shop sales were held. I didn't ask
what they thought the homeless should do for themselves. I
was afraid I'd hear that they should join a gym, get their hair
done or find a nice condominium.

I glared at these people I sometimes referred to as "my
kids." I'd teach them. Maybe they wouldn't find the Ghosts
of Christmas Present boring if they had to meet them, do
something for them. "Fine," I snapped. "No more *Christmas Carol*. You already know all about being Scrooge. Let's
see if you can learn something new."

Before the dismissal bell stopped reverberating, I was in
the principal's office, petitioning. In a school with no tenure,
one wants the administration on one's side. I was eager to
help, not join, the homeless.

I presented my Dickens-inspired idea. My tenth graders
would cook and serve a holiday meal at a soup kitchen. Maurice Havermeyer's eyebrows rose in horror. I loftied up my
pitch, improvising multisyllabic academese, heavy on "the
inherent necessity for community" and "endemic socioec-
onomic isolation," and by the time I invented "participatory

empathic responses," I had him so thoroughly confused that he stopped spluttering.

"Yesss," he said in his lockjawed fashion. I wasn't sure if his accent, that upper-crust Main Line malocclusion, was any more authentic than the imitation Phi Beta Kappa key he rubbed when he was nervous or the cryptic rosette he wore in his lapel. It didn't matter. The "yes" was very real. He sounded as surprised by it as I was. He experimented with it again, pulling at the word until it was long enough to wrap around his stomach. "Yessssssss."

I was not only surprised, I was worried. This was too straightforward and too enthusiastic. Completely out of Havermeyer's character. His little eyes glinted, increased their kilowatts. "The holiday season," he said. It was hypnotic fun watching him talk, lips and chin rigid, like a ventriloquist in search of a dummy. "Giving of oneself. Participatory empathy. The very image. Yesssss."

I could almost watch pictures form in his brain. A human-interest story in the *Philadelphia Inquirer*. A spot on the Six O'Clock News. A feature in the Sunday magazine. Reprints on heavy stock, glossy fodder for prospects. Increased applications, higher endowments. Bliss.

He was mentally drooling.

He walked to the long window overlooking the park and stood with his back to me. Then he turned with the expression God probably had when delivering the Ten Commandments. "Amanda, I admire your thinking. You have come up with the perfect vehicle to increase parent participation."

"Parents? It's students I—"

"And the one who immediately comes to mind, who would be a fine starting point, is Alexander Clausen. It is my impression that he needs no more than a judicious push to more fully identify with our aims and goals."

Pregnant pause. In the last few years, quiet Laura's father, Alexander, car tycoon, real-estate developer, political animal and who knew what else, had risen like our city's own star over Bethlehem. He was famous both for his personal success and for his acts of charity. He guaranteed that fame via a public-relations firm and an omnipresent photographer, both of whom documented his every generosity. No trees, not even saplings, fell in a Clausen forest without being heard. In fact, they were recorded in video and released to the press. Somehow, his rosy cheeks and largesse had even convinced media folk to adopt the nickname he used in his ads. Everybody called Alexander "Sandy" Clausen, Santa Claus. Now there was talk about running Santa Claus for mayor.

"Don't you teach the Clausen girl?" Dr. H. murmured.

"Yes . . ."

"Her father mentioned you. Said the girl is fond of you."

Havermeyer rhapsodized. "Clausen has a real flair for this kind of thing. I'm sure he'll have lots of ideas about it. And once he's more directly involved in the, ah, image and welfare of our school, well . . . He can be a very *giving* man."

I understood. I was the good elf who'd get Havermeyer onto Santa's gift list. "But the idea was for the students to give of themselves," I said. "People to people. A quiet holiday gesture, a learning experience, a—"

"We are never too old to learn, are we? Adults also benefit from giving." He paused. "And, I dare say, in this case, so might Philadelphia Prep."

Why be subtle? Or bother with poor people and students at all? Instead, why not sit outside Clausen's house crying "Alms, alms"?

And why didn't I express more objections instead of worrying about how I'd pay my rent if I thwarted Maurice Havermeyer?

On the way to my car, I passed Laura Clausen holding hands with a twelfth grader, Peter Shaw. They were quite a contrast. He was dressed to menace in all-black clothing, a wild mane of dyed black hair, and a scowl as dark as the rest. She was mouselike and much younger looking than her fourteen years, bundled in a baggy time warp—Peter Pan collar and fifties skirt. I inspected them with too much interest and for too long, and Laura noticed. I tried to hide my embarrassment by mentioning that I'd be seeing her father soon.

"Why?" Her pale little-girl face pinched up even more. "Did I do something wrong?"

She was so withdrawn, so young and naive looking and so bright and articulate when she wrote, that I'd forgotten she was another of Philly Prep's special cases. Her records spoke of slow social development, academic underachievement, periodic eating disorders, attempted runaway. Off the record, she was rumored to be either guilty of arson or the victim of a flammable accident that had seriously scorched her home. Whatever it was had also scarred her left arm.

"No, no," I said. "Your dad might work with me on a project."

I was wrong. Shortly after I made that remark, I came to realize that nobody works with Sandy Clausen. In fact, the very word "with" was not in his vocabulary. Neither was "listen." I rebelled, reacted, bargained and protested, but even so, my innocent plan mutated like something in a science-fiction movie.

"IT'S A FAIRLY SIMPLY PROJECT, MR. CLAUSEN," I SAID. We met in the teacher's lounge in the late afternoon. Sandy Clausen made it clear that he'd come back early from a business trip to keep this date. Dr. Havermeyer responded with reverence, almost scraping his forehead on the floorboards before backing out of the lounge, leaving matters in what he called, "your more than capable hands." I didn't think he meant my hands, somehow.

"Now, now. We're going to be working together, shoulder to shoulder, so there's no room for formality." Clausen's voice and face were so jovial I smiled back automatically. "I certainly want to feel free to call you Amanda, if I might, and I want you to call me Sandy."

He seemed an agreeable enough man. "Sandy. There are a few charity kitchens that are relatively close to school, and I thought we could pick one, then choose a night to cook and serve a Christmas dinner we'd planned. That's it, the whole thing. Nothing very fancy, of course, but substantial. The students could collect food donations and then—"

"Very interesting," he said. "Brilliantly simple and to

the point." He reached over and shook my hand. "I'm impressed."

I thought, foolish me, that shaking hands meant it was a deal. And it was, only not my deal. Or, as Sandy Clausen might have put it, it was my deal—with a few adjustments.

Because subsequently, without consulting me, he dropped the idea of having the students cook dinner. "Up for lots of possible legal problems," he said. "They aren't professionals, they could undercook or add something bad, or—"

"They'd be supervised, they'd be using recipes. Most of them know the basics of cooking, anyway, and those centers use volunteer cooks all the time, so—"

"They could burn or cut themselves, and they're our *children*." His voice was tender. Made you imagine tiny babes, wee urchins straining on tiptoe, not girls with half-shaved heads and black lipstick.

"But if we don't cook," I said, feeling suddenly weary and apprehensive, "then how do we feed people?"

He gave his Santa smile, all but patted the top of my head, told me not to worry and hired a caterer.

"A catered dinner in a shelter?" I asked. "Palate Pleasers? They did my cousin Grace's wedding! Their current specialty is nouvelle Indochine cuisine and, forgive me, I cannot imagine them in a soup kitchen!"

"Well, Amanda, I absolutely agree with you. In fact, I'm glad you brought it up, because I've had my people check out those three centers you mentioned, and in all honesty, it turns out they aren't in the best neighborhoods."

"Of course not! They're shelters for homeless people—"

"And I'm sure when you think it through, it will become apparent that we'd be subjecting our parents to a great deal of anguish about the security and well-being, both mental and physical, of their children. After all, most of our children are not what's called 'street smart,' not used to what they'd see and be around in those—"

"But that's the whole point of—"

"And why have we worked so hard to achieve so much if we're going to expose our children to the very dangers we've been fortunate enough—and hardworking enough—to escape?''

"But it's because these children have no idea of how privileged they are, of what real life is for most people that I wanted to—"

"And what, frankly, is festive about a shelter? 'Tis the season to be jolly, Amanda, and those places are downright depressing.''

It was like conversing with a steamroller.

"So," he said, "I've volunteered my own home, and Maurice Havermeyer agrees that that is a better idea. I promise you, I'll make it festive, a real celebration." He beamed another all-is-well-with-the-world at me, but I refused to acknowledge or return it, my own feeble form of passive resistance.

We continued along those lines. I couldn't back out and I couldn't move forward with what I wanted, so I wound up with an inflated, embarrassing carnival featuring handpicked poor folk. Need I say that it wasn't my hand that picked them, either? One more good intention paving the road to hell.

BY NOW, ENOUGH TIME HAD PASSED SINCE MARIGOLD MARgolis and Charles Dickens had started the thing two and a half weeks ago, for me to have moved squarely into Scrooge's camp, to have become Santa Claus's only nonfan.

Now, with the Sandy and Mandy show minutes away, the only Christmas spirit that interested me was waiting to be guzzled later, after the mortifying business was over.

With twenty minutes before lift-off, I ignored my snaggled stocking and screwed in earrings while I read compositions. I was beyond tired and the night was young. Right after school, I'd zoomed to the other end of the city to do my last "Rediscovering the Classics" class with a group of fortyfive retirees. I'd become "the Thursday lady" at Silverwood Retirement Community, subbing as a favor for a pregnant friend. Now that her baby was born, she would be returning to the once-weekly stint with the new year, and I was going to miss my retirees. What a change from my daily dose of adolescents. The old men and women, some reading in braille, some entering class on walkers, all so frail yet so resilient, were eager to think and discuss and appreciate or criticize. And what fun to teach without grades or assigned papers or tests—but with stimulation and an exchange of ideas. I'd learned a lot from them.

We'd all promised, teary eyed, to keep in touch, but I wondered if we really would. Two of the women had baked an assortment of Christmas cookies for me. I eyed the tin, but kept it closed to prove I was a self-disciplined and honorable woman.

More proof—I continued to read essays. I wanted to start the new year fresh, wanted everything marked and returned before vacation, which gave me fourteen hours before class began tomorrow. Minus a sizeable chunk for the wretched party. Minus a few much more pleasant hours if/when C.K. Mackenzie appeared later tonight. That depended on whether somebody decided to murder somebody else between now and the end of Mackenzie's shift. Talk about being out of control concerning the logistics of love, or like, or whatever one should call our condition. I had not yet become either adjusted or resigned to life as a cop's exceedingly good friend. Actually, I would never have met Mackenzie had it not been for a murder, but I wasn't always sure if that had been my good or bad luck.

I decided to believe that the criminal element would ease up and give me a break tonight, so I took papers to mark and the unopened cookie tin downstairs and ate crackers dipped into peanut butter. I literally had no appetite for the catered extravaganza that lay ahead. Peanut butter was fine, except for the unfortunate smears it left on compositions.

Luckily, the day's mail was so unimpressive, it couldn't seduce me away from my work. No interesting Christmas cards—no personal notes, not even a mimeographed annual letter full of exclamation points, babies, vacations, acquisitions and promotions. Only two bills, one ad and, in an unmarked envelope with a Florida postmark, my mother's missive. She had taken to mailing me articles about safe sex. I was sure that to her all sex was suspect, but she was trying to be contemporary, as uncomfortable as it made her. Hence envelopes with no return address and articles with nothing but "F.Y.I." written on them, as if we were spies.

I left it all in a wicker basket, unopened, and continued marking papers. In lieu of *A Christmas Carol*, the tenth grade had read poetry. Although poetry is the written equivalent of zits to most sophomores, the substitute unit wasn't intended as punishment. The students' responses, however, their unit papers, did seem punitive.

I thumbed through the stack for Laura Clausen's, knowing she would at least try to think about the subject. She didn't disappoint me. She'd chosen Auden's poem about Icarus falling from the sky. Her analysis of its structure was precise and intelligent.

The phone rang, but I ignored it. I had a brand-new, state-of-the-art answering machine to shield me from the outside world. After two rings, my recorded voice would take over.

Laura's paper turned unsettling. "Daedalus was a murderer," she wrote. "He made promises and wings, and they both failed. Instead of protecting his child, he sent him too close to the fire, to his death. Parents and children aren't equals or ready to do the same things, and Icarus shouldn't have been pulled into his father's fantasy which, in effect, murdered him."

The phone rang a third and then a fourth time.

"Nobody cared," Laura wrote. "Icarus splashed into eternity and the plowmen kept working. As Auden says '. . . suffering . . . takes place while someone else is eating or opening a window or just walking dully along . . .' Nothing has changed since then. Nobody cares about anything except his own life and concerns. Icarus, unnoticed, still dies every day."

I felt chilled. I read it through again, hoping the secret message that seemed embedded in it would come clear.

The telephone began again when I was halfway through. I cursed all machinery everywhere and my inability to comprehend it.

"I expected you to be out," my mother said. I wondered if I could convince her that I was. I am fond of her, but it is

fair to say that she was not far from my mind when I bought
the answering machine.

My mother is a woman with overwhelming energy. My
father has retired. She has not. She is president, founder and
namer of the Hava Little Hu-Manatee League, bent on saving
the gentle sea cows. She is active in Meals on Wheels, a
cofounder of the Elysium Condo Square Dance and Discount
Shoppers Association, a reader to the blind, a fairly bad but
enthusiastic golfer and the second-highest winner in the
Greater Boca Raton Perpetual Gin Game.

Any lesser woman would be too tired to closely monitor
my social life as well, but she fits it into her schedule with
amazing regularity.

The clock and Laura's composition pressed on me.

"Good news about your sweater," my mother said. I
cringed. A year and a half ago, after lusting for a hand-knit
number I could not afford in this lifetime, I bought expensive
yarn with which to make my own. And then remembered
that I had no knitting skill. On a visit north, my mother
commandeered the yarn. But she rivals Penelope for the
slowness with which she completes knitting projects. She
declared my sketch "too plain" and added sequins and vintage bugle beads. After delicate diplomatic maneuvering, the
glitz went back to her sewing kit and the yarn was pulled
apart and remade into something she called "plain," i.e.,
the sort of lumpy cardigan comic-book schoolteachers wear.
Again it was unraveled and again she requested my mea-
surements and again decided they were wrong. That attempt
yielded the perfect puffed-sleeve pullover for Bwana, the
orangutan. I'm not sure what virgin wool is, but I'm positive
that what we have is the woolly equivalent of an old, tired
hooker. Still, Mama knits on.

"It'll be finished by the time you're here," she said
brightly.

I didn't ask what "it" was in this incarnation. I was wing-
ing my way south for part of my vacation, because, as my
mother constantly pointed out, I had no reasons—such as
husband or children—not to.

My mother informed me that I had fallen further behind

in the marriage sweepstakes. Not only had one of her casual acquaintances' daughters—a plain girl, she said, nothing special—acquired a two and a half carat, gem-quality, emerald-cut engagement ring three days ago, but worse, the same evening, a neighbor's obnoxious, undeserving daughter snared an investment banker with only one ex, no children and an already paid lump settlement. A free and clean, barely used male.

I tried to make it clear that I couldn't talk, that I had to leave. I immediately regretted my words, the verbal equivalent of the doctor's rubber hammer tapping her knee.

"A date?" All reflexes in order.

"The school party. I told you."

My mother doesn't remember parties that don't have the prefix "wedding" or "engagement." She considers my job busywork, a waste of prime husband-hunting time. She even resents it when I call my students "my kids."

"Working nights," she grumbled. "Throwing away your life. Did you see the *Today* show this morning?"

"Mom, I leave for work at—"

"A report said it's never too soon to prepare for menopause."

"I'm thirty! Barely."

"Still seeing Chuck?"

"Who?"

"The detective."

"Oh. That Chuck." I had made up the name to give her a point of reference. I didn't know how to answer. Yes to the detective, no to Chuck? I couldn't say that while I knew C.K. Mackenzie in the biblical sense, I didn't know his first name. My mother would be appalled by both facts.

I said I was still seeing the detective. I didn't add that I wasn't seeing him enough, or clearly.

"A *U.S.A. Today* poll says marriage is back in style."

Maybe Mackenzie was afraid of trendiness.

I pushed us back to neutral ground. "You know, I'm running late. I just got home from that class at Silverwood. I told you I was teaching there temporarily, right?" I did another round of peanut-butter dipping while she complimented my kindness to the elderly. I eyed the cookie tin, but again resisted temptation. And remembered that there was something I should tell her—except I couldn't remember what.

A little more peanut butter restored a portion of my brain cells. "A woman in my class said she knows you, Mom." Except, I'd forgotten who it was. Jenny, the one who looked like the Pillsbury Dough Boy in drag? Harriet of the gruff voice and heart of mush? They'd both come up to talk to me afterward.

"Who? Who?" My mother sounded like an owl.

It was a short person, I thought. I was looking down while she said it. Wheelchair. Minna! "You know somebody named Minna White?"

In much less time than it would take a computer to do a similar search, my mother sorted her past. "Minna! Minna. Of course! Minerva White, from when we lived on Brooke Street. You must remember her!"

I was seven, if that, when we moved from there, and all I remembered offhand was a place I used to hide under the back porch, a girl with bright red pigtails who could spit farther than anybody, and how awful it was to have to lie still on a cot during kindergarten rest time.

"She had a fluffy white cat," my mother said, pulling the complete file out of her memory, "and a boy they called Junior. Nervous kid with a strawberry mark on his chin? Good friends with that freckled boy, Barry, the one whose father was a baker, that big fat man with a lisp who—"

Philadelphia has millions of residents, but to my mother, it is a tiny village and one of her self-proclaimed roles, even after relocating to the Sunbelt, is as its official historian.

"There was some trouble, too, with Minna's husband. At least I think so. Maybe it was Junior? No, he'd have been too young. This was before she moved away. When you were in elementary school."

Historian, yes. Accurate, no. She realized how wobbly her facts were and changed ground. "I heard from Mrs. Bloom that poor Minna isn't doing well. Is it true that she's blind from her diabetes and crippled with arthritis?"

"Afraid so," I said.

My mother tsked. "And is it true what she said, that Junior turned out pretty much a no-good? Mrs. Bloom said he never comes to see Minna, but he still takes money."

"I don't know about that kind of thing. We talked about *The Scarlet Letter* and *Vanity Fair*. She didn't even connect me with you until this afternoon."

"You know what I remember about her? She loved cannoli. *Loved* them."

"Which reminds me. I'm supposed to have dinner with sixty-five hungry people in ten minutes, and they are thirty minutes away."

"I *never*," she said, "*never* will understand how you get involved in such—"

I had been asking myself the same question nonstop for weeks. I had a chance to ponder it anew while my mother debated which of my father's genetic flaws accounted for my weaknesses. I also screwed the top back on the peanut butter, put away the crackers, and dusted off the counter.

"You're running yourself ragged," she said. "Teaching all day and after school, then giving an enormous party."

"It's not my party. I'm not doing much at all." Nobody was except the caterer that Santa Claus had provided, the public relations firm he kept on retainer, and the merchants who had donated gifts. "A parent's taken charge." It was obvious that my mother hadn't been reading her *Philadelphia Inquirer* thoroughly. Clausen had managed to get himself and his party onto the front page today, and there had been two other significant features about it this week as well.

The one thing I was supposed to do for the party was show up, and I was definitely late. And I still had unmarked compositions. Damn, if Mackenzie arrived tonight, I'd have to spend some of our time hunting run-on sentences and indefinite pronouns. "I have to leave," I said.

"You know, dear, next time you see Minna, do something for me—take her cannoli for old time's sake."

"I don't know if I'll ever see her again. The class ended tonight."

"But now that you know she's an old friend, Amanda!

The poor woman. It must be especially hard on her around the holidays.''

I vowed to enlist Mackenzie's aid in mastering the answering machine this very night.

"She isn't lucky, like me. Her child doesn't visit her. Think about it.''

From now on, when I expected a call from Florida, I'd have a therapist on standby. "I will,'' I said. "But right now I'm really in a rush.''

"Why? Do you expect to meet the wino of your dreams tonight? Listen, Mandy. I'm sure you're tired after a long day. Why risk pneumonia? Stay home. Take a bubble bath. Pack for Florida. Forget this party.''

Why, just that once, didn't I listen to my mother?

Two

DESPITE BEING LATE, I DID TRY TO ENJOY THE RIDE. AFTER
all, the city was twinkling away in holiday attire. The least I
could do was look.

I headed for East River Drive. There were, of course, no
crew teams out at this hour or season, but the park setting
was nonetheless picturesque. Every Victorian turret on Boat
House Row was outlined in white lights that glimmered off
the dark river.

Once off the drive, I passed tightly packed homes that I
knew had blistered, chipped paint, missing parts, visible
wounds. But not tonight. Not this season. Now they were all
red and green lights, candles, wreaths, Santa faces and messages of peace and love.

And then the houses became more splendid and the dec-
orations more subdued. I have a love-hate relationship with
Chestnut Hill. Once, I lusted for one of the many houses still
owned and rented by the developer's family, nearly a hundred
years after they were built, but the necessary interview—
checking everything from my lineage to my educational cre-
dentials—cooled my ardor and I gave up the idea before they
could order me gone.

Of course I was late. Since I didn't want to be there at all,
this wasn't a real problem, except that it made it impossible
to find a parking space. I circled the Clausens' block again

and again but the area was clogged with residents' cars, mini-vans from various agencies and a chartered bus unloading people of all known ages, shapes, sizes and races, plus a few who looked like new inventions. However different they may have been originally, their shabby clothing and wary expressions made them look united, or at least related.

I didn't blame them for being suspicious. I didn't know what any of this meant, either. I circled the block again, wondering whether the Innercity Services Van, the Septa Senior Charter, and the Palate Pleasers catering truck would occupy their parking spaces during the whole party, their drivers dozing over their wheels. "Give me a break," I muttered. "Sleep somewhere else." They didn't.

On the next pass, I thought I had a spot when a taxicab pulled away, but the car in front of me had also been waiting, and I set out again, wondering what variety of homeless arrives in a cab.

By the next go-round, I recited every parked vehicle's make and ownership as if I were putting a curse on them all. They still didn't budge. I was about to leave, to call in sick, when a neighbor, probably sure our gala was lowering his property value, took to the road. His legacy was a genuine parking spot.

The Clausens' place was perfection. Much as I disliked its owner, I admired his taste in domiciles. It was where you'd go after you met the prince and needed a place for the happily ever afters.

Tonight, the house was not only glorious, but packed. Round tables with green cloths and poinsettia centerpieces filled enormous nooks and spacious crannies.

Every wall and most of the polished wooden surfaces were decked with holly and evergreen, punctuated by crimson velvet bows. In discreet corners and on mantelpieces fat green candles threw off soft light and the holiday smell of bayberry. At the far corner of the living room, a towering tree shimmered with gilded and spun fantasies, straight out of my every childhood dream of Christmas.

I grew up with rather low-key and unenthusiastic holiday celebrations. Both my parents are half-somethings, representing most of the major religions, and they long ago decided on an ecumenical smorgasbord for their daughters. Interesting and democratic as it probably sounded, it translated into droopy, noncommittal holidays.

Such was not the case Chez Santa where dwelled the all-out, definitive spirit of Christmas Present and Past.

Aside from the handpicked needy, there was Maurice Havermeyer, a harried-looking press photographer, a tall, bearded observer of some kind, and my friend Sasha Berg, there by permission of S. Claus. She waltzed around the room, large and flamboyant in purple velvet, convincing people to sign model releases so that she could capture them for a photo essay on food. There were also three Palate Pleasers employees in checkered dresses and a dozen Philly Prep students who were, at my insistence, waiting tables. These students servers were my only victory over the Clausen-Havermeyer bloc, which had wanted professional waitpersons. But to achieve victory, I had sweetened the moral pot with extra credit that didn't involve writing or memorization.

Of course, Santa was also very much in residence, appropriately bedecked in velvet, tufting, beard and resonant "Ho-ho-ho's," glad-handing his rather stunned-looking guests.

The press photographer snapped candids and grabbed hors d'oeuvres from passing students. Alice Clausen, Santa's Mrs., intermittently peeked around a corner, smiled tensely and disappeared again, reminding me of those bobbling plastic birds perched on the rims of glasses. Maurice Havermeyer cleared his throat and searched the ceiling for inspiration. I estimated his endurance at forty-five minutes, and checked my watch to begin countdown. As for me, after I'd reassured myself that the Palate Pleasers could more easily run the kitchen and the students without my interference, and that Sasha was too engrossed stalking mouths and edibles to talk, I had little to do but become part of a human-interest story. I talked with, or listened to, a family of four who lived in a rusting VistaCruiser station wagon, a pugnacious man who mentioned 'Nam ever third word, sneered at the rich kids' school and the rich bastard who owned this house, and made spitting noises for punctuation, and to a woman in her sixties who nervously picked at her skirt and checked behind her every few seconds. I found chatting exhausting when what I really wanted to do was wave a wand and offer solutions. When the timid woman walked off, checking over her shoulder, I sighed with relief and leaned against the wall.

"Want some?" A bearded man held out a glass cup. He was well dressed and self-confident. Not a guest, obviously. The visible portion of his smile suggested that he was offering me more than punch. "Not good," he said, "but available." I assumed he referred to the punch this time and accepted.

"We were afraid to serve anything with alcohol," I said. "Given the crowd." It had been solemnly decided that liquid red dye was less dangerous than traditional gloggs. People wound up dead, but not sleeping on grates, from carcinogens.

"I'm Nick Riley," he said. "I'm writing a piece about Clausen. And you're Mandy Pepper, the English teacher." He rolled his eyes in mock horror. "Are you going to make red marks all over my copy?"

I detest the coy "Yikes! an English teacher" school of approach. I am also suspicious of beards, now that they don't make any political statement. Or maybe I'm jealous because no amount of equal rights will ever give me a man's ability to camouflage weak jaws and funny features with hair.

"I hear you thought up this shindig," he said, nodding toward Havermeyer. "So thanks. Made it easy to get to Clausen."

"I had a very different shindig in mind. Feel no need to thank me or mention my name in your article."

He cocked a brow above eyes the color of fudge. In all fairness, his visible parts weren't at all bad. Nice nose, eyes with a generous sprinkle of laugh lines, good cheeks. "A little hostile?" he asked.

I wasn't sure what he wanted from me, or I from him, so I began what I hoped was a discreet interrogation. "Who's the piece for?" I asked.

"It's on spec."

Nobody wanted it. There was something to be said for his

honesty. He could have lied and named any magazine he liked to impress me.

"Have you been writing long?" I asked next.

"Off and on. Mostly fiction. Sold some, but it isn't a living, so I have to stop too often, too long."

"Where's your fiction? I'd love to read it."

The vaguest hint of annoyance tightened his lips. "Oh," he said, "little magazines. I'm sure you haven't heard of them."

"Try me. I'm an English teacher, remember?"

He curled his lips into a smile, or sneer. "Okay—what's the last time you read *Fundies* or *Mercury Three* or *Oxlips*?"

"*Oxlips?* Like the animal's mouth?"

"Like the flower, I think."

I grinned. "Well, I think my subscription ran out. But still, congratulations."

He nodded.

"Why this kind of story, then?"

"Man cannot live by *Oxlips* alone. I make money in real estate, development. Here's Alexander Clausen, the king of developers, right? Or at least the prince, the heir apparent." I could almost see the blood speed up in Nick's veins. He gesticulated, cutting the air with his hand. "He's interesting, too. A mystery. They say he wants to be mayor, but who knows anything about him? His background? Where he started? How he did it? What's his secret?"

I certainly didn't have any of those answers.

"Nobody knows. So why not find out? I heard about this party, knew it'd be an easy way to meet him, set something up and maybe do both of us some good."

"You mean good for your writing career?"

"Good for my *life*. I'm being honest. Tonight's the start of something really big for me. Alexander Clausen and I are going to be important to each other."

I didn't understand how, but Nick's enthusiasm was contagious.

"What sort of real estate is it you've been involved with?" I asked, to make conversation.

He shrugged. "This and that. No names you'd recognize. I'm kind of a late bloomer."

He spoke with enthusiasm, moving quickly and almost constantly in a private charged electrical field. It was a startling, even exotic, up-tempo switch from Mackenzie's slow Southern beat.

"But—I am finally on the very brink of blooming," he said, and then he grinned wickedly. He was definitely attractive. "So," he said, looking around, "how'd you choose your guests?"

"I don't know where they came from, and it seems rude to ask. Sandy Clausen knew somebody who knew somebody else, and so it went. It's generous to open his house, but also, maybe . . ."

"Insensitive?"

I felt a tremor of kinship. "For people with no home, a palace like this could be depressing, I'd think."

"And how about those miniature quiches they're passing around?"

The house, or the hors d'oeuvres, or something, did appear to bother a sizeable proportion of the guests, who were solemn, scowling and sometimes muttering. However, it was hard to tell whether they were temporarily disturbed by the party or permanently disturbed by life. Still, it was disorienting watching Santa chuckle his way through a frowning, distracted, almost hostile crowd.

Nick dislodged his long body from the wall he'd rested against. "I'd like to interview you."

"I don't know Sandy Clausen."

"You've worked with him. You could give me an impression. I don't want his PR pap. I want the real stuff. You in the book? Can I call?"

I nodded, and he strode off. It was a story he'd been after, not me. I couldn't tell whether I was disappointed.

Sasha materialized. "Nice stuff," she said of the departing Nick. "Good going. Happy holidays."

"He gave me a cup of punch. Are you perhaps mistaking it for a betrothal?"

"I like him. I talked to him earlier. He's a better prospect than No-Name."

Sasha and Mackenzie have developed a mutual disapproval society for reasons that escape me. Sasha refuses to remember what it is Mackenzie does. Mackenzie grumbles about her artsy-fartsy photos.

"Who needs a CIA agent, anyway?" she demanded. Before I could correct her, she spied someone eating a cocktail frank and was off, camera at the ready.

The *Inquirer* photographer stayed through the first course. Havermeyer lasted eleven minutes less than my estimate. A reporter from the local giveaway rushed in late, flashed bulbs in the faces of our guests, and left. Nick hovered around the tables, pestering everyone about the gifts Santa distributed from his big bag. "Nice," they answered him, "I like it fine." He wanted more. He wanted to know the impact the muffler had on this one's soul, the meaning that one's cologne held for the future. He wanted cute epigrams, quotes to spark a sensitive narrative, the mark of an *Oxlips* contributor. He recognized insensitivity in Clausen, but missed it in himself, and so he badgered on.

Eventually, he became bored with grunts and monosyllables and let people eat in peace. The evening lost its rough edges, the guests lost their scowls and suddenly we had the basic, generic holiday party where everyone seemed to be having a moderately good time. I sat next to a man with splayed teeth and a spotty past he appeared proud of. The only homes he'd known had been prisons. He flirted outrageously with a woman whose thin blond hair was pulled like a bad hairnet over her scalp, and she giggled back, covering her mouth with her hand.

Sandy Clausen never settled down. He was everywhere all at once, overacting, patting shoulders, hugging, handing out color-coded gifts.

I realized the party could do very well without my monitoring, excused myself and headed for the powder room, my kidneys desperate to process and purge the pink punch.

En route, I nearly bumped into an elderly man. He stood

rigidly, leaning on a cane topped with a metallic duck head, scanning the room as if lost.

"Can I help you?" I asked. He looked disoriented.

He blinked and took some time to focus on me. Both his hands now clutched the top of the cane. After he'd seen what he needed of me, he looked back at the room, all in slow motion. "There," he finally said in a surprisingly strong voice. "Yes." He walked off like a wrinkled warrior, full of purpose, moving behind Sandy Clausen, who was talking to a large, ginger-haired woman.

"Alexander Clausen." His voice, though strong, sounded oddly hollow.

Sandy Clausen frowned slightly and continued his conversation.

"Alexander Clausen."

It seemed to echo, which was impossible in the crowded, carpeted room.

"Alexander Clausen!" The old man lifted his cane and down came the duck head on a red velvet shoulder.

Clausen turned, annoyance showing through his Santa beard. And then his expression changed to pure astonishment, and the skin of his face became almost as white as the whiskers.

The old man nodded. "Yes," he said, as if answering Clausen's unspoken questions. He pointed a finger at his own chest and then at Clausen's, binding the two of them as surely as if it had been rope passing from one man to the other.

"You'd think he sees a ghost," a woman near me said. She was gray—hair, skin, dress and shoes.

"Jacob," Clausen whispered.

"A ghost," the gray woman repeated.

I felt light-headed, almost faint. I knew *A Christmas Carol* by heart—at least the part about Marley's ghost. I could hear it now, over the babble of the party. "In life I was your partner, Jacob Marley." Then I regained my senses. I was caught in a Dickensian time warp that had nothing to do with this little scene. Dickens' Marley was indeed a ghost. And dead. This old man was very much alive. And Clausen wasn't Scrooge.

The powder-room door opened and it was my turn. I dawdled in place, although nothing more than pointing and staring appeared to be happening.

"Isn't this a line?" the gray woman behind me, she who had spoken of ghosts, said. Her priorities were straight, and besides, I couldn't admit to eavesdropping. I went in. When I emerged a few minutes later, the old man and Clausen were elsewhere, the drama over.

But another scene was beginning with an urgent grasp. "They told me you know him," a man said. He wore a blue suit older than he seemed to be, a suit so ancient it could break your heart.

"Who?"

"The man who lives here. Who gives away cars. *Talk* to him."

Dear God. This was a new level of naivete, believing late-night car ads.

"One," the man said. "That's all I need." He had a gravelly, used-up voice and pitted skin. "One. I'd sleep in it, live in it. Be able to leave this damn city. He has so many, he could easily afford to. I told him."

I looked for our host. This was his baby. I saw the man with the cane, but not Santa.

"He *chuckled*, like I was out of my mind. What is he, some kind of a liar? He's allowed to make promises he don't mean? On television? In front of everybody?"

Our host wasn't hard to find. He is one of those people who fills all the available space, and when dressed in red, shouting, "Ho-ho-ho," he was inescapable.

But Santa wasn't ho-hoing at the moment. He was fuming, fists clutched and cheeks unpleasantly flushed. Amidst all the bustle and good cheer, he must have failed to notice until now that Peter Shaw, Laura's presumed boyfriend, was one of the serving folk. You would have thought he'd be impressed by Peter's altruism. He was not in my tenth-grade class and therefore he alone was not receiving extra credit for his work. Sandy didn't seem to care. While I watched, S. Claus herded his waitress-daughter into the curve of the staircase.

"Lies!" the gravel-voiced man said to me. "People like him don't deserve to live, dammit! People like him keep people like me in the gutter!"

"Listen," I told him, "you two will have to work this out. Meanwhile, I'll get you some punch." Okay, it was feeble, but he seemed frighteningly near the edge, and the only other option I could think of was a discussion of advertising ethics, and that didn't seem appropriate.

He declared that he'd get his own damned drink, unless that had strings on it, too.

I was glad he'd decided to postpone approaching Santa.

Clausen's face was mottled above the white beard. He shook his head and sliced his hand through the air like a scimitar. Laura looked wispier than usual. I thought I heard the words "slut" and "trash" aimed at her.

Most of the nearby guests were trying, as was I, to act as if they weren't eavesdropping, weren't hearing a word. A few watched, openmouthed.

Laura stood immobile, as if paralyzed, but her eyes were frightening. Peter, at a wary distance, looked ready to strike. I tried to disperse the gapers, urging all stragglers back to the tables for dessert.

"The whole reason I came here," a familiar bumpy voice behind me said, "was I figured Sandy Clausen would give away a car. One lousy car. He says he gives 'em all away on TV." He tried modifying his rough voice so that it sounded like Clausen's. " 'You know me,' " he mimicked, " 'I'm Santa Claus! Let me tell you what we're giving away today!' Damn," he said in his normal voice, "I can get a free meal at the shelter. I want a car!"

I turned to the man and made more soothing noises.

"*One*. Even a subcompact."

"You know how ads can be . . ." It was time for Clausen to leave domestic squabbles and deal with truth in advertising and whatever else was erupting out of this man.

"Why shouldn't I have a piece of the good life? I ask you— why?"

"You should." I peeked at the hallway. Sandy Clausen had reinvented himself once again. Gone was the irate father.

Now he lounged with one arm on the wall, the other chucking his daughter under the chin, patting her shoulder, touching her hair, as if the earlier confrontation had been my hallucination. He leaned over and kissed Laura's forehead, and took her arm in a courtly gesture, as if to lead her in the grand cotillion.

Laura remained rock eyed, expressionless and mute. The alarm I'd felt reading her paper returned, and I wished in vain that we could find the privacy and time to talk about it now. We definitely would tomorrow.

Abruptly, Laura shook off her father's arm and pulled away. Her father grabbed her shoulder and turned her back to him, stared at her, then released her as if she were burning his fingers.

She left. He stayed by the stairs, lighting a cigarette and smoking it, dark with anger.

It wasn't violent, it wasn't loud, but it was so intense that it was embarrassing to witness.

I'm not sure how long I stood there, worrying over what I'd seen. But Sasha tapped my shoulder and broke into my tangle of thoughts. "You can't be a wallflower at this kind of party," she said. "It's illogical. The action is in the living room, behind you. Give a listen."

The decibel level finally sank into my consciousness.

"Yeah," Sasha said. "It's a party."

We were finally perking. The cliché of holiday spirit had indeed become fact.

"Gotta go now," Sasha said. "They're pretty much finished eating, and I'm in a rush. Thanks for the chance to shoot. I think I got some good stuff."

"Stay. We haven't talked yet."

She ran her fingers through her jet-black hair. "Can't. Got a date."

"Shall I ask about him?"

"What's to say? He's new, stunning, rich, perfect."

I shrugged. "Just another guy, is that it?"

She had gone into the hallway, to the back wall where the coatrack stood, and had extracted an ancient, rubbed to the nap, black velvet cape. She put it on and flipped the hood up. Little Black Riding Hood. Or the witch, to mix a fairy tale or two. "That face in there?" she said as she went to the door. "That Nick? He's got style. My money's on him. Go for it." And she left.

Twice married, twice divorced, Sasha nonetheless adored men and they reciprocated. The affairs inevitably came to sad endings, but as bright as she was, she was sexually dyslexic and didn't learn a single thing from any of the disappointing encounters. And that was half her charm.

I turned my attention back to the party, and found myself actually enjoying it. There were moments that were gifts when the eyes of a Philly Prep student met those of the homeless person he was serving and he stopped and looked, and honestly seemed to take note. To feel. Conversations started, questions were asked on both sides. Students forgot about clearing up and sat down to talk with guests. I wanted the photographer to verify this miracle, but he was long gone. I hoped Nick would write it down for posterity because otherwise it would be too hard to believe.

The tree sparkled, candles twinkled, people bubbled.

I tiptoed, afraid to break the spell with a normal tread. There was a vacant spot on the living room sofa, and I sat down to drink in the vista instead of more punch. I tried, in fact, to dispose discreetly of my cup on the end table, but it was fully occupied by a poinsettia in a red-foiled pot and an ashtray. I had to admire the planning that had so filled the tiny wooden top that nobody could possibly add anything—including water rings. Still, it left me holding the bilious red liquid.

A middle-aged woman sat next to me, carefully, slowly, unwrapping her shiny package in a long charade of anticipation and pleasure. Her excitement was contagious.

"I do love presents," she murmured. "When my Thomas was alive . . ." Her hazel eyes looked almost bruised with fatigue.

Carefully, she pulled the tape off the cardboard box, disengaged flaps, removed Styrofoam pellets and finally, lifted her prize out of its nest.

And then those tired eyes stared, dumbfounded, at what I

had last week declared the very worst of the gift donations, a porcelain figurine of a man in lederhosen. It had annoyed me for its stupidity—as if the homeless carry knickknack shelves around. But all the same, when the student who had solicited the donation looked hurt, I left it in the pile of gifts. I had meant to remove it later, but had forgotten.

The woman bit her bottom lip. Her long fingers played with her unkempt hair and her eyes welled up.

I felt responsible for her grief. Intentionally or not, I'd let the idiot thing pass. Merry Christmas—here's some insult to add to your injury.

"There's been a mistake," I said, trying to save face for both of us. "That figurine didn't belong with—certainly wasn't intended for—there are so many other things. Scarves, gloves. I'll find you another—"

"This isn't mine?" she asked. "I wasn't supposed to get it?"

I was so ashamed of us.

"I didn't steal it."

"Of course not. I didn't mean—"

She cupped her hand over the little man's head. "Your Santa gave it to me. Please don't take it." She looked as if she might crinkle up into herself.

"But—"

"The other gifts," she whispered, "they're for people who don't have anything and never will. But this—" she pressed it to her, "this makes me know I'll have my own place again someday. This is a real Christmas present. For a real person. I had a house, you know. Before Thomas . . . before my luck turned."

"Tell me," I said, and for a long time I heard how a once-solid woman, Gladys, her name was, could shrink through disease and bad luck and loneliness and confusion and age until she was no more than a statistic falling through the cracks. Not all her connections to reality seemed too secure, but she was very optimistic. We talked intently until a voice booming "Merry Christmas to all and to all a good night," surprised me soundly.

It had no effect on the crowd. The room was so flooded

with goodwill there were high-water marks on the walls, and nobody wanted to pull the plug.

However, I had late night with Mackenzie as an incentive plan for moving on, so I said good night to Gladys and stood up, the first to go.

I wasn't the only one leaving. Peter and Laura were at the front door. Peter had his coat on and presumably, Laura would have also been bundled up and away, but Santa had her shoulder in a vise.

Alice Clausen had emerged. She stood by the door with her fixed and anxious smile, as if she saw nothing odd in the taut little drama before her. In fact, as if she saw nothing, anywhere, ever.

They were like a bad, slow-moving silent film. Peter waited, tense and dangerous as a doberman, and Laura stood limply as if all her bones had dissolved. Her father, in disgust, released her, turned and walked back into the crowd.

"Larkly parny" Alice Clausen said, breaking the silence. She giggled. "*Lorvely* parny. *Party.*" She hiccuped. Her eyes crossed, and she peered at me, leaning closer and closer, until I realized the rest of her was also tilting en route to the floor. I put out my hands to stop her at the same time Laura grabbed one of her arms and Peter the other.

"Can I help?" I asked.

Peter shook his head. "Laura knows how to handle it, but thanks anyway."

"I'll—I'll see you both tomorrow," I said.

Still propping up her mother, Laura turned and pierced me with a look so dark and intense it felt like a scream.

"Save me," her eyes cried. "Save me."

I would like to think that if I'd known for sure how to save her, and from what, I would have done so, instead of standing there gape-mouthed, convincing myself that what I had really seen was a desperately embarrassed teenager whose privacy I was violating.

If I had known for sure, I would have stayed.

That's what I'd like to think.

Three

AT HOME, I MARKED COMPOSITIONS AND LISTENED TO SEA-
sonal selections on the radio until "The Little Drummer
Boy" became the holiday equivalent of Chinese water tor-
ture. In silence, I continued working. Macavity the cat
slurked over, on the prowl for moving ballpoint pens. I
looked at Laura's paper again, sighed, tried in vain to find
my way through to its secret heart, then put it aside. There
were other papers to grade.

Macavity immediately sat down on her composition, purring, poised to thwack my pen the next time I used it.

I had a few pleasant surprises that began with "I never
thought I'd say this, but . . ." and went on to express actual
pleasure in the experience of poetry.

Not enough, though. The numbers were on the side of the
maddening fakes who numbly regurgitated my words, my
least favorite species of student.

Forced to make a choice, I'd take the depressing but honest
variations on "Why All Poems (Especially the One You Assigned) Are Incredibly Stupid and Boring." For example,
from the pen of Clemmy Tomkins: "A person should say
what he means so normal people could understand without
a teacher. Who cares anyway because mostly its about sym-
bols and images and dumb things no normal person cares

31

about anyway except love maybe but even then it isn't love like for a normal guy so its still dumb.''

I fixed his punctuation, suggested changes in wording and then gave up, since brain transplants haven't yet been perfected, and I could think of no other method of improving Clemmy's writing. I put the paper aside for Mackenzie, who thinks of himself as a normal guy even though he's known to show off with a line of poetry from time to time.

There was only one paper to go when I heard C.K.'s knock. I took that as a sign that we were almost in sync—emphasis on the ''almost.''

We have developed a discreet, efficient system. He knocks, then uses his key. If I am otherwise occupied—so far a hypothetical situation, since I have chosen not to be since meeting him—I use the chain lock as well, and he retreats into the night. This is rather ornate, but it accommodates my independence and his unpredictable working hours.

Before he finished knocking, I opened the door and felt the happy rush the sight of him inevitably produced. C.K. Mackenzie is a fine specimen of manhood, but not tritely Hollywood or Madison Avenue handsome. I am dangerously overfond of his salt-and-pepper curly hair, light blue eyes, slouch, drawl and all the ephemera that make up his style.

Actually, I am overfond of him, period. At least, I think so. He's never around long enough to be sure. Certainly we are not career compatible. I don't know if it goes deeper than that, because his job interrupts, disrupts, dictates and generally keeps us at arm's length, so who knows which part is Mackenzie and which is The Detective?

Mackenzie says that I have artificially separated the two, and that, not his job, is my problem. He claims that the man and the job are one and the same, and I have some kind of learning disability.

It isn't as if I'm pushing for an ultimate commitment. I'd panic if a major life decision loomed. But lately I feel as if I'm part of a movie, stuck in a freeze frame. I'd prefer a hint as to what's going to happen. Even a promise that something, anything, eventually, will.

This year, Sasha, who never worries about the longevity

of love but insists it be painted in primary colors while it's around, gave me an early gift, a photo of a man and woman completely out of focus and dimly lit. She titled it, "C.K. and Mandy, Wherever at Last."

"Feels so fine to be here," he said after the initial kissing and hugging. He meant it, because his accent deepens under the press of emotion, and he was almost unintelligible, mushing his way through "fahn" and "heah" in a soft slur. He retrieved a beer from the refrigerator and hunkered down near me.

"One more paper," I said.

"No problem," he murmured, but all the while, his hand greeted my anatomy in ways that did not facilitate concentration.

"Be amused." I passed him Clemmy's paper.

He read, chuckled and sighed with exasperation and then, having exhausted the nuances of Clemmy Tomkins' world view, resumed distracting me.

"Two seconds," I said. "If you're bored, please decipher that damned answering machine for me." Then I remembered Laura's paper. "Wait, read something instead, would you? I want to know what you think."

He settled in again, long legs crossed as he studied her paper. One of the many traits I admire about Mackenzie is his ability—very rare, very sexy—to give the subject at hand his full attention. "Showed me her stuff before, haven't you?" he said after checking her name.

"This feels different."

I read an airball essay on "Thanatopsis," frequently glancing at Mackenzie, monitoring his reaction. I had never before realized how poker-faced he could be. Finally, my eyes rested on Laura's last paragraph, waiting for him to join me there. "Nothing has changed since then," she'd written. "Nobody cares about anything except his own life and concerns. Icarus, unnoticed, still dies every day."

Mackenzie looked up. "Want a fire?" he asked. "You're shiverin'."

"What do you make of it?" I asked.

"Must be hard for her to be in the same class as that Clemmy," he said. "I'm impressed, is what."

I waited for more, but Mackenzie was eyeing the answering machine, as if revving his motors to begin the trek across the living room.

"It's not her writing skills that concern me. Something's wrong. I wanted to talk to her about it tonight, but . . ." I described the evening, the tension, the cryptic scenes, the sad end. Laura's eyes. *Save me.*

He slouched back into the sofa pillows. "Don't read too much into it. She's brighter than your other kids, is all. Maybe this is about the homeless, kind of a meditation about what you'd been saying on sensitivity and caring."

"There's a second essay in there, Mackenzie, but it's in invisible ink. This is written in code."

"Don't go overboard translating." He stretched. "You wanted something with the machine?"

"I keep messing up."

He shuffled over to the counter that divides my downstairs room into living and kitchen segments. I followed. "Her conclusion wasn't part of the assignment. She didn't have to write anything like that at all. She veered off into that— that—"

"That what?" He upended the machine and pushed buttons.

"I don't know." Indictment? Warning? Cry?

Save me.

"Teenaged girls tend toward hysteria. That is not sexist, that is fact. Everything's a matter of life and death. What you saw tonight is probably nothing. A daddy annoyed by his little girl's boyfriend. You said the boy's older, fierce looking, troubled. Who wouldn't be upset?" He beckoned me over. "Look here, Mandy, push this for incoming calls. Adjust the volume here."

"What about her mother?"

"Ah, that sure sounds sad, but it has nothing to do with Icarus. Now this here memo button is like a tape recorder. Say you have an idea, you press it down, see? Records what you say, for as long as you like."

"You don't think her paper means anything?"

He'd perfected his shrug into a Gallic-by-way-of-New Orleans trademark. He used it now. "Give her an 'A' and relax."

"But—"

"Now this changes your message. Push it down, wait for the light and say what you like. Only please, don't make it cute."

"I felt like this before about a composition. Turned out the girl who wrote it was pregnant and suicidal."

He turned his head to me. "Killed herself?"

"No. I called her as soon as I'd read it and we talked and she got some help."

"How come that time you knew what to do, knew for sure what you'd read?"

I shook my head. Maybe the message was clearer, or easier.

"Here's how you pick up your calls from another phone." He went over the code, and it sounded logical and easy. It had sounded that way when I read it in the manual, too. It had not worked that way when I tried it.

He checked his watch. "Goin' on midnight. Too late to do a thing about Laura or her family now, anyway. It can wait till morning."

I wasn't sure whether he was motivated by logic or lust. "If you could have seen her eyes—" I began.

"This threatens to get real boring. The language of eyes is nice and literary, but I never did hear of an eye confession or anybody's collected eye writings or somebody's dirty looks being called pornography, did you? Eyes don't really speak, and that's why we had to go and invent tongues."

"I'm sure—"

"Where'd you learn to read 'eye'? Maybe you speak a different dialect, or you're mistranslating."

"But—"

"Because if you really can read eyes, how about mine?"

His were easy to decipher. Even so, it took a while to let go of the first part of the evening and embrace its remainder. Once I did, in the way of such things, I stopped thinking about cryptic compositions, half-glimpsed domestic strife and much of anything else.

Until the next morning, when the clock radio declared reveille. My alarm, which sounds like a Nazi storm trooper's klaxon, terrorizes me every workday. Once I'm hyperalert, heart beating double time, I'm ready for the newscaster's announcements of the imminent end of life as we know it. And then I'm ready for Philly Prep.

Mackenzie's shift didn't start for hours, so he selfishly made inviting morning sounds, sleepy, wistful moans and mewls. He attracted Macavity, the cat, who left his voyeur's post on the chair next to my bed and snuggled in, but I was made of nobler fiber, and I left, staggering into the bath-room.

When I emerged, sans stratospheric heart rate and morn-ing mouth, I dressed as serenely as is possible given that a delightfully rumpled alternative beckoned across the room. I felt jealous of my own cat, and wondered who cared whether I made it to school the day before vacation. Who was waiting desperately for his or her graded poetry paper? Why was I so determined to leave? Why not give a substitute a break— a real testing, the day before Christmas? The announcer pro-claimed the wind-chill factor, and that almost did it, except I had mentally uttered the word "Christmas," and that yanked back the night before and Laura. I had to talk with her.

I pulled on my moral cloak along with a boot and spoke sternly to Mackenzie, or myself. "No morning games. I have to leave."

"Shhh," he said.

"If our situation were reversed," I explained, "you wouldn't like it if I—"

He pointed at the radio. "Clausen."

"Another commercial?" I frowned.

Mackenzie shook his head, and the way he did it made my pulse skyrocket all over again.

"—flamboyant business style, then for his involvement in the city's welfare and development, a prominent philanthro-pist, the prime mover behind the massive Liberty Harbor project, and widely held to be the front-runner for the office of mayor, Mr. Clausen had hosted a Christmas party for over seventy needy Philadelphians in his home hours before his death. He was still in a Santa Claus costume.''

I sat down hard on the bed, still holding a boot. "What do they mean, 'still'? What happened?"

"A fire," Mackenzie said. "Clausen died in a fire."

Fire. I saw Santa's ruddy cheeks, white beard and red outfit, all charred.

"—cause of the conflagration remains undetermined and is held at this time to be accidental. However, officials stressed that the matter is still under investigation."

What did that mean? And what happened to the rest of the family? Alice Clausen—passed out somewhere? And Laura— had she left with Peter? I hoped she had—I hoped it desperately.

"Mr. Clausen's wife and daughter as well as a houseguest were alerted by a smoke alarm and escaped to safety."

I felt both relief and fear. Laura was safe. But she'd been in the house during the fire. Laura. Fire.

"Feelin' guilty, right?" Mackenzie yawned and stretched. "No cause, Mandy."

"I knew . . ."

The newscast droned on, listing Clausen's charitable works. If only he were still alive, he'd be ecstatic over the amount of airtime he was getting.

"What? What did you know?" He sat up straight and ran his fingers through his hair. "It's sad, that's all."

It was more than that. I got up and hobbled downstairs, one boot on, one stocking foot, to my stack of marked papers.

And there it was. "Instead of protecting his child," she had written, ". . . he sent him too close to the fire."

Icarus flew too close to the sun, Laura. Not to a fire. Why didn't you say it the way everybody else would? I stared at the phrase, at the paper, reading it for what I had always known it was—an indictment of more than Icarus' father, an indictment of all of us for not caring, not saving him. Or her.

I thought of her burn-scarred arm, of the stories about her, of other papers about destructive dreams. "Purgings," she'd called those fantasies. And "safe murders." And there'd been fire in them, images of burned zones and sooty remains, fire storms and wildfires. And she'd written about Joan of Arc, about a martyrdom that burned everything but the truth of her away. Of course, she'd also written innocuous papers, lyrical, soft, meditative and gentle papers, but right now, they seemed only rest notes, quiet spaces inside her true song.

"What're you doin'?" Mackenzie asked a few minutes later as he, too, came downstairs.

I bit my lip and said nothing, Laura's paper in one hand, my suede boot in the other.

"I don't think that composition's what they'll want from you," he said. "Fellow on the news says they're searchin' for a guest list. You have it?"

The guests! I hadn't thought of them. But then, why should I have? Why should the police? Except that it felt so good—almost wholesome compared to the alternatives. A stranger, an unknown, not a wide-eyed fourteen-year-old girl who looked twelve. And the guests hadn't comprised the most stable group. Muttering, frowning. Pulled in from the fringes for one night only—angry, perhaps? Envious, enraged? The man who'd wanted a free car had sounded close to the edge. And what about the spitting 'Nam vet? They were floaters, drifters, disenfranchised unknowns. Anyone of them could have had a secret agenda, could have wanted something badly enough to kill for it if refused. They might not even have known they wanted it until they saw it in Clausen's opulent house, heard it in Clausen's jolly laugh.

There were sixty-five possibilities. Strangers. I felt relieved.

Except that I had no idea who they were, and I told Mackenzie so.

He pointed his thumb up the stairs, to the radio. "Accordin' to one Dr. Maurice Havermeyer, it was your party."

"So I can cry if I want to? Damn. Why would they want the guest list, anyway?"

"That's not a real question, now, is it?" he said, almost

sadly. He took Laura's composition out of my hand. " 'Cept
we know the list isn't where they should look. Pity. A good
mind, all messed up.''

"Don't even think that."

"Radio just said there was a fire in that house last year."
He stretched the word fire into "fahr," somehow softer, more
bearable. "You know about that?" He didn't wait for my
answer. "Remember that paper you showed me about Joan
of Arc? How fire cleansed her?" He shook his head.

"Imaginative writing. You said so yourself. Besides, she
wrote others that were as ordinary as can be."

"And a big fight between the two of them at the party."
He was almost musing to himself. "Front of everybody.
Doesn't look too great."

"If you met her, knew anything about her, you'd know
she couldn't possibly—"

"I hope you're right. Listen, I know this hurts, Mandy,
that you care a lot about those kids, even if you won't always
admit it, and she's real special. Nevertheless, you have to
consider the possibility that—"

"She isn't the kind of person who'd—"

"You're a teacher, not a wizard. You can't save the world.
It's hard when somebody you're fond of—"

"Listen, Mackenzie, it was in the papers, that first . . .
lots of people knew about that other . . . about the . . ." I
couldn't say it.

"Fire?"

I nodded. "Anybody could have set her up."

"A motive would be nice. You suggestin' that one of the
homeless, sleeping in his newspaper found the story, got
himself invited to her house a year later and torched the
place?"

I felt ill. *Save me*, her eyes had begged. She'd let more of
herself show in her papers than was safe because she trusted
me. And I'd shown her secrets to a gentleman caller who
happened to be a homicide detective. I'd given him ammu-
nition with which he could now prejudge and damn her.

My sick guilt increased. Maybe I couldn't have stopped
anything from happening, but I could have taken some ac-

tion, called for help when I heard that silent scream. I could have tried to do something, and I hadn't. The most guilty sort of innocence—sitting on the sidelines.

I realized that although I denied Laura's possible guilt to Mackenzie, I was privately assuming it. Otherwise, why was I thinking about what I could have prevented?

"Another suggestion," Mackenzie said. "After you find that guest list, back off. Laura can make you sad, break your heart even, but the fact is, if she becomes police work, she doesn't concern you."

"Of course she concerns me! I'm very concerned!"

"I'm not playin' word games. I'm givin' you sound advice. She is not your job."

"I know what the *C* in your name stands for, Mackenzie. For callous. Or is it cruel? Or maybe creep!" I pulled on the other boot and stormed to the closet.

"Where you goin'?"

"To my job!"

Let him take that any way he liked.

Four

THE DAY BEFORE VACATION IS ALWAYS A BLACK HOLE EDU-cationally, so I couldn't blame its draggy disjointedness on the Clausen fire. In fact, the tragedy had been accepted with a level of indifference usually reserved for academic work. Sorrow and concern were expressed, but only for a moment. And then vacation plans took over and the classroom was all tropical isles or ski resorts.

Except for the eleven erstwhile waitpersons. They were like people who miss the plane that crashes. They told and retold the story of how little time had elapsed between their leave-taking and the conflagration and how they had almost decided to stay longer, might have been burned themselves.

Laura, of course, wasn't there to add her point of view. Nor was she at her house, which was no longer inhabitable. I was so informed by a semifriendly, semisuspicious policeman who was on duty when I called during lunch. The fire had not touched the phone lines, so I could also be informed that the police were doing their job and, frankly, that the world would be better served if I did mine. Mackenzie's message in a new mouth.

Peter Shaw was also absent, so I couldn't find out what had happened after I left. Which was probably lucky, because I wasn't sure on what grounds I could legitimately ask.

Maurice Havermeyer, Ph.D., was present, however, and

41

since he had told the press that I would produce the guest
list, he spent a great deal of his day trying to convince me of
the same, humphing and throat clearing and suggesting where
I might have placed it. I reminded him that I had had nothing
whatsoever to do with finding the attendees. I had never even
been told precisely how they were selected or from where.
Besides, what on earth would a list say? John Smith, grate
outside First Pennsylvania Bank? Molly Curtis, Baimbridge
Street, various doorways? I tried to express that concept in
patient, nonthreatening terms. I suggested that he tell the
press the truth—he had erred. Sandy Clausen, not I, made
up and kept the list, if there was one. But admitting fallibility
was not Maurice Havermeyer's strong point.

He looked discouraged. There was a reporter in his office,
asking about Laura's history of arson. This was not the kind
of media attention Havermeyer had intended.

"I got there late," I said. "Did someone check names at
the door?"

Maurice Havermeyer pantomimed deep thought. Obviously, he hadn't paid attention and didn't know, but he grap-
pled with how best not to say so. "I walked right in," he
finally managed.

"I'm sure there were some controls. The group looked
too handpicked, too fresh and clean and basically sane to be
a random street selection. I'm sure there's a list."

"I certainly hope it's found quickly." He scowled and
fiddled with the imitation Phi Beta Kappa key. "There are
reporters all over, rumors and speculation about one of our
own students, about our motives for the party, all in all, the
worst publicity this school has ever endured. This project,
this party of yours was supposed to be a pleasant expression
of the holiday spirit. How did you allow this to happen?"

The bell rang for the next class, thereby preventing me
from garnering additional unpleasant headlines by murdering my principal.

MIDAFTERNOON, DURING MY FREE PERIOD, I TRACKED DOWN
Mackenzie at the station and managed to have a phone dis-
pute. The school secretary, Helga the Witch, gleamed with

malicious delight at my strident, unhappy sounds. I kept my back turned and my words as cryptic as possible, but every time I peeked she was staring, unabashed, and smirking.

"Mackenzie here." A babble came out of the receiver. Shouts, calls, bedlam.

"It's Amanda. I was wondering. Is it your case now or—what is that noise? A riot? A jailbreak?" I flashed with fear—who would you call if the police were in trouble?

"Christmas party. You were sayin'?"

"Is it your case?"

"Which is 'it'?"

"You know very well which one."

"Oh. The *fahr*. It's not in this department. Yet. This is homicide."

"It isn't one, then?" I felt enormous relief. Of course the fire was an accident. Of course Laura was innocent—but all the same, nice not to have to prove it.

"Don't know yet."

"But you have no connection with it, right?"

"Not at the moment."

"Then don't do anything. You weren't supposed to see those compositions, have any special knowledge about anybody."

"But I did see them." The cop party sounded as if it were going to have to be broken up by citizens' arrests.

"Only because I was indiscreet."

"What?"

"I was indiscreet!" Helga's prurient-interest meter went off the chart. I hunched over the receiver. "You didn't take a vow to tell everything even when you don't know if what you know means anything." The ruckus in the receiver was overpowering.

"What's it mean—'dake a cow?' Sounds unsavory. You sure I do it?"

"Take a vow, not dake a cow!" I zoomed around and yes, her hooded eyes were wide open and very interested. "Don't say anything!" I shouted into the phone. "Don't *tell* them! Don't theorize!" The roar of manly chaos was taking over, a tidal wave of sound. "You have no moral responsibility."

Let Helga have a heyday with vows, moral responsibility and indiscretion.

He slurred something. It didn't seem worth asking for a translation. But I did ask if I'd see him later. It was, after all, soon to be Friday night. As in Thank God It's.

He produced one of his noncommittal, frustrating and infuriating answers, the verbal equivalent of his shrug. I know he can't predict his hours. I know that the first forty-eight hours after a crime are the most important and that Mackenzie and Company will work nonstop as long as they can and that it's for the common good, et cetera. I know all that and it still annoys me. Especially on a weekend night. And my annoyance annoys Mackenzie.

"Never mind," I muttered.

"How's that?"

Useless. First the Philadelphia Police Force would carouse on my tax dollars, and then Mackenzie would work late. I hung up.

Bah. Humbug.

MY LAST PERIOD CLASS BEHAVED LIKE POWs SIGHTING THE armies of liberation, and Havermeyer had forbidden early dismissals. By the time we were all released, I felt bruised, inside and out.

At home, I realized I'd stormed off without feeding the cat that morning, and I apologized profusely while I fumbled through the catfood cans and Macavity strolled, purring, to his dish. "Yummy giblets," I murmured, and then I saw a note propped against the can opener. "I fed the feline. Don't let the little glutton bamboozle you."

Life is really bleak when your own pet tries to rip you off. I put the catfood away, downed aspirin and made herbal tea that promised serenity. Then I sulked unserenely on a tall stool at the kitchen counter.

The cat settled in silky contentment on my lap as I flipped through late catalogues, cards from businesses and a manila envelope from Silverwood. I peeked inside and found a mimeographed collection of stories called *Mining Silver*. Some of the women who'd been in my Rediscovering the Classics class had also been in the Tuesday Creative Writing class, and they'd asked me, shyly, if they could send me their "book." I put it aside for another time, wrote out two greeting cards and stalled on the third.

"I ask you, Macavity," I said. "Is it worse to mail factory-signed, computer-labeled completely impersonal greeting cards or *mean* to send cards with wonderful, personal messages, but never complete them?"

Instead of answering, he began worrying the top of my stack of unmailed missives, tapping gently, experimentally, until the top card slid off. Satisfied, he began on the next card down. Tap, tap, a furry scientist conducting an experiment. "But why," I asked, "must I arbitrarily use this particular New Year's, after all?" I decided to choose another New Year's as a deadline. The Russian Orthodox was too soon. Maybe the Chinese? Or the Jewish—that gave me till next autumn.

I finally remembered to listen to my phone messages. Mackenzie said he'd call later if possible. That he was glad to see that I had mastered the machine. That he was pretty tied up, so maybe tomorrow. Or late tonight. But I shouldn't count on anything.

Live or on tape, the man said the same damn thing.

"Miss Pepper? This is Jenny Crittendon? From Silverwood?" The Pillsbury Dough Grandma's voice sounded sixty years younger than she was. "We're so upset because we forgot to invite you to the Tuesday group's holiday party. It's this coming Tuesday—of course!" She giggled. "The day after Christmas. Cookies at one. And we thought, since you're on vacation this week, maybe you could be part of our daytime group this one time? We'd *really* like you to come. *Really.* Please? Oh, I hope this isn't too late. They'll be so mad. I was supposed to ask you last week! We all hope to see you. Tuesday. One o'clock. In the dayroom. Oh, and we sent you that copy of our stories and we hope it doesn't get lost in the Christmas rush and we all hope you enjoy them." She sounded out of breath by the end.

There was certain disadvantages to a machine, I now knew. If I had never gotten the message from Jenny Crittendon, then I wouldn't feel uneasy about an invitation I hadn't sought and wasn't overly excited about. I liked those people, certainly, but I'd be busy getting ready for Florida next Tuesday and Silverwood was across the city. I wished I hadn't heard how eager Jenny sounded, and I wished I wasn't now wondering about how her Christmas was going to be with her children two thousand miles away. Minna White was in that class, too, and I wondered if the dreadful Junior would visit her or whether Tuesday's party was going to be the event of the season for lots of the people at Silverwood.

The tape continued. "What's this? A machine?" My mother's feelings were audibly hurt. "I called to see how your party went, but . . . well, a machine! This feels like talking to myself. So, ah, good-bye." Pause. "Oh, yes. This was your mother. Beatrice Pepper. And oh! You wanted the time, right? It's—it's—Amanda, I don't have my glasses on and I don't know where they are, and my watch is—why do I have to tell you the time, anyway? I taught you how to tell it yourself twenty-five years ago. Call me."

I was so bemused by my mother that the next message almost escaped me. I ran the tape back and listened again. "Miss Pepper?" It took a second to realize it was Laura Clausen. We had spoken so infrequently, and on those few occasions I had prompted and begun the conversation. Laura sounded as surprised as she sounded timid. "The police— they said you called my house? I'm at my aunt's in the city because—well, you know, the house is . . . and I'll . . ." I could hear her breathe, could almost hear her deciding what she wanted to say. "I guess you're still at school, so I'll call again. Tomorrow, because I have to go out now." Silence. Then, "Uh, good-bye," and a click.

No number to call. I had planned to be out all the next day, doing a blitz of just-under-the-wire Christmas shopping, but if I were gone, Laura and I might never connect. I wasn't going to ignore her signals for help ever again.

My feet and head both still hurt, but I hauled myself up and pulled the boots back on. With Mackenzie detecting elsewhere, I had a long Friday afternoon and evening ahead to get my shopping out of the way so that I could wait for Laura's call tomorrow. Maybe I'd finish my Christmas cards.

I wandered toward Wanamaker's men's department. The big shopping problem was, of course, none else than Mackenzie. It was important to find the absolutely right gift for our first Christmas. Something loving—but not so intensely so that it produced a fight-or-flight response. Something that meant a great deal—but not *too* much. Something much more in focus than we were.

My headache increased in the damp wind, but through its little lightning strikes of pain flipped a mental catalogue of menswear. Men's gift options were limited, expensive and subtle. What's the male equivalent of good, but noncommital costume jewelry? C.K. wasn't of the gold chain, pinky ring or cuff links variety, and tie clips didn't say much.

He had a good wallet. He didn't wear cologne.

All dress shirts look alike, and didn't you have to measure arms and necks, anyway?

Belts, braces, socks, even cashmere; handkerchiefs, even of the finest weave, were impossibly boring—or overpriced.

Men's games were an obvious choice. Things that clicked, whirred, shifted gears and went from zero to a thousand in a second. Prizes for the testosterone set. And out of my price range.

Robes were nice, but his mother gave him one every year. He didn't wear pajamas.

Ties were the ultimate cartoon-strip gift. Besides, every man I've known fixates on one pattern—paisleys, amoebas at play, tiny ducks. Mackenzie was a stripe man. Debating green stripes vs. blue seemed a major nonevent and surely receiving the final choice would be the same.

I found a cable-knit sweater the color of his eyes, but it cost too much. I touched it, loved it, imagined it warming and cozying his flesh, and it still cost too much. If only I had learned to knit like everybody else.

When I found myself fondling a soap-on-a-rope, I knew I needed a break.

I felt better as soon as I left the land of slacks and socks and was surrounded by the soaring central court, nine stories of gilded columns, and shoppers who looked much less impatient and discouraged than I. There was something permanent and comforting in the old, space-wasting, extravagant architecture. It gave a benediction to shopping as did the rich Bach cantata that poured out of the massive pipe organ, flooding the court and sanctifying our purchases.

I gravitated toward the enormous bronze eagle, the city's designated meeting place.

And bumped, literally, into a very startled Laura Clausen.

"I'm sorry!" she said after a moment. "I didn't see you. I was . . . thinking."

We stood there awkwardly. I, too, apologized for not paying attention, then finally asked a potentially rude but real question. "Are you . . . shopping?" I didn't expect her to rend her clothes or keen, but still, it seemed odd to be in John Wanamaker's less than twenty-four hours after her father was incinerated.

"No." Her voice was tiny and fearful, and I was sorry I'd asked. "My mother—I had to walk her to the doctor." She looked at her watch. "She'll be a while, so I came here." She shrugged. "Sometimes I think better when there are lots of people I don't know around." I saw a flicker of the *Save me* terror, and then it disappeared.

"I got your message," I said. "I'm not in any rush."

She shrugged again. Here she was in the heart of the great emporium, completely out of style in her baggy Doris Day good-girl togs. The essence of innocence, and so small. She was delicately made, fragile, peering out of enormous dark eyes with such intensity that I felt guilty for all I didn't know or have to offer.

"I called you back a few minutes ago," she said, "to say never mind. That first message, well, it was just a mood. Now I'm okay."

She definitely wasn't. "Then how about a soda, or coffee?" I said.

She checked her watch again, and reluctantly agreed.

I'M SORRY ABOUT YOUR FATHER." WE WERE ACROSS THE street, on stools at Woolworth's. I love the aroma of five-

and-dimes—pressed powder, hot-dog casings, goldfish and laminated menus.

Laura acknowledged my condolences with a twist of her mouth. She had a milk shake. I had black coffee. Saving calories for the madcap whirl of holiday parties the magazines promised me.

Laura seemed engrossed in tracing lines down the side of her water glass.

I leaped in, both feet first. "Laura, maybe this is a dumb time for it, but I wanted to talk about your paper. About Icarus—about Auden's poem."

She did a sequence of softly spastic body motions that seemed to translate into: Yeah, great, who cares, so what?

"It . . . troubled me," I said. "There's a great tension, a—"

"It isn't good?"

"It's marvelous. Exceptional. The best in the class."

She looked relieved, then slumped over her milk-shake straw.

I spoke slowly, picking my way carefully between the words. "But I had the feeling you were talking about more than Icarus."

She sipped. "I'd better go," she murmured.

I looked at my watch. Five thirty-five. I took a chance. I was sure it was the sort of doctor's appointment that has a set time. Like a fifty-minute hour. "Doesn't she have fifteen more minutes?"

Laura pursed her lips.

"I don't mean to make you uncomfortable," I said. "But sometimes it helps to talk to someone."

Deep in my brain, I heard a voice from the past. "You're their teacher," my department chair had said the first day I arrived at Philly Prep. "Not their friend, not their pal, not their psychiatrist. You won't serve them well if you ever forget that." I still didn't know if you could so neatly slice up the many roles of a teacher, but I knew I had been treading out of bounds, so I backed off. We would share a fifteen-minute respite, then go our separate ways.

"I'll talk to my mother's shrink." She sounded defiant

and frightened. "He'd like my dreams, wouldn't he? You've seen them. The safe murders. The fires. He'd eat them up."

So much for proper professional reserve. Laura was being deliberately provocative, obviously in need of a reaction. "You still have those dreams?"

"I think so."

I busied myself with a second cup of coffee, stirring in sweetener, and I made what I hoped was a wordless but sympathetic and encouraging sound.

"I'm not always sure if I'm asleep." She sounded in a dream state at the moment. "So are they dreams, or what?"

"Everybody has daydreams." But of course, that wasn't what she was talking about. She was talking about wide-eyed nightmares. Insanity.

She picked up her purse and stood.

"Laura—where can I reach you? We could talk more. I'm not trying to be your psychiatrist. I just want you to understand that you aren't out there alone."

She stood behind the row of stools, staring down at a ring she wore. It had a tiny blue stone. She twirled it around and around her finger. "I did it, you know." She was barely audible.

No. I won't listen. I refuse to hear.

"It wasn't an accident. I killed him. I'm not sorry, either."

My mouth pursed, and a soft windy noise came out, but no words.

"The other time, they say it was an accident, but it wasn't. I let it burn."

"What happened last night is terrible, very sad, but why think you had anything . . ." She was pulling further and further inside herself. And yet she stood there, testing whether I'd follow her lead.

"Why?" I asked again. "What do you think you did?"

I hadn't followed her lead at all. Instead, I'd taken the wrong path through the maze and dead-ended. She shook her head. "Doesn't matter."

I thought about Daedalus and Icarus. "Then tell me," I said. "Who is Daedalus? What did he do to you?" In the silence that followed my question, I became aware of the impossible contradictions between our conversation and our surroundings. We were talking about a possible murder while a nasal voice on the loudspeaker announced a special on artificial snow.

Laura turned away. I paid the bill and followed her through tinsel-edged aisles. She paused in cosmetics, oddly trans-fixed. I remembered how soothing, how promising Wool-worth's nail-polish display had been to me in my teens, symbolizing the infinite possibilities of womanhood and promising that with the right lacquer came the right life. But I had never been grappling with Laura's kind of problems.

"Maybe you had one of those dreams," I said.

She shook her head. "He's dead, isn't he?" She examined a shrieking red bottle. Her own nails were unpolished.

"What's your aunt's name?"

"Alma." She held fluorescent purple polish to the light, as if it were a gemstone.

"Alma Clausen?"

"Leary. My mom's sister." She was so small and frail. "My dad doesn't—didn't—have any relatives. Except for me, I guess. Lot of good it did him."

"It was an accident!" I insisted. "Why even think you had a part in it? It's not in you—it's not who you are!"

"Of course it is," she said. "Everybody knows how I am. He certainly did. I wanted to do it. I thought about it all the time. And I did it. That's how I am." She looked at her watch again. "I have to go. My mom—she's pretty wobbly." She put down the polish and walked out of the store.

I hurried behind, then walked beside her. Tiny strings of lights glimmered against the branches of the trees on Broad Street. They reminded me of last night, of the lights along the river, of the twinkling candles all over Clausen's house. "Laura—why did you call me today?"

"I was going to tell you before the police. I don't know why. Then it seemed dumb. I changed my mind, but look how it turned out—I told you anyway. Things I imagine have a way of happening for real, like I said." Her nose and cheeks were ruddy with the cold.

"Please," I said. "Don't tell anybody else. There is no reason, nothing to be gained from it. Tell your mother's doctor if you have to talk about it. I think you're hysterical, Laura, or feeling guilty about the quarrel last night, or feelings you've had. Accidents happen, and they remain accidents even if you imagined them, or thought about them. Don't put yourself in jeopardy. Please?"

She looked puzzled. She also looked exhausted. We paused at the corner near a thin Salvation Army Santa ringing his bell. "She's in there," she said.

I had to negotiate further. "Before you say anything to anyone official, call me. Talk to Detective Mackenzie."

She shook her head. "Who's that?"

I did some calculations. Mackenzie's investigations at Philly Prep had been eight months ago, in April, before Laura enrolled. Longer ago than I realized until this moment. A long time to tread water with a man. I shelved that thought for another, more appropriate, time. "A good friend. He could advise you how to proceed. Okay? Promise?"

She nodded. Not because of my persuasiveness, I was sure. Not because of her own common sense or natural self-protectiveness. She was simply too tired to do anything but agree and go retrieve her mother.

I hadn't gotten a single thing on this expedition except Laura's dubious promise, but I had no energy left to find anything beyond my way home.

I LISTENED TO MY MESSAGES WHILE I HEATED SOUP, AND Macavity, not sure if something he considered delicious might be brewing, hugged my ankles like fur leg warmers. First I heard Laura's retraction, the one she'd mentioned.

Then Mackenzie. "Doesn't look good for tonight," he said. "There's a new lead." He did not sound thrilled. "Probably as useless as the last few thousand." He'd been working on a particularly revolting homicide involving a John Doe found, bit by bit, in several dumpsters in Oak Lane. I heard him sigh slowly, with feeling. Well, a night alone avoided further ethical dilemmas. I didn't want to talk about whether Laura was an arsonist, whether her compositions meant anything, what she had told me today. By tomorrow, it would all be over, declared an unfortunate accident, and we'd all live happily ever after.

"And a postscript," he said. "An update for your ears only. We are trying to keep it out of the news for a while." I wished I hadn't learned to work the machine, because I was suddenly sure I didn't want to hear what came next. "There's no ash in Clausen's throat."

I turned off the burner and left my soup. Macavity stalked back to his own dinner.

"Which means he wasn't breathin' by the time of the fire. So it wasn't a cigarette killed him, which is good news for the tobacco lobby." He took a deep breath and then continued. "Unfortunately, not so good for us. Tests bein' as slow as they are, compounded by holiday schedules, and such, we're gonna have a while to ponder the little but nagging question of what, and who, did in Santa."

Five

SATURDAY WAS THE SORT OF MORNING THAT MAKES ME WISH I could paint, or at least be in a better mood. Knife-edged winter light slanted across the living room and lit it from within. I tried to warm myself in a beam, but I still felt chilly and gray.

Alexander Clausen had probably been murdered. Unless he had a conveniently timed heart attack while smoking, pulled down the Christmas tree, ran to the sofa and died before the cigarette ignited the boughs—he was murdered.

Laura Clausen insisted she had murdered him.

I was pretty sure that I alone knew both these things. What I didn't know was what to do about them.

So I took up residence in that shaft of sunlight and drank coffee, giving inspiration time to reach me. Three cups later, I was wired, but the caffeine connections sputtered and failed before reaching my brain. I had no idea what to do. I needed a second opinion. More accurately, I needed a first.

Sasha's answering-machine message was infuriating. "I'm off doing something so marvelous," she said, "it would make you sick with jealousy to hear about it, so don't even ask. Instead, leave your—"

I hung up. Just as well. Sasha is empathetic, quirky and bright, but apt to sacrifice discretion for the sake of a good story.

54

I didn't have anyone to tell. I was alone with my questions and caffeinated bloodstream.

So I housecleaned. Cleanliness is not next to godliness in my book. It is, in fact, way down below world peace and brotherhood, lagging behind courtesy and compassion. And trailing even small civilities. But while cleaning was not an inspired option, it was virtuous and full of motion and purpose. I could fool myself that I was getting somewhere as I pulled furniture away from walls, books off shelves, cans out of kitchen cabinets and impressive mold growths off refrigerator containers.

But disposing of sprouted carrots and dust bunnies couldn't help Laura. I needed to talk to her.

I looked up Aunt Alma. There were enough Learys to populate a hamlet, but none were Alma. No initial A. either, that feminine disguise which is about as protective and as transparent as the emperor's new clothes. I wondered if C.K. Mackenzie got lots of phone calls from heavy breathers and peddlers of obscene dreams.

I was determined to find Laura, so I began Leary-dialing. One after another. Alphabetically. The Learys, I learned, were a mixed group. There were cordial Learys, snarling Learys, Learys who were out promptly on this last Saturday before Christmas and slugabed Learys who were not overjoyed by my wake-up call.

Midway through the alphabet, I found an amused Leary. "Alma?" Kevin Leary asked. "She's Zack's wife, not mine. Who's this?"

"Amanda Pepper, and I'm trying to reach—"

"Amanda. Amanda. Slips my mind where we met."

"Actually, you—" My finger ran down the list of Learys until it found Zachary.

"But how could you confuse us? Zack's hair is much thinner, didn't you notice?" He chuckled again. "After all," he said, with the pacing of a man fondling a favorite threadbare joke, "I'm the baby. Zack's three minutes older, and it shows."

My turn to laugh politely. I wasn't sure how many other twin jokes he had in waiting. I spoke quickly, confirming the number I saw in the directory, thanked him profusely and sincerely, because getting to the Z's on my own would have meant another hour and lots more snarls.

Alma Leary sounded both protective and suspicious when she told me that Laura was out, taking one of her walks. "You're her teacher?" she said. It provoked a rush of words in the background, a "just a second," from Alma and the transfer of the receiver.

"Miss Pepper?" She was out of breath. "This is Alice Clausen. Laura said she—I guess she told you where we were—she isn't here now. Is there a problem?"

Her husband was dead. Her daughter was convinced she herself had done him in. Alice and her daughter were homeless.

Was there a problem?

Before I could respond, she heard the echo of her own words. "I mean," she said, still sounding like someone who'd just finished a marathon, "besides the . . . the problem."

"I wanted to offer condolences and to see how you and Laura are doing. This is such a terrible time for you both." I was afraid to say much, unsure whether Alice Clausen knew of her daughter's homicidal claims.

"Yes," she agreed, panting. Either she was jogging in place or dangerously anxious. "I'm sorry she isn't . . . I . . ." She left an auditory parenthesis that needed filling.

"Mrs. Clausen, is there anything I could—"

"Alice," she said.

I wasn't interested in the nuances of social address at the moment. However, I started over. "Alice, I'm concerned. Can I be of any—"

"Would it be out of line—could I possibly . . ."

"Ummmm?"

"Could we—could we talk? In person? Would it be too much of a—you were so kind Parents' Night, at school." All that I remembered of her visit were her repeated apologies for her husband's being out of town. "Is that—would that be—am I being—"

"That'd be fine. Is today good for you?"

We settled not only on today, but immediately. She was five blocks away.

I pushed cans back into cabinets and the sofa back against the wall, flicking dust rags and racing in circles with the vacuum, making fun of myself all the while. Alice Clausen was not arriving with white gloves to inspect the premises. She was not a woman who saw clearly half the time, anyway. Still and all, I tidied and made nice. My mother would be proud.

My mother! I had to return her call. But as I remembered that, my own caller arrived.

Alice Clausen was so glazed, my furniture could have been upside down and she probably wouldn't have noticed. I was surprised she'd found the house. I helped her in, took her mink coat, scarf, hat and gloves, one by one as she remembered and located them, led her to the sofa, poured coffee for both of us and settled across from her in the suede chair. She had classic good looks—fine, quiet features, a delicate frame and straight pale blond hair. Still, as she sat facing me, she looked like a life-sized sculpture. Almost human. Almost alive.

I put on a tape of Vivaldi's *Four Seasons* because I believe that baroque music induces sanity.

I cleared my throat. Recrossed my legs. Asked if she wanted another cup of coffee, then realized she hadn't touched the one in front of her.

"How about a fire?" I regretted the words as soon as they were out of my mouth. Nonetheless, they represented action, a project and more heat, so even though she didn't visibly react, I fixed the logs and lit them.

Then I waited for a lead. Eventually, I began to fear that we would sit silently through the new year. "You wanted to talk," I reminded her gently.

She blinked, inhaled, then slowly deflated as the air escaped.

I smiled encouragingly.

"Laura told you," she finally said. Her eyes filled. She clenched her hands. "I know she did."

I admitted nothing. I didn't know what the mother-daughter relationship was, aside from the sorry scene at the Christmas party. Perhaps this was the person who had convinced Laura that she was innately bad. I waited for the point.

"Have you told anyone else?" she gasped out, and when I shook my head, her relief was overwhelming. "Because she—she gets confused." Her breathing eased, some anxiety dissipating. "Sometimes she isn't sure if she dreamed something or imagined it or did it." Her eyes were large and dark gold, the color of good Scotch whisky, but rimmed in red. "I thought she needed help about that, somebody to talk to, a professional, but Alexander . . ." She slumped into silence.

Her brief burst of energy seemed over. "She's never seen anyone?" I asked.

She shook her head. "I thought when she ran away, or after the fire—the first one . . . But he wouldn't, he—it was an accident. She didn't mean to, but she was so upset, all the time . . ." The first fire. I had tried to forget Laura's history as a suspected arsonist.

I went in search of tissues.

"And I was . . ." She still faced my chair as if unaware that I had vacated it. "I didn't . . . .I knew something wasn't right. She was such a bright, happy child and then . . ." She accepted a tissue and blew her nose. I settled back in.

"Prying quacks, he called them. Thought it was shameful, getting that kind of help. He'd even get angry at television shows if they had psychiatrists helping people. Turned them right off."

The doctor's appointment the day before had probably been Alice's first session with a psychiatrist. Alexander had to die before she could start to heal. Maybe she'd come calling for both my silence about Laura and validation of her seeking therapy. "Your husband was wrong," I said. "It's smart and important to get help."

Who was I to put the stamp of approval on anything, and who was she to look so grateful and surprised when I did so? It was becoming obvious that Santa Claus had preferred to walk all over his family instead of his lush carpets. Both Laura and Alice were almost mashed flat.

"To be honest . . . I have a . . . little problem," she said.

I nodded, not agreeing, not implying that I was aware of her problem and that it didn't seem little to me. Obviously, she had no memory of the night of the "lorvely parny," or of pitching into me. Nor had she been in any condition to notice, as I had, how unsurprised Laura was to see her mother pass out.

"I have . . . bursitis," she said.

I had never heard it called that before.

"And it hurts, so sometimes—even the doctor said a drink could help. But sometimes it doesn't, it takes more, and I . . ." She studied her hands. She had long fingers and beautifully manicured nails. "Bad nerves, too. I can't get steady. It isn't all my fault. I wanted to be a good mother."

I was trying hard to fill in the gaps between her visit, Laura's confession, bursitis and her effectiveness as a parent.

"Sometimes I wasn't . . ."

I settled back, hands folded across my midriff as if I were Dr. Freud until I remembered that my turf was dangling participles, not exposed ids and mangled egos. Even if I figured out what she was saying, I had no idea what to do with her revelations.

"I didn't *listen*," Alice Clausen said. "I didn't—"

I interrupted. "Nobody can listen all the time. Every mother thinks she could have done more. Don't be so hard on yourself."

"I turned away. My shoulder hurt. I didn't listen."

"You know, that idea of talking to a trained professional is a good one. I think somebody like that could be very helpful." I left my shoes on the floor and curled my bare feet under me as a reminder that I was very untrained and barely professional.

"Should I tell him, then?" she asked.

"Tell who?"

"Because if I don't, maybe it'll be listed as an accident. Why not? Why shouldn't it be? Would it matter?"

I tilted my head, hoping for a clearer view of what was going on.

"If I told him, would he keep it secret? Is that how that works? I'm afraid to ask him."

My neck would only stretch so far, and even sideways, she wasn't making sense.

"But if Laura rushes to the police, even to your friend, I'd have to do something."

"Mrs. Clausen?"

"Alice."

I took a deep breath. "Alice, what are you saying?"

"I have to *do* something!" She was suddenly agitated. Her expensively kept hands flapped like rags in a strong wind. "I never do anything! I never *listen*!" She stood up, a reedy woman trembling in the winter light. "She protects *me*!"

I, too, stood up, at the ready, even though I wasn't sure what was coming. What would I do if the woman had a psychotic break? My only medical knowledge was first aide and whatever was the residuum of a long-lost summer fling with a medical student. My pulse accelerated as I followed her. She looped around the room, bumping into furniture, hands flailing. I moved a pot of dried flowers to the center of the coffee table, put our coffee cups out of danger in the sink, and picked up the still-unread sections of last Sunday's *New York Times*, which she'd bumped onto the floor. She paced and I followed. "I *have* to!" she said abruptly.

I stopped her, put my hands on her shoulders and spoke calmly. "What do you have to do?"

She gave an exhausted sigh. "Tell them, of course."

"Tell who?"

"The police."

"No, wait. We agreed that we wouldn't say anything to them yet."

"Laura isn't supposed to. I have to."

"Why? What do you have to tell them?"

She looked surprised I'd ask. "That I did it," she said. "I murdered my husband. Finally."

I lowered my hands and sat down abruptly. I didn't believe

her, but then I hadn't believed Laura, and I believed even less that Santa held his breath until he died.

"Laura is so used to *covering* for me, that she'll say she did it. And they'll believe her, because of . . ." She perched uncomfortably, tentatively on the arm of my mother's old sofa, as if she might take flight any moment. "Because there was that . . ."

"Other fire?" When she nodded, I continued. "But you said it was an accident. In fact, I thought both fires were."

She examined her manicure.

"Well, for the sake of conversation, then, how did you, ah, do it?" The room temperature plummeted forty or fifty degrees. I put another log on the fire, but it made no difference.

"I don't remember," she finally whispered. "I was . . . having a bad night. I was upstairs, asleep, hating him, and then I was downstairs, so angry, and he was dead and I was glad." She studied her nail polish again. "Sometimes I . . . don't remember. Even when I'm awake. It happens."

"Maybe you woke up, went down and found him already dead? And you were sleepy and confused, so you thought you had done something?"

She shook her head.

"But the news said you were asleep when the fire started. I assumed—a smoke alarm woke you up, didn't it?"

"I don't think so."

"Did you and your husband quarrel?"

She shook her head.

"So for no particular reason, you—"

"I had reasons."

"Such as?"

"You think he's so nice. Everybody thinks he's so nice." She looked at me darkly. "He was evil."

"How? In what way?"

"I don't want to talk about it."

"So you woke up, went downstairs and—did what?" I made a deal with myself. If Alice Clausen mentioned fireplace pokers or baseball bats or poison or knives or any weapon, if she screamed until he had a heart attack—

anything that would have made her husband die before the fire, then I'd contact Mackenzie immediately. If, instead, she said she put a match to him like kindling, I'd maintain my skepticism and silence. "What did you do?"

"I don't want to talk about it."

"But the police will want to know."

She shrugged.

I changed course. "If what you're saying is true—"

"It is!"

"Then why is Laura saying that she—"

"I told you! To protect me!" The arms windmilled. "You don't understand how it was! You don't understand anything!"

She was right on the mark. Not only that, but with unrepentant, wobbly confessions from both wife and daughter, I wasn't overeager ever to understand how it had been.

"Still and all," I said, "there's no need to talk to the police yet, is there?"

"What if she does, though?"

"Laura?"

Alice Clausen nodded woefully.

I slumped into a lethargic and heavy confusion. Alice perched like a nervous bird on the arm of the sofa, and we'd probably still be in those positions if the telephone hadn't rung, breaking the spell.

It was Mackenzie. "Mandy?" I knew from his tone this wasn't going to be an invitation to party.

"You're still at work?" Maybe the thirty-six-hour shifts of medical residents are necessary, but why should homicide detectives work that way? After all, their clients are already dead.

"Again, not still. Actually, I'm supposed to be home sleepin'. I'm on four to twelve. Didn't I tell you? I juggled it around so we'll have Christmas Eve and Day. Didn't I give you my schedule?"

"Schedule? You have one? I thought you were indentured." He didn't chuckle.

"Maybe real late?" But he was yawning by midsentence, so there went Saturday night.

"What you doin'?" he asked.

I was doing finger exercises on the scales of justice, but I saw no need to tell him.

"Remember that Clausen business?" he asked, idiotically. How could I forget it—even if its players hadn't been rushing to confess to me? "Surprisin' thing happened about it just now. A boy, Peter Shaw, called."

"About . . . that?" I didn't want Alice to go on alert.

"You sound weird. Is somebody there with you?"

"Uh-huh," I said, relieved.

Mackenzie's voice grew cold. "Didn't realize you were entertaining. Sorry to interrupt. Get back to your guest."

"Oh, for the love of—" I gave him three more seconds to fantasize my romantic suitor, and then I opted for honesty. "Alice Clausen's here."

With no sound of grinding gears, Mackenzie switched suspicions. "Why?" he demanded.

"For a chat."

"Sure." He grew silent, ruminating, meditating, speculating.

"You called because . . . ?"

"Peter. Says he got my name from you. You talk to him?"

"No. But the kids at school remember you from last spring. Besides, nothing about a teacher's private life escapes them."

"He hasn't spoken to you about this?"

"I haven't seen him since . . . that night. Why'd he call?"

"You know him, though?" Mackenzie, unlike me, gets the answers he wants.

"Taught him two years ago, if that counts."

"What was he like?"

"Then? Going through a rough period. Punky, arrogant. Acting out."

"You think he's violent?"

I took a deep breath. He had been. Definitely. Also provoked. His father had been an alcoholic who beat up his wife. Peter had intervened, attacked him back, and the father had pressed charges, trying to have Peter institutionalized. Ugly, stupid case that was eventually dropped when the mother filed for divorce. I knew of no further incidents. I chose my words carefully. "He went through a bad time, but it's long since over. He looks scary with the hair and the muscles and the black clothing, but it's all adolescent show. Why did he call you?"

"Said he heard I was an okay guy, so he picked me. I thought for a while he was asking me out on a date."

"Picked you for what?"

"I told him it wasn't my case, but he didn't care. He was on his way over and he wanted me. Flattering, I guess."

"Wanted you for what?"

"To wrap things up with this Clausen business. The kid says he had a fight with Alexander Clausen. Says he killed him. And says he's not one damned bit sorry."

Six

MAYBE CONFESSING HAD BECOME TRENDY. I'D HAVE TO ASK my mother.

What bothered me most was that while everybody seemed ready to be named a murderer, not one of them even mentioned remorse or sorrow about the act. In fact, they seemed chilly and proud of having done the deed.

That made it sound like a group effort, but nobody claimed membership in a club. Not a one of the trio had spoken of collusion or cooperation. Each had acted alone, yet nobody is killed three times.

Either one had done it and two were lying, or all three were guilty of conspiracy and were playing with the truth. Or, and this was my theory of choice because I wanted it so, all three were innocent, lying for reasons I didn't yet know.

I wondered if anyone had found the missing guest list, or if anyone would even care about doing so now that Peter had confessed.

Alice Clausen sighed jaggedly, startling me. There was something pathetically forgettable about her, a sense that she hadn't made much of an impression even on herself. "That was your policeman friend, wasn't it?" she asked anxiously. "What's happened?" She cringed in anticipation of my answer.

"I'm not sure." That was the truth, pretty much. Besides,

if Alice was confessing to protect Laura, she might react to news of Peter's confession by retracting her own. Or, worse—if Alice was confessing because she honestly did her husband in—would Peter's confession let her remain in unpunished, guilty silence?

I didn't know what to tell her and, more importantly, I didn't know what I should have told or should now tell Mackenzie. I had made a few side steps, for good reasons, and now my feet were so pretzel-twisted I couldn't move without falling.

"Did Laura?" Alice Clausen asked. "Tell me. Did she tell him? She promised she wouldn't, or I wouldn't have let her out, but . . . that's why he called, isn't it?"

"He didn't even mention Laura."

She looked at me suspiciously, then stood up. "Laura's probably back at Alma's. It's too cold to keep walking this long. And Alma's so busy with Christmas and then they're going to Antigua, and we're in their way and . . ." She began to cry again.

I located the tissue box, patted and clucked sympathetically.

"And of course there's the funeral . . ." She blew her nose. "If they ever finish those things, those tests they do." She paused, and I could almost hear her gears shift again. "It's so *hard*!" She shuddered. "Alexander took care of things, not me!"

A part of me registered, with distaste, that she was blindered, drugged, dependent and willingly ineffectual. Not my image of womanhood. But another slice of my consciousness knew that I should stop ticking off a list of character flaws. They weren't a person. Alice Clausen was, and after watching her synapses wave idly like sea anemones, connecting only by chance, I knew she needed help. And quickly. She was out on an emotional ledge, one foot poised for a dive unless somebody skilled talked her down.

I wasn't that person, but I could try coddling and the little psychological first aid that I did know. "Let me walk you back to your sister's," I said. Once she was settled, I would do my Christmas shopping in one wildly efficient swoop. I thought about the wind-chill factor and the Alice-induced ten-block detour, but realized that aside from humanitarian considerations, I also had no choice on a pragmatic level. If I didn't help the woman on to her next destination, she'd sit in my living room until she became a nervous fixture, something to be fed and maintained along with the cat.

Alice Clausen looked grateful, embarrassed and suspicious. "I can't let you . . ." she said. "It's out of your way. You mustn't . . ." I waited, but she didn't finish it.

So I armored myself against the great outdoors in Sherpa chic—boots, an extra sweater, coat, scarf, hat and gloves—until I could barely move.

Macavity, the original, definitive "house cat," jumped onto the sill, verified that the panes were still frosted and returned to the hearth. Smart cat.

Alice layered slowly, pausing in indecision and puzzlement before each new garment. I waited, thick of limb and fat fingered, temperature rising so rapidly that I began longing for the frozen tundra outside.

The telephone rang. Of course. And of course I had forgotten to switch on the machine. "Ignore it," I announced from behind my muffler.

"It could be Laura," Alice said. "She worries about me." She tried to look perturbed by the idea, but it was a pose. Alice Clausen adored her own helplessness.

A mental picture of Laura, undersized in baggy clothing, listing dangerously under the weight of her mother's leaning made me ache.

The phone rang for the fourth time. Alice Clausen begged with her eyes.

I pulled off one fur-lined glove and picked up the receiver.

"Mandy Pepper? Nick Riley." I recognized neither the voice nor the name.

"Laura?" Alice asked.

"A telemarketer. Sorry," I snapped. "This is a bad time and there will never be a good one. I don't buy by phone, and I don't do fake polls."

"The Clausen party."

I remembered. Late-blooming Nick of the *Oxlips*.

"I wanted to talk about Sandy Clausen."

"You're still working on it?"

"It's only been two days! I'm writing as fast as I can!"

I took a deep breath. "I mean, does this seem a good time?"

"Well, Christmas makes getting interviews hard, but—"

"Not that! Because your subject is, ah . . . you know."

"Oh!" he said. "That. Actually it's made it a hotter topic, if I can bring it in soon. You know, who was he, how'd he live and how'd he die. In fact, it's pretty much presold to *Philadelphia Magazine*."

"Sounds promising." I itched inside my many layers. I'd be the only Philadelphian to get prickly heat in December.

Lest I overheat to the point of spontaneous combustion, I began unbuttoning. "Remember when I said this was a bad time?" I asked. "It really was—is. So congratulations on the sale, and good luck."

"You said I could interview you."

I couldn't remember. I still felt like Three Mile Island just before meltdown.

"They want it as soon as possible—while he's news; you understand—so I was wondering if you have any time today."

"I'm on my way out."

"Later?"

"Don't think so." Frivolous as it was compared to homicide, the fact was, Christmas would arrive no matter who had done what to whom, and I had more gifts left to find than hours in which to do so.

"Then when's good for you?"

The next few days looked just as congested. Unless Mackenzie defected once again, in which case I'd need time to kick walls, rip up his photos and recuperate. But I wouldn't count my missing chickens until I had to. And beyond the Mackenzie days, Florida loomed. There was simply no time. I gently suggested the same.

"I know it's Saturday and all," he replied, "but is there any chance of your being free for dinner?"

I squelched an automatic refusal. I could spend my post-shopping Saturday evening with Lean Cuisine, those unfinished greeting cards, and TV shows designed for thirteen-year-old baby-sitters. Or I could be with an attractive and very acceptable companion. Besides, somebody was ringing my doorbell. So I accepted.

After I'd hung up, I was able to untangle and remove my coat and the extra sweater as well. Then, finally comfortable, I answered the door so that the Canadian cold front could blast directly into my veins and sinus cavities.

"Laura!" Alice Clausen said, because that is who ushered the next ice age into my living room. "Where were you?"

"Aunt Alma said you were here," Laura spoke in her classroom voice—an almost inaudible murmur. "I hope it's all right that I came over, Miss Pepper."

"Did you go to—you didn't, did you?" Alice wrung her hands.

Laura frowned.

"Did you? Where were you? What were you doing?"

"Walking. Thinking."

"Outside?"

"I went into stores."

"I meant—did you talk to anybody about . . . anything?" I almost reminded Alice that there was no point to her awkwardly disguised questions. I knew what she meant. But she wasn't remembering who knew what, only that there was a frightening secret that mustn't be shared. I wondered whether my own illusion of shielding someone from harm was equally misguided.

"I called Peter," Laura said. "But he wasn't home."

"Nobody else?"

She shook her head, and Alice Clausen's muscles visibly unknotted. Mine, on the other hand, tightened. What should I say about Peter's whereabouts? I gnawed at the question while the Clausens dealt with their own concerns.

"You spend too much time with him," Alice declared. "Up till all hours last night. Alma thought it was disgraceful. I had to keep explaining." Alice adopted a pose of despair that didn't rationally correlate with Laura and Peter's late hours.

Laura looked at her shoes, nice penny loafers, a little scuffed, but not terrifically engrossing. Alice studied the rug. That didn't seem much of a grabber, either.

So I made hostessing noises, mentioning that we'd been just on the verge of walking to Alma's house, asking if anyone wanted anything before setting out, emphasis on leave-taking.

"Could I use your phone?" Laura whispered. "Maybe by now, Peter's home." She slipped off her coat.

I had gnawed the issue down to the marrow and couldn't think of a reason why I had to keep Peter's mission a secret from Laura. "He won't be," I said. "He's at police head-quarters."

She dropped her coat, pressed a fist to her mouth and shook her head back and forth, as if forcibly containing a scream. "They arrested him?" she finally said.

I shook my head. "He went to them."

Alice Clausen stood where she was, confused and fearful.

"I have to go," Laura said. "Now." She picked up her coat off the floor and was almost at the door when both her mother and I shouted "Where?" and, at the same time, began regathering and rebuttoning sweaters, gloves, hats and coats.

"Don't!" Alice said.

"I know what he's doing there. He's lying. He's saying he did it." Laura's back was to us and her hand was on the door.

"Why?" Her mother was swaddled in dark mink now, and for at least the tenth time that morning, I wondered how a woman could be so finely groomed and outfitted and still be such a mess. "Why would he?"

The words penetrated Laura's coat, hit her between the shoulder blades. She turned around, looked at her mother with disappointment. "To protect me," she said. Her voice was suddenly strong, almost belligerent, very un-Laura. "Can you understand that?"

WAY BACK IN MACKENZIE'S PAST THERE WAS A TRAVEL agent who was either tenacious, forgiving, or incapable of

updating her Rolodex. In any case, she still sent annual regards via a lush calendar, and Mackenzie therefore spent
every working day near a full-color photograph of a glorious
place he's never seen.

This month's geographic delicacy was a Tahitian beach.
There was a Christmas bauble on a palm frond. I sat near
his desk, imagining the slap of waves on sand, the rustle of
palm fronds, the distant ocean roar.

My fantasy world was drowned by Alice Clausen's snif-
fles, Laura's hesitant, muffled half-sentences and C.K.
Mackenzie's repeated "What?" and "How's that again?"
and "This is the damndest . . . ." He shot me a barrage of
accusing glares, as if I had orchestrated this entire business,
put the players up to their merry pranks. I shot back pure
innocence. It wasn't my fault that Servino, whose case Clausen was, had to sit by, annoyed and huffing, as a sort of
auxiliary, paternal extra. It wasn't my fault that Mackenzie
was the confessor of choice.

We were well past the recitation of rights. Mother and
daughter had passed on lawyers, against both Mackenzie's
and my advice. Peter had been booked and Mackenzie
seemed definitely put out by the idea that the swift hand of
justice was receiving a smack and a reprimand.

"Let him out. He lied. He was protecting me," Laura
said for the third time.

The word "protecting" had cropped up once again, once
again reminding me of Laura's composition. I almost knew
it by heart now. *Instead of protecting his child, he sent him
too close to the fire, to his death.*

Mackenzie nodded at Laura. "And now you're protectin'
Peter." His tone was soothing, compassionate, dangerous.

"No. I'm telling the truth. I did it."

"With him?"

"Alone. All alone."

"No she didn't! She's mixed up, I tell you! *I* did it!" Alice
insisted. "And alone!"

Mackenzie closed his eyes and breathed deeply. Then he
opened them and looked at the clock. "Now I've asked you
before, Laura. And you, too, Mrs. Clausen, but all I've got-

ten is answers like 'he deserved it' which aren't answers at all. So I'm askin' again and I'd sure appreciate something real this go-round." He leaned closer to Laura. "We're talkin' about your father, your daddy, not some abstract idea. You're tellin' me you killed your own dad, and I'm askin' you why."

Laura's eyes widened. She swallowed.

"Why that night? What did you and your father quarrel about at the party?" he demanded.

Information about the quarrel was compliments of my big mouth. I felt as sick to my stomach as Laura looked to be.

"Peter," she whispered.

"What about him?"

"Everything. That he was there. That we spent time together."

"Her father thought she was too young for boys," Alice said. "He had his ideas." Her head dropped forward, as if someone had smacked it from behind, and she sat in a position of complete dejection.

"Had you fought about it before?" Mackenzie asked Laura.

"Not really." She looked at the detective. "He didn't know until that night. Peter never came over or called the house."

"You kept him a secret?"

She nodded.

Mackenzie stood up and looked down at her, looming. "So," he said, "your father was real angry about your boyfriend. That's one kind of thing. But we're still talkin' murder here. Why?"

Laura was again engrossed in her penny loafers.

"Now if your daddy was so angry about his visitin' the house at all, why was Peter still there after everybody else had gone? Why was he there in the middle of the night?"

Laura's mouth opened and shut, a little guppy in a police station.

"Why?"

"I asked him to stay."

"With you?"

She nodded.

"For how long?"

"Till morning."

"In your house? In your bedroom? Overnight?"

She nodded again.

"Even though your daddy didn't even want you datin', you asked a boy to spend the night?"

Her nod was more like lowering her neck for the guillotine.

Mackenzie returned to the chair facing her. "Why is that?" he asked gently. "Why'd you do that?"

She looked at him gravely, leaned toward him, as if pulling to the truth, as if willing herself and her secrets into his hands. "I thought about it all the time," she said. "All the time. That other fire—that was an accident. I think. But I remembered the flames. Burning it away. Like in hell, like where the devil . . ." She stopped and shrugged, as if she'd said nothing much.

"What did you need to burn away?" Mackenzie spoke softly.

Laura looked surprised, as if she'd forgotten where she was. She swiveled to see the room, Mackenzie, her mother, me, and then she stood up suddenly, pale and shaking. "I'm going to be sick," she said.

Mackenzie pointed in the direction of the women's room. Then he looked at me, but I had already gotten up to follow her.

From behind us, I heard Alice Clausen's moans and weeping interspersed with Mackenzie's low, slow questions.

Laura splashed water on her face and stood breathing deeply over the sink. She clutched its lip as if to keep from falling down. "Why won't he believe me?" she said.

"Maybe because you aren't telling the truth. Because you didn't do it. Because none of this makes sense."

"Why won't he let Peter go?"

I took a deep breath. She looked so tiny and innocent in the white glare of the bathroom. "Laura, why do you insist that you killed your father? You have no motive. Who are you protecting?" There it was, that word again.

"No—" She shook her head. "I—" Her hands left the sink edge and clenched into fists. She stammered, flushed with frustration and conflict, then stopped trying to speak. Instead, she stood crying, hands at her sides, not even bothering to wipe her tears or running nose. As if that would be a waste of energy. As if everything was.

I was her teacher. She was my pupil. Until now, we'd had a lopsided, limited communication through her essays and my speculations. But it was a defined relationship. I knew what to do with it.

No longer. I stood back, afraid of crossing some line into the forbidden or inappropriate, wishing I knew the ground rules.

Laura continued to cry.

Icarus, unnoticed, still dies every day.

I noticed. She had to know it. Forget the rules—there weren't any except the fundamental one that I was an adult and she was a child in pain. I walked over and held her. She was as fragile and lost inside her baggy clothing as a loosely joined pipe-cleaner doll. "He has to believe me!" she said into my shoulder.

"He needs the truth."

"It is true. I did it."

"He needs to know why, to make sense of it." She shook her head and pulled away, but I held onto her. "I can't," she said. "Never. It'd kill her."

"Her?"

"You've seen how she is! She's worse than that. She can't—she won't—"

"Did you ever try? Sometimes people are stronger than you think they are."

Laura shuddered and stopped crying. "I tried," she said in an emotionless voice.

I took a deep breath. I could finally read Laura's paper, see through the mask of Icarus and Auden to Laura's face and message. Laura had tried to tell me that she was in grave danger. She wrote it in code, didn't spell it out, couldn't use the words because, while an adolescent might be willing to complain about almost every perceived oppression, there are some secrets, some problems so central, so mixed with guilt and warped love, shame and confusion that they make one mute. But very few.

She had tried to tell me. And with all good intentions, I had backed off as neatly as her mother had. I let Mackenzie tell me my instincts were off, or exaggerated. Let him because I didn't want to force out a truth that frightened and revolted me because it reversed the natural order. The most basic law—that adults protect their young. I behaved like all the other adults she knew. And so finally, Laura had nobody to turn to except another child, Peter, her only defender, asked to help her through the night, not as a lover, but as protector.

Parents and children aren't equals or ready to do the same things, and Icarus shouldn't have been pulled into his father's fantasy which, in effect, murdered him.

A part of me cried halt, warned me I was galloping to conclusions. But what else could it be?

Her father's fantasy! How could he do such a thing! I was nearly shaking with fury. And how could *she* let him touch her daughter! Mr. Wonderful, Mr. Charity. Santa Claus for God's sake! Poor Laura, flesh and blood, bright mind and long future twisted around the pain of protracted, silent victimization. The long slow murder of her childhood.

Her parents had failed miserably to protect their only child. Both of them. For how long had she been pulled into her father's profound sickness, and felt murdered, nightly or however often he claimed her? For how long had her mother made herself deaf and blind with the help of a bottle? I took another deep breath. Impulses came from every direction, clashing midway. I didn't want to add more pain or put Laura in further emotional jeopardy by forcing out the truth. But if my suspicions were right, and I was sure they were, then I'd be multiplying her pain just as her mother had if I remained silent, consciously ignoring her signals. I had to say something. I had to drag it out, disinter it, because it wasn't dead.

"It's time to be concerned with Laura," I said. "Nobody else. You've been terribly abused, and the idea that you can't tell the people who could help you is part of the damage he did to you.''

I watched her confusion and slow comprehension. Her secret was out, exposed to light and air, without her having said it. Then her expression turned to horror. Terror. Surely there would be a thunderbolt, the apocalypse. It had been so much easier, more permissible, to confess to murdering the man than even to whisper why she had cause.

''Not one bit of it was your fault,'' I said. ''You have nothing to be ashamed of. Nothing to be afraid of now, either.''

She looked at me bleakly. It was going to take a lot more than her English teacher saying things were okay before she realized the guilt was not hers. Her father had done his twisted work well.

''And your mother knows, too. She just doesn't know what to do about it.''

''She could have stopped him!'' The words ripped out of her throat. As terrified as she'd been of exposing her secret, I was sure it was equally terrifying to let out any of her anger. ''She's my *mother*!'' The fury drained away almost as quickly as it had come, and her head returned to its bowed, defeated position.

''He was sick, and she's a very frightened woman.'' My rational tone surprised me. Inwardly, I felt homicidal rage against the senior Clausens.

Perhaps some of the violence I felt showed, because Laura crumpled. If I hadn't caught her, she would have fallen to the floor. As it was, I held her, again aware of how little weight she carried.

She doubled over, clutching her stomach, visibly hurting deep inside.

I held her and eased us both down onto the floor. And there we sat, crying, holding each other.

I don't know when it was that Mackenzie, worried, sent in a policewoman to check on us. Susan Bertram, her name was, and I will honor her forever, because when I explained, as obliquely and gently as I could, what had happened, she looked as if she herself had been wounded. She sat down next to Laura on the cold tile floor and put her arm around her and made it clear that she had all the time and intention in the world to stay with her and keep her from falling.

I knew Laura's mind was numb with old griefs and new fears, but I hoped that on some level, through her tears, she'd notice that there were some safe harbors, even if you sometimes found them on a ladies' room floor.

Seven

ONCE WE EMERGED FROM THE WOMEN'S ROOM, OFFICIAL
wheels spun. Servino, the man assigned to the Clausen case,
asserted himself and talked with Laura, Alice and Peter in
rapid succession, then repeated the process.

Susan Bertram, the policewoman, talked with Alice and
Laura separately and together.

Mackenzie talked with Peter again.

I waited. Ever since I was a kid, I'd been intrigued by the
two circles joined by a curve that make up the Philadelphia
Police Administration Building. It almost looks like a plush
resort, or multiplex stadium for games and concerts. But
inside, whether or not the curved walls covered with corrugated paneling made for efficient use of space, as touted,
there was a definite lack of graciousness, and you'd never
confuse it with a pleasure palace. I had a choice between a
hard chair squeezed between file cabinets and detectives, or
a bench in the municipal court waiting room. The latter at
least had a little more elbow room and a view through a dirty
window of people being booked.

I found and read an ancient, tattered *Sports Illustrated*. I
paced. I managed to feel both mentally agitated and brain
dead. What did everything mean? I was no longer positive
about Laura's innocence, although more than ever I wanted
it to be true so that she could get on with her life and healing.

Still, if that brief glimpse of what she'd lived through made me feel homicidal, how could I not allow her the same impulses? I was no longer positive about Alice or Peter, either.

More time passed. I thought wistfully and irrationally about how cigarettes had once helped make blank times like this bearable, serving as little measuring rods.

This would have been an eleven-cigarette wait.

Mackenzie appeared, rubbing his neck and sipping something that resembled crude oil. It was different, seeing him on the job. Once upon a time, when we met and I was a suspect, Mackenzie had been attractive, but less than endearing. Now, watching from the innocent sidelines, I realized there was something breathtakingly elemental about his methodical search for truth and justice. If I squinted, I could almost see him atop a white horse, plumed helmet, pointed lance and all.

And that's one way women get seduced into unworkable, undefinable and mangled social lives. Not me. I blinked three times and Lancelot turned into one tired cop slouching over a Styrofoam cup.

"What a mess," he said, sitting down beside me. "And how'd it come to be my mess, anyway? It's not even my case."

"I thought you all helped each other out. One for all and all for justice, or something." I patted his free hand. "Feel flattered. Those kids trust you. And Alice trusts those kids."

"Damn depressing," he said. "Inconclusive. Infuriating. Any one of them could have done it. There's motive, opportunity . . ."

"But do you think so? Do you really?"

"Three different versions, but not a one mentions how it was done—and we don't know ourselves."

"When will you?"

"It hasn't even been forty-eight hours yet," he said, looking stunned by my foolishness.

"Still, you told me they have all those snazzy tests, computerized equipment. They've had two whole days. What have they been doing?"

"Mandy, there are usually clues to tell you where to start.

Marks or discoloration. You kind of know whether he was clubbed, or stabbed, or poisoned. But here . . .'' He shook his head and slumped on the bench next to me. ''Wouldn't you think a guy like Santa, who has to go down chimneys, would wear a flameproof suit?''

Alexander Clausen must have ignited like a torch.

''Anyway,'' Mackenzie said, ''his skin's . . . well, they have to start from zero. I mean they'll figure it out by internal evidence, but some tests take a week or more. Plus—''

''I know. It's the holidays.''

''Even cops deserve a personal life. You wouldn't believe how angry some women get when we have to work nights,'' he said gravely.

I sniffed; disdainfully, I hoped.

He finished his coffee. A gritty triangle of grounds stained the side of the cup. ''I don't know, I thought maybe Peter hit him with something. But we checked the fireplace poker, and it's clean. No hair, no blood, so I just don't know.''

I enjoyed concepts—murder, guilt, weapon—more than particulars like hair and blood. I wanted, inappropriately, to change focus. It was, after all, the season to be merry. Someone had even pinned red and silver garlands on the walls. It helped soften the sight of four furious and handcuffed teenagers being charged behind the glass partition.

To the casual observer, Mackenzie looked unaffected by everything, slumped as usual on his spine, long legs relaxed. But his normal slur had faded into an unintelligible swamp of vowel sounds. He cared. Good man.

''Ahknowkidslahn.''

He was really upset. I pulled apart the sounds. There was time, because his pace decreased as his drawl increased. What had he said? I. Know. [that?] [the?] kids [are?] . . . [a] kid is? . . . Lon? Who was Lon? Kid has long? Lawn?

''Thall ur. Feelt mah gut.''

I said it all to myself again, pushing at the words the way he did, and it finally cleared up. Not lawn, lying. The kid, Peter? was lying—and they all were. C.K. felt it in his gut. So did I, only I spoke Philadelphian and could understand me. ''Three questions,'' I said. ''Why is he lying? What will you do with Peter? And could you either talk Northern or provide an interpreter?"

He crumpled his cup almost angrily and sat forward on the shellacked bench. "Ah talk fahn," he said. Nonetheless, he did trim the edges of most of his words. "Can't hold any of 'em. Mother's completely out of it and Laura's almost as vague. She doesn't remember much of anything, ever. I don't know if it's trauma or mental problems or what. And I sure as hell don' know why they're all doin' this. Why step forward to do so much lying?"

Again he made it sound like "lahn." Soft, cushiony. So much less offensive than "lying." It's what he did with "crime" and "fire" as well. My twangy homegrown accent made everything sound worse.

Laura had told the policewoman and me that she had nightmare after nightmare of revenge, shapeless methods, misty punishments. But after the first fire—accidentally started with an overturned candle but then deliberately allowed to continue—flames filled her dreams, made them clear and definite, as if the candle fire had been a sign. Fire cleansed and punished. Wasn't it what God had chosen for sinners in hell?

The night of the party, she'd asked Peter to stay in her room, as a protector. My hunch had been verified. "He cares about me," she'd said. "We don't . . . we weren't . . ." Then her voice dwindled to a whisper as she approached the topic of her father. "He loved parties, people paying attention, saying he was important. And then he'd . . . he'd want to . . . later, to . . . keep feeling good." She had covered her face with her hands. "He said it was my fault. I made it happen. He made me dress like a baby, hide myself, because he said I was so . . . He said it would kill my mother if she knew what I was really like."

Later, when she was calm again, we had asked if her father had come to her bedroom that night. Peter was asked the same question, separately. Both said he hadn't.

"I went downstairs before he could," Laura said. "I killed him before he could. Pushed the tree down, set it on fire."

"Why leave your room where you were safe with Peter?" I asked.

She looked even more uncomfortable. "I heard him. I thought he was upstairs, but he wasn't. Maybe I got afraid of his seeing Peter or . . . I don't know. I just went downstairs."

"She sleepwalks," her mother had said in her interview. Alice Clausen gripped her purse so hard that her knuckles were prominent and white. Her hands were so elegantly tended, and so out of control, shaking with a life of their own. I imagined Alice, wealthy and passive, turning body parts over to someone for updating and maintenance checks, barely noticing what was done. "She's sleepwalked since she was a baby. Started out in her crib but ended up asleep all over the house, and never remembered how she'd gotten there. Mixes things up."

We sat in silence.

"Mackenzie?" I said now. "I know why they're lying."

He raised one eyebrow. An endearing, if skeptical, gesture.

"Laura truly believes she did it."

"Go on."

"So do the other two. I mean think that Laura did it, and they're covering for her."

"That's how you figure it?"

"She probably was downstairs when the fire alarm went off, sleepwalking."

"Bumped into the tree, huh?"

"Probably. After Clausen was dead, you see. And Peter found her there."

"Mama, too?"

"I don't know. Alice might still have been out cold. But maybe. In any case, she knew. That night, that fight at the party—she knew for sure what she'd known and denied for a long time. So later, when she realized that her husband was dead and she thought Laura probably did it, because Laura kept saying so, she confessed out of shame at her collusion, as a way of making it not so, finally making her the good mother."

Mackenzie squeezed his crumpled coffee cup.

"And Peter has the same reasons," I said. "Laura told him her story, and he was enraged, protective—finally to the point of defending her the only way possible, by confessing. So! Now that it's obvious those three didn't do it, it's time to find the somebody else who did. Like one of the guests. What is happening with that list?"

He shook his head. "Clausen's secretary said the PR firm handled the event. The PR firm says they advised him against the whole project, but finally found a church shelter that only admits the sober and drug free. The pastor of the church says they sent the first thirty, no names asked, no history. 'We are all brethren,' he says. That gives us thirty unnamed from there and thirty-five completely unknown from other sources. That's all I know. They're still looking, but it's—"

"—the holidays, right?"

"Would you ease up? Anyway, it's not my case. But if it were—I wouldn't worry too much about that list. And what made you think that quote it's obvious those three didn't do it end quote?"

I had mistaken noncommittal grunts, yawns and brow raises for agreement. "I can't believe you don't see it," I insisted. "It *is* obvious that they're innocent!"

"Uh-huh," he said. "That's just it. How hard would it be to conspire to look like they didn't conspire?"

"I don't get it."

"Ah'm talkin' funny again?"

"Conspire" had indeed been aspirated mush, but that wasn't what I meant. "It's your logic this time."

He spoke as if to a dunce. A Yankee dunce. Slowly, with exaggerated precision, snapping off syllables. "Any one of them could have done it alone or with the others' help. They're all happier with him dead. Then the next thing they'd do is confuse us all. Disagree on particulars. Never mention anything the papers haven't said first. We've all seen enough TV shows where the bad guy knows too much and blurts it out. So this group's careful. They'll sound upset that the other one's confessing, seem like they never talked it over together. Look like well-meaning, amateur bumblers, in fact. Confession crazies.''

"Come on!"

"Hey, it's real smart. Look guilty, claim guilt—but be dumb, unpolished, like your claim's an obvious lie. Knot up the force, tie up our hands. Have to let 'em go until something links 'em in a conspiracy or implicates one of 'em."

"That's ridiculous. Too Machiavellian—so complicated and silly!''

His eyelids lowered in disdain or boredom, I couldn't tell. "Silly? *Silly?* You saying they don't have motive, every one of them? And cause? That the urge to kill and the reason for it wasn't running real hard in their veins? Especially Laura. My money's on her. With a little help from the boyfriend.''

"Great. Why not just take her out and hang her, right now?''

"There are mitigating circumstances. She'll get an easy sentence, maybe probation. Treatment. Psychiatric care. It's not the worst. You know what they did to parricides in ancient Rome? Whipped them, sewed them in a leather sack along with a live dog, a cock, a viper and an ape, and then threw them into the sea. Things have improved.''

I had no answer. Mackenzie's work had frayed his view of mankind, and I didn't like what he saw out of those pale blue eyes. He seemed contaminated. On the other hand, I seemed stupid, my theory naive and as porous as cheesecloth. We sat under the tinsel, glum together. He was angry that he couldn't prove their guilt. I was angry that he couldn't see their innocence. The tension built without our doing one more thing. Look, Ma, no hands.

"Cheer up," he said. "Soon you'll be a thousand miles away in the sun forgetting all about it.''

The remark fed my growing hostility. I had been waiting for three weeks, since the moment I mentioned the trip my parents kept requesting as their Christmas gift, for him to say, very simply, "Don't go. Let's be together.''

He had a few days off, too. It was our first chance, or could have been, to spend a leisurely time together, to begin to know each other like normal people.

Never once did he say "Don't go" or any variation thereof. Instead, he expressed nonstop delight at my good fortune. Florida in December, what a treat. Oranges, flamingos, sunshine, palm trees. Sometimes I hated him.

He stood up. "I'm followin' your lead, flying south, too. Haven't seen my folks in a long while." He nodded, agreeing with himself that his trip was a great idea. He stretched and yawned. "So," he said, "you might as well go." He picked up his crushed plastic cup and raised his arm in the classic, inevitable male rite, the wastepaper toss.

Of all the arrogant, insufferable pronouncements! Freeing me—giving me permission to leave town because his wonderful self would be in New Orleans! I might as well go? "I *will* go, dammit!" I snapped. "I have my tickets! Or did you think I was sitting around waiting for you to offer me an alternate plan?"

My outbreak messed up his aim. He walked over and picked the cracked Styrofoam off the floor, rubbed his shoe over the wet grounds, spreading the grit over the linoleum. Then he peered at me as if I were a new and mutant form of life. "Merely meant there's no need to stay here at the station any longer. What got you in an uproar? What tickets you talking about?"

I fumbled with my coat, hoping he couldn't see my embarrassed blush.

"Sue Bertram's givin' them a ride home. All of them. They win this round."

My face no longer felt like I had sunstroke, so I looked at him. "I'm glad," I said. Mackenzie seemed overly impressed with his own largesse. Saint C.K., freeing the innocent. "And very surprised," I added nastily.

"You think we're monsters? Lack all Christmas spirit? Ready to lock them in leg irons? Sometimes you disappoint me. Anyway, what'd be the point? There's no case. They'd be out by nightfall, and we'd look like jerks. Newspapers would love it, wouldn't they though?"

"However you feel about their guilt or innocence—"

"Hers."

"Laura? You insist on Laura?" He said nothing, so I finished buttoning my coat, disgusted with him.

"By the way," he said, "Susan talked to the aunt, who's calling the shrink so Laura can get some help. This is kind of unusual, the abuser being dead and all, so normal practice, separating the two and such, doesn't make a whole lot of sense. Besides—"

"I know. I *know*. Holidays."

"Well, then, everything's taken care of." He checked his watch. Case closed. "Any more questions?" He thought he was endearing, irresistible. Instead, he was insufferable.

I had an attack of S.S.S. The dread Sudden Stranger Syndrome. I looked at this man I'd known for months—my lover and boon companion—and deep inside, a shocked voice asked, "Who the hell *is* he?"

It was not a new experience. The longer I am single—and the more it happens, the longer I'm going to stay single—the more familiar S.S.S. becomes. It generally speeds the newly perceived other into the past tense.

"I do indeed have another question," I said. "So should you. Like—who really killed Alexander Clausen?"

"Ah," Mackenzie said. "Yay-uss. You would say that."

Three hours later, I was back at home, dropping packages on the sofa, throat scratchy, cheeks hard with cold, sniffling and thinking of nothing except a warm bath. A hot bath. A boiling bath.

"Why," I asked Macavity, "are all the hot tubs in California, where nobody even understands what freezing means?" The cat, who had contempt for all water, anywhere, and presumably for people who steeped themselves in the wretched stuff, yawned.

I glanced at the mail, then tossed the lot of it into the wicker basket by the phone, to be reexamined, someday. Three cards with institutional return addresses and two premature postholiday sale announcements. No more safe-sex mailings from Mom. Maybe she knew that sex wasn't an issue I had to deal with this evening.

The day that had begun in icy radiance had long since dimmed into blustery, bone-cracking frigidity. "Too cold for

snow,'' a salesman had said. ''Too bad. No white Christmas.'' I suggested that we fake it by lining up all our frost-
bitten body parts.

''Who are you, Scrooge?'' he'd asked—after I had paid.

I was. And not only that, but I had a Dickensian ailment
now, the ague. Whatever that was, I felt it in my bones.

I wanted brandy and a hot tub, followed by a quick flight
to the Tahitian beach on Mackenzie's calendar. I wanted
Mackenzie to say ''Don't go to Florida.'' He could slur the
words all to hell. I'd understand.

Only the brandy seemed possible. Until I remembered
that somewhere in the fat little portfolio that was supposed
to organize my personal and professional lives, there was
still an entry on the page labeled ''Domestic Errands.'' ''Buy
brandy,'' it said. However, having written it down, I then
forgot about it. I wasn't even sure where the Organizer Portfolio itself was, and my life was as rumpled as ever.

Eventually, I noticed the blinking red light of my answering machine. I still wasn't used to the idea of being on call
whether home or away, let alone used to the machine itself.
First, I pressed the memo button by mistake. It recorded my
irritated mumbles. Then I pushed fast forward. Finally, I
found playback.

There was a worried call from Alma Leary, asking her
sister's whereabouts. I didn't need to answer that one since
Alice and Laura were long since home.

An anonymous message—''Damn machines!''—from
someone even less in tune with the times than I was.

Sasha was terse. ''More telephone tag,'' she said. ''But
I'm off to Atlantic City to gamble. Spell that g-a-m-b-o-l,
please. Shake loose No-Name and join me.'' However, she
left no number.

Another confused message from the Southlands. ''This is
Beatrice Pepper,'' it began. ''Your mother.''

Even Macavity, warming my ankles with predinner rubs,
looked amused.

Beatrice Pepper continued. ''I don't like this. It's confusing. Oh! Yes. I'm supposed to tell you the—it's three—ah,
three fourteen—no, fifteen. Saturday. But why does that mat-

ter, Amanda?'' She allowed herself a histrionic sigh so I'd
know how selfless she was to put up with my eccentricities,
then continued. ''Your sweater was coming along just fine
until Daddy said the arms looked too thin and I listened to
him, even though what does he know about things like that?
So I redid them, and then I realized that they weren't thin.
They were right. The rest was huge. I think maybe I got it
mixed up with Beth's maternity sweater. And I wanted to
give it to you next week.'' A sigh as large as the sweater must
be. Then her whole tone perked up. ''But of course you won't
need it here, it's so warm and sunny, so it doesn't matter if
it's a little late. I'll measure you when you're here. Although
the wool is getting a bit frayed, dear.''

I was amazed the wool was not yet pure lint.

''It doesn't feel right, talking to a machine. Call me. We
can't wait to see you. Oh and—is there time left to talk more?
I'll try.'' She spoke very rapidly now. ''Good news—Molly,
the lady across the courtyard who took ceramics with me?—
her son just separated from his wife—a terrible woman—and
he'll be here the whole time you are. A podiatrist. He's no
movie star, understand, and he has a little stutter, but honestly, after a while, you hardly notice.''

I wanted brandy and all I had was vanilla extract. I wanted
Tahiti and was being offered a condominium pool and a
homely, stuttering foot doctor. Probably my longed-for hot
tub would translate into the water heater's exploding and
flooding the basement.

''Consider this official confirmation, all right?'' the next
message began. No salutation, no identification. ''Eight
o'clock tonight at Lissabeth's. Meet you there.''

A wrong number, alas. I'd read a profile of Lissabeth's.
Peach and jade decor and Philadelphia Renaissance cuisine.
Enticing.

Mackenzie and I seldom dined. We ate out spontaneously
and at his odd hours. Most of the time, we ran to South Street
and brought back cheesesteaks. With fried onions. Ketchup.
Oil dripping from the rolls. Or hoagies. Very Philadelphia.
Very good. But not at all Lissabeth's, where mention of the
peasant excess of a Philly Steak would induce the vapors.

Maybe I should go anyway, claim the meal by right of answering-machine message.

Macavity nibbled experimentally on my ankle, reminding me that he was a hungry carnivore and domestication went only so far. I walked around the half-cabinets that demark the kitchen, performed culinary wizardry with a can opener and dropped the results into the cat dish. When I straightened back up, I saw a slip of paper on the counter and the message, "Lissabeth's—8:00." In my handwriting.

This wasn't déjà vu, but what was it? Bad science fiction? Hadn't I read this story? Seen this show? Wasn't that Rod Serling walking out from behind the sofa?

I stared at the paper until my memory jump started and I remembered writing the restaurant's name, twisting out of my coat while I talked on the phone. The doorbell had been ringing, Alice had been confessing and Nick-from-the-party had been offering to swap food for interview data.

So I wasn't in the Twilight Zone, after all. In fact, I wasn't in such bad shape. Lissabeth's wasn't Tahiti, but it was a lot closer and a lot more possible. And I was glad to give Nick a second glance, especially as viewed through the gaping holes in Mackenzie's character. Saturday night was looking up.

THE SOUP WAS LIQUID YIN AND YANG SIGNS SEPARATED BY julienned beets. I prodded it daintily, loath to deface a work of art. I noticed that Nick also ate carefully, using his arm gingerly. "Tennis," he said. "A friend belongs to an indoor club. We've been playing a lot. Unfortunately, my elbow is nearly as bad as my game."

Modesty, I was sure. The man vibrated with energy. He'd be a whiz on the courts, a blur of action.

We exchanged histories so that I knew he was a native Philadelphian, nearing forty, divorced, no kids and "into real estate." I got a sense of a few lucrative deals punctuating long, dry periods. He lived in South Philly in a small house he'd fixed up and was an avid cook. The combination of quirky, energetic entrepreneur, homemaker and *Oxlips* fiction writer had potential.

After a time, Nick returned to his task, asking me if I'd liked Alexander Clausen and what kind of person I would call him. Anything like his public image? Did I know anything about his history or background? Where had he come from? How had he gotten the money to buy his first franchise?

Since I knew nothing, it was easy enough answering. Or not answering, as the case more often was. We had already done a little dance around the subject of Laura's personality, psychology and alleged pyromania. I was glad Nick Riley didn't know me well enough to recognize how uncharacteristic my terseness was.

"Frankly," he said, "it isn't hard to read between the lines and find out there isn't any Santa Claus. Or wasn't."

"Is this some kind of exposé, then?"

"I don't know. It'll be what it turns out to be."

"I thought you admired him. The other night, you were so on, so enthusiastic about him."

He shrugged. "Admired his empire, his accomplishments, not him. I didn't know him. What about you? What did you think of him?"

"I didn't know him enough to have an opinion." I had become a sanctimonious hypocrite and liar. My dislike of Sandy Clausen was set in granite. I simply didn't want to see it set in print.

The salad was a chicly arranged culinary punishment. A tart dressing coated arugula, bitter cress and a wrinkled, pursed mushroom that was either an exotic rarity or rotten.

"Have you been teaching ever since college?"

"Before I started at Philly Prep, I copyedited, tried PR, and wrote speeches for a banker, among other things. It wasn't exactly clear career tracking."

"Do you enjoy teaching?"

"No. I do it for the money."

His high-wattage smile escaped the confines of his beard.

"What about you?" I said. "Are you indeed in bloom?"

"Pardon?"

"At the party—don't you remember? Something was just about to happen, and you were so excited it was contagious.

You called yourself a late bloomer, and I thought you said the blooming was imminent. As if it were about to happen right before my eyes.''

He studied his empty salad plate. Then he beamed out that smile of his. ''Guess I'm still a bud. One thing about being a late bloomer, though—there's no rush.''

The waiter deposited a dish of angel's hair pasta in front of him.

My veal scallop was the size of an unostentatious earring. The vegetables were all baby somethings. I felt like the Jolly Green Giant committing infanticide, whomping down in one swallow a thumb-sized ear of newborn corn, a generation of toddler carrots, a fetal eggplant. A bundle of anorexic stringbeans was tied with a pimento bow. There was a great deal of lovely china plate visible even before I began eating. I was still hungry when I finished.

''You should write about the places they grow these crops,'' I suggested. ''Dollhouse farms that might fit under this table. Tiny tractors the size of my hand.''

The lovely smile again. ''Which reminds me—I already have an article to write.'' He lifted a hank of angel's hair. ''Laura started that fire,'' he said abruptly. ''I'm positive.''

I reminded myself that his was pure speculation. So far, the papers were talking about an accident. I frowned.

''Come on,'' Nick said. ''Somebody told me you have a policeman friend. What's he think?'' The grin invited common sense. ''I won't quote you. What's the statistical probability of a family's having two major, accidental fires?''

''I don't know about statistics. I know about Laura.''

''You're overly emotional, subjective, about her.''

''She's my kid—my student. Of course I care.''

''Your kid's a pyromaniac. Now, a murderer, too.''

Mackenzie thought so. Now Nick. Everybody was going to. Even without her compulsive confessing.

I ordered dessert out of pure hunger. What arrived was a miniaturist's dream. Three tarts, each no bigger than a fingernail, one filled to the brim with half a single grape, one stuffed with a sliver of kiwi and one straining to contain three blueberries. Nouvelle dieting.

"What made you pick Clausen for your article?" I asked. "There are so many more interesting, more important people in the city."

Nick had a thimbleful of chocolate mousse, the bud in a sauce-painting of a flower. "I don't think you understand how much power he was accumulating. He was on his way to owning and running the city. That's what's interesting, the power."

"How'd you know about him?"

"Everybody knows about him. He made sure of that. But, a more interesting question is whether we just ate dinner or a round of tapas, or appetizers? You know, I'm a terrific cook. I should have done it myself."

I had taken a cab to the restaurant because I couldn't bear the idea of walking from my parking lot to my no-parking street in the freezing dark. I was going to take another cab home, but Nick drove me and, to my relief, declined my offer of coffee or drinks. I was exhausted. And hungry.

I thanked him for dinner and the evening. "That cop friend of yours," he said. "How serious is it?"

"I have no idea." Sometimes I actually told the truth.

"Then could I call you again?"

"That would be nice," I said, again as honestly as I could figure.

"Great. I'll cook for you next time."

I was not going to give Mackenzie the key to my social life and have him let it rust. He was a difficult man with an impossible job, and I was hard pressed to remember what, aside from pure lust, had ever attracted me to him.

Once inside the house, I felt a depression I'd been ignoring drape itself over my shoulders like a heavy cape. Sorrow over Laura and her story, Alice and her miseries, Peter's bewildering involvement, fear of what would happen to all of them, confusion as to where the truth lay, and anger or sadness over the slippery, evasive Mackenzie leaked down inside of my skull.

There was only one message on the machine. The drawl was in place, and loving. He was oblivious to my disdain, damn him.

"You all right?" he asked. "I'm worried 'bout you. I'm worried about all of them, but you understand, I have a job. But I was thinking—you'd recognize a guest list, or notes about the party in a way nobody on the force would. So would you consider—it's not exactly the holiday spirit or a date—but I've talked to Servino about it, and he agrees, so all the same, would you snoop at Clausen's with me tomorrow? Try an' help your kid? Or will that make you angry because it could be called work on my part, even though it's my day off? What do you say?"

I say it's turnabouts like that that trick a woman and weaken her resolve. Make her say what the hell, I can stand his weirdness a little longer.

Make her remember what it was, aside from pure lust, that attracted her to him in the first place. Make her remember the pure lust, too, more's the pity.

Eight

SUNDAY WAS THE TWINKLY SORT OF WINTER DAY THAT makes defectors to the Sunbelt miss the seasons. Yesterday's winds had forced all airborne flotsam and jetsam into Jersey. The hitching posts on my cobbled street were decorated with holly, doors trimmed with wreaths, and windows filled with ornate trees and potted poinsettias. We looked like a colorized Currier and Ives.

And a small but definite miracle had taken place. The Sunday *Inquirer* was where it should be. Not stolen. Not in the gutter, not on my neighbor's step, not ripped, not wet.

My relationship with current events was tenuous. Often, by the time I bought replacements or dried the pulpy offerings I'd found, official statements had been denied, rumors renounced, scandals settled and small wars ended.

But now, finally, the delivery boy was listening to my pleas. There was hope for mankind.

I was euphoric until I noticed an envelope attached to the paper. "Second notice," it said by way of address. Inside was a card with a snow-laden evergreen and a plaintive message reminding me of my carrier's labors on my behalf and that the meaning of Christmas was giving.

I hunched over my coffee pondering what I should "give" the wretch. What came to mind ranged from garden-variety nastiness to acts Torquemada would have admired.

Then I wondered if I was crotchety and tyrannical a few decades ahead of schedule. "Set in her ways" used to be shorthand for old maids' peculiarities. Now that they didn't even say old maid, what did they call our peccadillos?

"Who are you, Scrooge?" the man in the store had asked. Contemporary mean-spiritedness knows no gender boundaries. Maybe he'd been right more ways than not. My holiday spirit had been polluted by Mackenzie's thick-headedness, the specter of New Year's with a stuttering podiatrist and the unbearable sorrows of the Clausen family. Still, I wasn't exactly Scrooge's twin yet. My nightgowns were sexier, I didn't wear a funny cap in bed and I had no Jacob Marley, no partner living or supernatural.

My thoughts doubled up, as if cramped. I went back over them. Something snagged like a hangnail on pantyhose. I muttered "paperboy" but nothing happened. But when I tried "Scrooge," "Marley" and "ghosts," I felt that gritty discomfort. I sat immobile, waiting for the idea to articulate itself, but it was as insubstantial as Marley himself, and after tickling around between my ears, it disappeared.

I grew tired of sitting in place and decided that activity might help. Forget the impenetrable and focus on something easy. Wrap gifts. The newspaper could wait. It always had before.

I packaged the "bonus" gifts that I'd bring to Florida for my parents, sister, brother-in-law and niece. I had even found an antique silver rattle for the still-unborn niece or nephew. I had long since mailed off the major family presents. I wrapped a book I'd bought on impulse for Laura, a collection of poetry by young women. I was counting on the chorus of voices inside the covers to have something to say to her.

Finally, only Mackenzie was left. Of course I had spent too much, rushing to Wanamaker's yesterday after the police station, pressed for time and inspiration, and buying, as I always knew I would, the too-expensive, sufficiently unthreatening hand-knit Mackenzie-blue cable sweater. He would be irresistible in it, and I looked forward to not resisting.

As if reacting to the mere hint of unwed carnal joy, the telephone rang. My mother's dismay, however, had nothing to do with sex and, equally surprising, nothing to do with knitting. "It was Alexander Clausen!" she said. "That's who you were working with, and now look—he's murdered! I can't believe this. I missed Friday and Saturday's paper. Your father can be very inconsiderate, lining Herman's cage with papers I haven't even read, leaving others out by the pool. But why didn't you tell me?"

"Mom." I tried to make a hospital corner with stiff red-lacquer paper, but gift wrappers are born, not made. "I haven't spoken to you since before the party."

"You sound funny."

As well I might, with the telephone squeezed between my shoulder and chin. I had hoped my clenched diction sounded aristocratic, very Main Line.

"Something wrong with the your mouth? You hurt yourself?"

"I'm fine." I retrieved a prefab golden bow from Macavity, who'd been playing soccer with it, stuck it on my ineptly wrapped box and attached a card addressed to Cecil. My mother told me my sister Beth's flight plans and more about the speech-impaired divorcé while I wrapped the second-hand, leather-bound and illustrated copy of *Sherlock Holmes* and taped on a card addressed to Caspar.

"Amanda? You there?"

"Right here." With my jaw free, my brain activated itself. My mother had said "murdered." I knew that and the police knew that, but how did Beatrice Pepper in Florida know that?

"I can read," she answered my question. "It's on the front page. Who did it?"

"I don't know."

"Doesn't your policeman tell you anything?"

I swallowed the impulse to correct her usage. The possessive form was not appropriate. There was no such creature as "my" policeman.

"Mandy," she said, "are you . . . do they . . ." She coughed, started up again like my car in winter. "They don't think you—it's not like the last time, is it?"

"Nobody thinks I did it, if that's what you're asking." Besides having no motive—even Scrooge didn't murder casual irritants—I had a truly fine alibi. I had been in bed with the law at the time. However, I kept that to myself.

I walked the full length of the telephone cord, then stretched until I had the first section of the paper at my fingertips. I strained and scratched at it until finally, I had to let go of the receiver and grab.

"—then, thank goodness, you're not involved at all."

That wasn't a question, so I didn't answer or correct the assumption. I was too busy, anyway, skimming the story headlined "Clausen Death Declared Homicide" and subtitled "Who Killed Santa Claus?"

"Far be it from me to speak badly about the dead," my mother said, revving up to do so, "but if you had told me that it was Alexander Clausen you were having that party with, I'd have warned you about him."

"I didn't know you even knew him."

"Well, I didn't. Not really. Actually, not at all. But I heard things. I'll bet some people aren't crying about this news. In fact, you know one of them."

I knew more than one, but I didn't know which one my mother meant. "Who?"

"Your new friend, Minna White."

"The lady at Silverwood? Gee, Mom, are you suggesting that she's our killer?"

"*Minna?*"

"That was a joke."

"Not that she wouldn't like him dead."

"Why on earth?"

"Because he did something bad to, ah, somebody. He wasn't nice. I forget precisely how."

Another definitive news report from the world's best-meaning, least-accurate historian.

But that seemed to wrap it up for my mother. "Are you taking Macavity back to that nice vet?" she asked. We went from the cat to Mother's physical complaints, to the logistics of a coffee she was organizing for a Gray Panther candidate for State Senate, to untitillating gossip about a distant relative. And then we were out of material. I thought.

"By the way," she said as we were hanging up. "Did you set a time to take Minna those cannoli?"

"Mom, I said that if I could, when I could, someday, I'd—"

"Because you know what? After you told me where she was and how poorly she's doing, I called information for Silverwood's number and gave her a call, and I told her you'd be there."

"You told her what?"

"With cannoli."

"You actually promised I'd be there?"

"She's thrilled. Tuesday, I said. The day after Christmas. The day before you come down here, so you can tell me all about her. And Mandy? Get the cannoli at the Italian Market—you know, that little store that has the best."

"Do you think I'm becoming a Scrooge?" We were in Mackenzie's car, which always smelled of popcorn, driving up Germantown Avenue. We bounced so hard over a section of paving blocks that "Scrooge" came out as a squeak.

"Why'd you ask?"

"I'm getting cranky. Grumbling. I didn't give the paper-boy a Christmas tip. He didn't deserve it. He's wretched, arrogant and incompetent, but maybe that's just my warped perception. Maybe Scrooge felt that way about Tiny Tim, you know?"

Mackenzie scratched his head.

"And my mother is currently obsessed with my visiting a woman I taught at an old-age home, a former neighbor of hers, and I know it would be a nice thing to do, and I could even also see some other people who've invited me to sort of a party as well, but all the same . . . What's happened to my Christmas spirit?"

"Dead," Mackenzie said. "As a doornail. Isn't that how it goes?"

"That's how Marley goes, or went."

"Speaking of doornails, or dead," Mackenzie said, "the lab is fairly sure Clausen was killed by a blow to his head. Luckily, it cracked his skull."

"Luckily?"

"For us. That kind of mark survives a fire. There's internal evidence, too, even after the fire. In fact, that kind of cooked his insides, so—"

I was not eager to hear any more. I was, however, eager to clarify something. "That surely eliminates Laura," I said.

My boon companion shook his head.

"Oh, I forgot. The conspiracy theory. She got her muscleman to wield the weapon, is that it?" I folded my hands to keep them from punching him.

"I don't know what it is." He sounded weary.

We were in Chestnut Hill now, passing tiny row houses originally designed for servants, now occupied by folks in transit on the fast track. We moved onto the streets those servants once served, avenues heavy with turreted and furbelowed Victorians and gracious, imposing Italianate villas. Finally we were in front of Clausen's fieldstone palazzo. The boarded-up living room window and soot stains made it look like an unshaven pirate with a patch. There were fragments of barbecued furniture outside on the frozen grass.

Mackenzie crouched over the wheel, a hunter stalking a parking space. I remembered my repeated block circling the night of the party, how annoyed I'd been by the waiting drivers snoozing by the curb. I was definitely curdling into something persnickety. Or maybe it was a chronic condition, a birth defect, and I'd only now noticed it.

THE OUTSIDE OF THE HOUSE HAD LOOKED BRUISED, BUT NOT beaten, but the inside was nothing even the homeless would call shelter. At least not the entry and living room, which had been trashed both by fire and firemen. I knew there were reasons for axing furniture and walls, but the resulting destruction still grieved me. Charred party decor was still visible in the general mess. A skeletal wreath form with blackened wooden berries lay on the keyboard of a grand piano. I pushed down a key. Nothing much happened. A tinny plink, like a dime-store guitar's, sounded. I peeked—the innards were partly fused, partly broken, all damp. No more music.

"You know," I said, "the first time I came to this house for a meeting, I decided that this was the place for the happily-ever afters. I wish I hadn't been so far off the mark. I wish some of it were true. I still want to believe in it."

"Aren't you supposed to be saying 'Bah, humbug'?"

We wandered around, getting a sense of the house. It was an enormous sprawl, and only the front rooms seemed touched by the fire. The dining room was slightly trashed where flames had licked the Persian carpet and mahogany table legs. The butler's pantry's paint was scorched, but the glassware and china were intact. The kitchen seemed close to normal. It was, however, a depressingly small, dark space designed in an era when only the help would work in it. It had been modernized and bumped out a bit so that there was an eating area, and there was a tiny hallway leading to a freezing-cold addition, little more than a lean-to, with a washer and dryer, a spartan maid's room with a portable heater and an icy bathroom. The house had been democratized, but only to a point.

Mackenzie and I pulled open all the kitchen drawers and doors, as improbably as it was that they'd contain a list of guests. I was impressed by how much the Clausens owned, but I kept wondering when they used it. Did Alice entertain from within her alcoholic cloud? Had hiring a caterer been second nature for Alexander because that's what he had to do whenever people came to his house?

Everyone I know uses the refrigerator as Message Central. There's an entire industry devoted to cute magnets. But the Clausens' refrigerator was pristine. No dentist's appointment reminders, no theater tickets awaiting the date, no message pad, no flyer announcing school holidays, no beloved snapshots. Nothing.

If the kitchen was the heart of a house, this place was on a respirator.

Poor Laura. I'd call her tonight. Again I remembered the advice of that older teacher. "Be their teacher, not their friend," she'd said emphatically. "You cannot be both." I knew what she meant, and that she meant well, but I'm equally entitled to make up rules. Besides, there's a difference between needing to be a pal and wanting to be a friend.

We walked upstairs. There was a sewing room that showed no signs of use, a large and old-fashioned bath with a claw-footed tub, a pink and flouncy room that must have been Laura's, and signs that the master bedroom had been used only by the master. A more modern bath joined it to a very feminine boudoir. There was also a guest room I was willing to bet had never been occupied. This was not a family that could welcome close contact.

We were heading back to the ruins of the living room when Mackenzie paused at the dining room window. "I'm worried about the car," he said. "If somebody comes around that corner too fast . . ."

His point was well taken. However, the spot had seemed the only one between here and Manhattan. Everyone in Chestnut Hill was entertaining. I imagined rooms full of the glimmering dresses the magazines considered de rigueur for holiday parties. I didn't think I'd ever been to a party where such costumes were appropriate—except Halloween.

Mackenzie and I stood side by side, regarding the gracious street, lined with old trees that, even in their winter undress, seemed to guard the stately homes with dignity. The windowpanes we looked through were old glass, wavy and imperfect, hazed with a film of smoke that clouded our view.

I felt uncomfortable and displaced. It was probably no more than a matter of being back in a house that had bred and nourished misery. Now, a sign in front of the door said, "Stay Away. Unsafe," but it had been unsafe for a long time.

I wished I'd never read *A Christmas Carol*. Never suggested the party. I had upset the status quo, put something in motion. Without the party, maybe Laura and her family could have been saved. I could have talked to her about Icarus, found out, intervened. Nobody had to die.

The fact that I'd meant well made it sadder. "I'm going to visit that woman, my mother's friend," I suddenly said. "And go to that class party at Silverwood. I was pretty pious about being kind to the less fortunate—as long as it was my students' responsibility."

"You'll never make it as Scrooge," Mackenzie said. We kept looking outside.

I could understand why they brought people back to the scenes of crimes. Memories returned and clarified as if the indestructibility of matter included afterimages. All it required was a bit of on-site excavation.

The street was filled with cars, as it had been that night. But it didn't look the same. There had been other shapes. They slowly clarified as I mentally circled past again and again. I remembered their colors and what I had mumbled to myself.

A Septa Charter, an Innercity Services Van, Palate Pleasers Caterers. A taxi. "Mackenzie!" I said. "We have a lead. Besides that teetotaling church. There must be lists of which bus went out and where the pickup points were. Something." I was wildly proud of the discovery-memory.

"Any more?" We walked across the hallway. It had been immediately obvious to me that there was no point in digging, literally, through what had been the living room. If there was a list, and if it had been brought in here that night, it had long since met the same fate as the master of the house. I made this point to Mackenzie.

Nonetheless, he poked around with childlike delight. Instead of a mud puddle, he had a whole room of ash to muck about. He stood near what had been the bay window. Now it was blind boards. The room was dim, lit only from the far-off dining room windows. "There was the most beautiful tree I've ever seen in front of that window," I said. "All gold and silver and crystal ornaments, some that were pretty unusual. Antiques, probably." No trace of the tree was left.

Mackenzie kicked through a black tangle of carpet and carbonized something. "I see bits of some. Maybe Laura'd like them?"

I hoped that Laura would turn toward the future with relief, and suspected that she wouldn't want many souvenirs of this house and its past. But I didn't see the harm in Mackenzie's sifting out remnants if that gave him the illusion of accomplishing something. I watched him dive for glitter. Within minutes, he looked like he was wearing gloves and he had a broad sooty swatch from his forehead to his ear. He picked up a buckled metal wafer. "Probably a snowflake once," he said. "Maybe."

I looked around. My mind had been smoke damaged the last two days. Whenever I'd thought about the party, it had been a rushed and confusing blur. But now, back inside the living room, my mental landscape cleared until I could remember specifics, faces and moments. I could see where I had sat with Gladys and the porcelain figurine, and where I'd been waylaid by the man who wanted a free car. I wish I knew how Sandy Clausen had ultimately handled him. Or the spitting veteran. I could see the green-covered table rounds, the plates full of turkey and dressing, Santa with his bag of gifts.

And Marley's ghost.

There it was, the shred of an idea that had teased and refused to be remembered until now. The old man with the cane and the loud voice.

"There was a man," I began. Mackenzie stopped digging and looked interested again. "He was . . . different. Old, too. Said 'Alexander Clausen,' three times, as if he were tolling the name, tapped him on the shoulder with his cane. Clausen knew him. Called him 'Jacob'—but he was very surprised to see him."

"And?"

"I got this weird feeling. He made me think of Marley's ghost. His name was even Jacob, like Marley's."

"Yes?"

"He pointed to himself, then Clausen, as if there were a bond."

"And then?"

That was it, except for residual unease.

"Anything else happen?"

"I don't know. It was my turn to use the powder room. There was a line."

"You couldn't let somebody ahead of you?"

"Mackenzie, I was eavesdropping and trying to be subtle about it. I couldn't just stand there crossed-legged and gape, could I?"

He shrugged. "Any idea who he was? His last name?"

I shook my head. You'd think he sees a ghost, the lady behind me had said, but what's to be made of a cliché? The more I thought about it, the less significant the whole thing became. I was filled with so-what's and of-courses. Of course I thought of Marley—he was Jacob. A common enough name for men that age. Somebody suggested ghosts and it was a Christmas party. So what if the old man called Clausen by his first and last names? A million people felt like his familiar from his obnoxious TV ads. Of course Clausen was surprised. He probably hadn't heard the old man's call, and then he got bonked from behind. I'd be shocked, too, given the circumstances.

"Sorry," I said. "That's all there is, and the more I think about it, the less it becomes."

Mackenzie, fine lines of disappointment around his mouth, returned to his archeological tasks.

"Tell you what," I said, "I'll go move the car." I, too, needed the illusion of achieving something, no matter what.

FOUR BLOCKS AWAY, I FOUND A BETTER, SAFER PARKING SPOT, but as I walked back, I didn't feel any particular sense of accomplishment.

I walked up the flagstone steps toward the Clausen house and suddenly faced a tall, gaunt woman, faded patrician face inside a mane of gray hair, eyeglasses attached to a thick brown cord, and pruning sheers in her hand. Sixtyish, she wore vintage slacks, a nondescript cardigan and a Chestnut Hill Academy warm-up jacket meant to be worn by a football player.

"Who are you?" she demanded. "A plainclothes*woman* or something like that? What now? What on earth *did* that man start with his foolishness?" She pursed her lips and scowled. "I told him. I said, 'Alexander, this is an unforgiveable mistake.' And I was right. Advertise your house number for anyone to see and what do you expect?" She crossed her arms. The pruning sheers stuck out like a lethal beak. It was a little chilly for gardening.

She saw me eyeing the shears. "Work in the greenhouse

whenever I can. Live next door. Saw you two arrive a while ago, then *you* left and I wondered, and now you're back. I don't like to pry, but has anything else happened? Lord knows, we've had a fire. Riffraff. A murder, the papers say. What will this do to property values? He wasn't very considerate. Not at all neighborly. I warned you, you know.''

"Me?"

"You people. I put in a complaint the second I read about that—that *event* in the paper.''

"I'm really sorry, but I—''

"You'd think you'd listen to a decent citizen. I never called you pigs. Never demonstrated once. Voted straight Republican my entire life.'' She assumed a chin-up, self-congratulatory posture.

"Ma'am . . . I'm not who you—''

"And what do I get? Blather about freedom of assembly. I said, 'Young man, to whom do you think you're speaking? I know my Constitution. I'm past-president of the D.A.R.' —who did he think he was?''

"What exactly is your complaint?'' I asked, as politely as I could.

"I know my unfortunates well as the next. I am on the boards of several charities. I've opened my house, too, when it was appropriate. But not to that kind. I warned him. I warned the police. Nobody listened.'' She pursed her lips until she looked like a drawstring had pulled her shut from inside. "Gave me insomnia, it did, worrying about them being right here, right next door. Prowling around.''

"There were people outside?''

"I called you people. You think anybody cared? A patrolman came in his own sweet time, but of course by then the prowler was gone.''

"When was this?''

"During his *party*.'' She said the last word as if she'd been talking about obscene revels. "Twice.''

"You called two times about prowlers?''

"Three times.'' She nodded, shaking her hair. I could suddenly see a spirited young woman whose best feature was rich long hair. The habit of using it for punctuation, of making certain everyone noticed it, had persisted.

"Not that they even responded the third time. Maybe if they had, they could have stopped the fire sooner."

"I don't understand." She was going to have to get to the point, if there was one, soon, or I'd forget that I was trying to be a nice person.

"Why shouldn't there be three prowlers when that man next door imported a herd of lowlifes?"

I was glad that she hadn't been invited to any of the gala holiday parties in the neighborhood. Even her own kind was rejecting her, and I felt there was some justice.

"That rude man of yours talked about the boy who cried wolf, can you imagine? Told me to go back to sleep. But I saw them. I certainly couldn't sleep."

"Ummm," I said. "And what was it they were doing?"

"The first time he was prowling around the front here, but of course you people waited until he was gone to arrive. The second time he was prowling all the way around back. And the third time he was rushing pell-mell down those very steps."

"Maybe they were guests, a little confused as to where they should be." I was sure the woman was paranoid, so afraid of "them" that she made ghosties and goblins out of stragglers.

"How will we ever know? You people—you said if I didn't see anybody on my own property, I shouldn't worry. Try to be a good neighbor and see where it gets you!"

"I'm sorry for your troubles," I told the woman. "We try our best, you know."

"Then come when I call."

I tried to look understanding, if not repentant, and turned to go inside. And then remembered something she'd said. "What did you mean we could have stopped the fire sooner if we'd come?" I asked.

"Well, you'd have been here, then. That last one? The one rushing out? It was only minutes—less than that—before I saw the house light up. Who do you think called the fire company as it was? Not that anybody's thanked me. Not once.''

"This person who was rushing away—was it a man or a woman?''

The long gray pageboy bobbled as she shook her head. "Wearing pants, who can tell? It was night. Dark. It's your job to find out more, not mine.''

We seemed out of chitchat. I thanked her and looked toward the house.

"If you ask me, and nobody has, that was the one started the fire,'' she snapped. "Maybe the one murdered Alexander!''

I thought so, too. Mackenzie had to talk to her, even though I was fairly sure I'd heard everything she had to say, except for more harsh opinions of the police and assorted riffraff.

"But you didn't even answer my call!''

Despite her fine features, she resembled a hag, an out-of-season Halloween witch, gray hair flying in the chilly wind.

"And now,'' she said, waving her shears at me, "it's too late!''

She was right. I apologized once again, and meant every word of it. My feet dragged as I went into the house.

Nine

"FOUND ALL KINDS OF STUFF," MACKENZIE SAID, KICKING up dust.

"There's a woman next door," I said. "You'd better take a statement from her."

"The witch?" he asked, still digging around. "Servino talked to her, and so did five other guys."

"She said nobody did."

"She calls every day. Maybe every hour. The precinct and headquarters. She is not an easily satisfied citizen."

I was no longer amused by his ridiculous digging. "We're looking for a list, not liquified ornaments," I reminded him. "And I was thinking—Sasha took pictures that night. Even if we can't find the list, maybe some of the people in her photos could be identified. What do you think?"

"Worth asking her. Why haven't you?"

"Because she's out of town."

He looked at me as if he knew she was somewhere she shouldn't be, doing things she shouldn't be doing, with someone she shouldn't be with. I was tired of his attitude toward her. "I'll leave a message tonight," I said. "Now—enough fun and games in the dirt. Clausen had a study somewhere. He went to get something from it when I was here for a meeting. It seems a more logical place to look."

He shrugged and sighed. He was having fun and I was

spoiling it. "They aren't all ruined. Some are real interestin'. Look over there where I put them."

The needlepoint cover on the piano bench had become history, but its frame made a nice nest for Mackenzie's treasures. "I know what your pockets must have been like when you were a little boy," I said, lifting shapeless lumps and bumps of metals, precious and otherwise. The golden ornaments had been paint. I should have realized that all along, but the house had overwhelmed common sense. Now the Mackenzie collection featured hardened puddles of tin and lead.

"Mackenzie, this is silly. Clausen's study or his night table would be better hunting grounds."

"You have no patience," he mumbled.

"It's junk. Who wants melted drummer boys? And if anybody does, let them pick through themselves."

"What about this?" he asked.

I shrugged. It was a crystal, with its wire hanger burned away, but who cared? Who cared about any of it—a gray snowflake of something like iron? A colorless lump that might have been anything? An oversized duck head?

Is there such a thing as a double think, as in a doubletake?

"Mackenzie?"

"You're right." He wiped his filthy hands on his jeans. "Time to move on. That was fun, though."

"About this duck."

"Must have sentimental meaning. Kind of funny looking. Heavy, too, for an ornament."

"It's not an ornament. Not for a tree, anyway." I turned it over. The base of the head, the duck's neck, was hollow.

Mackenzie shook his head. "Body's missing?"

"Not a duck body. Something long and round that burned."

"Like a cane," he said softly.

"Exactly like a cane." I could see him, the ghost, tapping Alexander Clausen on the shoulder. He had held the cane up high and used the head of it—I remembered a flash of silvery metal, maybe even a beak.

"Maybe it was ornamental," Mackenzie said.

"It wasn't. He could stand without it, but not walk." The morning's queasy anxiety flooded back.

We didn't theorize. Instead, we found the richly paneled study and searched the drawers and shelves. I checked out his books, a compulsion of mine. This was a pip of a library, featuring gold-tooled editions of Reader's Digest Condensed Books, the twelve-volume autobiography of one Hon. Alfred Pettywell, a book on diseases of the ear, a two-part religious autobiography of a Welsh woman and the bound proceedings of the 1948 conference on maritime law.

"He bought books by the yard," I said. Another act against humanity on his part.

"Or by binding. Notice that they're all brown and green?" Mackenzie was fiddling with the computer, looking for disks or file directories with something suggesting guest lists.

"I give up," he said. "I never thought we'd find anything, anyway."

"This trip was to humor me?"

"Also to charm you, seduce you into remembering how honorable and fahn I am. Things like that. You've been pretty testy lately."

"You weren't really looking for anything? Just enjoying play digging!"

"That's what I mean—did you always have this temper? Are you sufferin' from holiday stress?"

"Damn, Mackenzie, you're so hung up on your stupid theory that Laura did it that you're never going to look any further. Even that lady next door—"

"My, my," he said. "I think you're letting your emotions cloud your vision. Like maybe I wasn't looking for something, but I at least know that I probably found something."

"Like what?"

"Like why do I have to tell you, Sherlock? You losin' it? Listen, I am dyin' of thirst. Let us wend our way back to the kitchen, and maybe I'll tell."

"What did you mean?" I asked as we headed for the sink.

"When still attached to a cane, a duck would be a pretty effective head-basher, don't you think? But you were supposed to think of that. You were supposed to get Nancy Drewish, whoop it up and win your sleuthing medal. How come I have to say my lines and yours, too? You must be stressed out. Florida's going to do you a world of good."

"The old man did it, then?" I felt lighter than I had in days.

He turned the faucet. Nothing happened. "Turned the water off," he said. "Drained the pipes."

"Forget it." I wrapped my arms around him and kissed him solidly. "I'll buy you a drink. Let's go."

"What's the occasion?"

"You are at last considering the idea of an unknown killer. You have actually broadened your line of vision. A holiday miracle."

"Right. My vision's now broad enough to notice that you look like Al Jolson singing 'Mammy.' Talk about doin' something dirty. That kiss set new records." He looked like a miner himself.

I touched my face, and he grinned even more. "Now you have streaks, too," he said. "Go the other direction and you'll be plaid." My hands had ashy deposits on every finger. "Interesting. You should see yourself. No place you'd want to be is going to let us in. And we don't have water."

I remembered the laundry-room lean-to. There should be some rags that could help remove the grit.

"Do not think I don't appreciate the return of your admiration," Mackenzie called out. "But in all fairness, there is still a problem."

The laundry room did indeed have a box of authentic rags. And surely even servants were given a small mirror in their bathroom?

"Because," he said, walking into the shed and shivering, "if the old man did it—where'd he go?"

It was bothering me, too. Marley couldn't have been the "prowler" rushing away, not if his cane were still inside the house.

The bathroom's amenities were as minimal as I'd expected them to be. Bare linoleum floor. Tub with white plastic curtain. Toilet, sink, a thin-looking towel, a small square of mirror and a window that looked out at the unlandscaped, utilitarian part of the grounds. I stared through it, wondering, while I worked on my face.

So Marley wasn't the rushing-away prowler. Maybe there hadn't been any interlopers, not in front, not in back, not on the stairs. Maybe they were a variety of upper-crust delerium tremens.

My mood wasn't sparkling to begin with, but the view from the maid's bath was not designed to lift it. What a switch from the cultivated grounds I'd seen at the entrance and from the bedroom windows, whence, even in the dead of winter, the view was organized and planned. All the unfortunate tenants of these quarters would be able to see in any season were trash and garbage cans, an unused dog run, a clothesline and a storage shed. Even the prying neighbor was spared the dismal sight by a high hedge. I shook my head, mesmerized, watching a gust of wind make the clothesline shudder and the door of the storage shed bump open and flap closed.

No, not closed, because something was out of place, lying on the ground, partially out of the shed. Bad housekeeping, to leave gardening tools exposed that way to winter.

"Well, your soot is evened out," Mackenzie said, coming into the small bathroom with me. "Now you are exotic and dusky skinned."

"Look," I said. "Over there."

He looked and shrugged.

"The door's unlatched."

He looked at me quizzically, his frown lines accentuated by soot.

"Mackenzie, there is absolutely nothing out of place in this house, except for fire damage. The kitchen drawers were perfect, the cabinets, Clausen's study, Laura's bedroom. But that—" I pointed at the window. "That is gross mismanagement. Everything in there is going to rust, or decay, or whatever form its ruination takes. I can't quite make out what it is blocking the door, but I think—"

The wind blew again, and again the dark object, partly shiny, partly dull, was visible. We leaned toward the window and squinted. And then, without saying anything, we hurried out the back door.

"I have a terrible feeling," I said, my feet crunching on frozen grass.

He nodded.

"She said there was a prowler out back. But of course, she could have been mistaken. Probably was."

"Uh-huh," Mackenzie said. "And probably, some people store shoes outside for the winter. With socks, and legs, still in them."

And then we were at the shed, and Mackenzie opened the door and there he was, a frozen sculpture of a crumpled man, contorted as if someone had tried to shove him onto a shelf, mouth open, expression confused.

"Marley," I said. Definitely. And definitely as dead as a doornail. Perhaps this wasn't the year to try for seasonal joy. The season certainly wasn't doing its fair share. It was hard to manage even a feeble "fa-la-la."

On the plus side, which was harder and harder to find, it's good to be with a cop when stumbling over corpses. Saves lots of official pestering and suspicion.

I stood on the frosty front lawn, near the remnants of the sofa on which Gladys and I had relaxed three nights ago, and on which Alexander Clausen had been immolated later that same night. I watched uniformed police transport poor frozen John Jacob Doe to a wagon, and then to the morgue, and sighed for his ignominious end, for his anonymity, for the whole wretched mess. Mackenzie stood at the curb, talking to the neighbor woman, who had swooped down on us, this time carrying a trowel and shouting "I *knew* it! I just knew it!"

I stayed out of it. The police hadn't hassled me, hadn't questioned me, hadn't intimated that I had placed the old man in the toolshed. I was with Mackenzie and my virtue was a given. I tried to take comfort from that, but even now that he was out of our hands, no longer our concern, the man I had referred to as Marley's ghost haunted me. Perhaps that's who he really was.

I tried to perk up on the ride back into town by searching

for clever or imaginative Christmas trimmings, but the spirit of the season eluded me. Maybe I needed to do something more active about it. If I couldn't be jolly, I could at least give.

We parked, washed, changed and, at my request, walked the five blocks to Laura's aunt's apartment. It was early. I didn't think we'd interrupt dinner or whatever Christmas Eve plans they might have. Besides, the book of poetry was a good excuse to touch base with Laura again.

"Be careful," I said as we rang the bell. "Tread gently." Mackenzie looked annoyed. "Sorry," I said. "You didn't need to be told that. I just needed to say it."

Laura answered the door, looking even less substantial, more swallowed by her clothing than was normal for her. Maybe I'd take her shopping when the sales began. We'd get her out of her father's camouflage and into something that let her look real.

She ushered us into a spacious, rather spare living room. It was all colorless gleam—bare waxed floors, subdued fabrics, sepia prints in metal frames, clear surfaces with no ornaments, souvenirs or books. The decor was chic and generically correct, but not a style that went well with flesh, let alone human imperfection and unpredictability. A Christmas tree, small but green and with brightly wrapped packages below it was the only oasis of color.

From somewhere in the far reaches of the apartment, I heard the splutters of a television set. In this room, all was silence, except for Alice Clausen, who sat sobbing on a gray flannel chair. She murmured hello and returned to heavy sniffling.

"She hasn't been . . ." Laura said. "Since yesterday, she's . . ."

"This must be Laura's teacher and the detective." A vigorous version of Alice strode toward me. Her hair was a darker blond, her eyes a deeper blue, her voice and step surer, the whole bone structure a shade less fine. I couldn't determine whether she was the older or younger sister. "I'm Alma Leary." She extended her hand. "And I hope this isn't official business."

"I've brought a Christmas gift for Laura," I said.

Alice buried her face in her handkerchief, but I still heard unhappy squeaks.

"However, ma'am," Mackenzie said, "since we are here, I hope you won't mind discussin' a few points with us." Alma and Laura looked at him intently. "See, it appears there is a new problem. Somebody else," he said in his slow, unthreatening manner. "An unidentified elderly gentleman."

"What about him?" Alma demanded. "Wait—what do you mean unidentified? Is he—you mean he's—"

Mackenzie nodded. "Dead, ma'am." He spoke with no hint of urgency, but Alice Clausen swiveled her head and changed her focal point to the detective.

"Somebody else? Another dead person?" she wailed. "Where? Who? What are you talking about?"

"We don't know who. He was, ah, in the toolshed."

"The service port?" Alice looked stunned.

Alma took over. "Inside it? But I know where it is—and it's shut up, isn't it? Didn't we talk about keeping it locked, Alice? People steal mowers and leaf blowers and things. Didn't the gardener take care of it? How would anyone get into it? And why?"

We were still all standing in the middle of the sterile room. Alma edged closer to Mackenzie. She was either belligerent or protective, I couldn't tell. She looked at Mackenzie in a manner that made him seem shorter than she was. "He must be a homeless person who broke in, went to sleep and died. Froze, or something. You always read about such things. Could have happened at any time. It's been a cold winter." She didn't actually brush her hands together as if wiping away that topic, but that was the effect. You got the idea that Alma solved things. And quickly.

"Interestin' theory," Mackenzie murmured. "However, this man was at the party. Miss Pepper here remembers him. White haired, with a limp. Used a cane with a duck-head handle?"

Laura nodded. She remembered him, too, murmuring that

he hadn't eaten his dinner, and she'd joked with him about it.

"Sit down," Alma said. She was a rather brusque hostess.

We obeyed, settling on an unyielding sofa covered in pinstripe. "You have a housekeeper living in that room, Mrs. Clausen?" Mackenzie asked. There had been no sign of life in the tiny cell-like quarters.

Alma nodded vigorously. "Marta," she said, answering for her sister, who was preoccupied with sniveling. "Nice girl, if a little slow." She paused, wrinkled her forehead and turned to Alice. "Wait a minute. Where *is* Marta? Where did she go? Where is she living now?"

It seemed a little late to think about a woman who had presumably been wandering around, homeless, for days.

Alice shook her head. "Oh. I remember. She quit." She wiped her eyes. "Wouldn't live there. Not even with a TV in her room. Left last Monday, but don't tell—" She looked stunned, then almost smiled. "I was going to say don't tell Alexander. He gets so angry when they quit, and they always do. It isn't my fault, either."

"So your husband would have assumed this Marta was still there?" Mackenzie asked.

"Well, not on Thursday night, it was her night off. She came back Friday mornings, but yes, he would have assumed she still lived with us."

"Do you know who the man in the toolshed was, Mrs. Clausen?" Mackenzie asked abruptly.

Alice gasped. "Of course not! Those people he brought in—all those people, they weren't the kind that I'd—of course not! Why would I—why would you ask?"

Mackenzie smiled, rather sheepishly. "I don't know. Your husband seems to have known him. Called him 'Jacob,' in fact."

"Alexander knew everybody. He was famous. Important. I wasn't."

Mackenzie seemed satisfied. Then, looking as if the idea had just this second come to him, as if it were indeed still coming in dribs and drabs, he leaned forward and spoke, slowly. "I'm wonderin', is it possible, do you think, that maybe somebody wanted to hide him?"

"The man in the toolshed?" Alice said. "Why? Why there? From whom?"

Mackenzie shrugged in apparent bewilderment. But his shoulder movement jogged my brain, and I could see from Alice's face that it had the same effect on her. I wish I knew how he manages to turn slouching and relaxing into prods.

Because who else would the man need to be hidden from but Alice, Laura or Peter? Who else was there? I tried working on why.

That they would recognize him seemed obvious, but necessary to say.

Laura had already remembered him with no particular emotional response. And Peter would have seen him as well, while waiting tables. And so had Alexander, definitely. So the man wasn't being hidden from him.

He had to be hidden from Alice.

My brain ached. I was close to my capacity for mulling, but I pushed on, trying to be logical.

Who'd hidden the old man? Not the person who'd killed Clausen, because why not leave his body where it could burn up along with Santa? Where, indeed, it could have been assumed to be Clausen's killer.

Mackenzie stretched, long legs way out on Alma's polished floors, eyes half-closed. He was deep into his poor-Southern-boy act, forcing us to think our way through to the conclusions he had long since reached.

If it wasn't Clausen's killer, who was left but Clausen himself?

Alice snuffled and sighed raggedly. Why would Clausen fear that pathetic, sniveling, unhappy, drunken woman? Must have come downstairs after the party. Come to, wanted something. Maybe stumbling, falling, giving notice. Scaring Clausen, because Alice knew the old man. Even drunk.

All of this took seconds, as if the various components and half-ideas had been accumulating all day, waiting for one good shake to fall into place.

Laura stood up. "Excuse me, please," she said.

"She's calling him again. That boyfriend," Alma said as soon as Laura had left. "On the phone with him every single minute he's not here in person. Something upsets her, pleases her, frightens her—anything, doesn't matter. Jumps up and calls." She tapped her finger on the chrome arm of her chair. "Isn't right. A girl needs to hold on to her dignity."

Alice whimpered.

"It's hitting her, finally," Alma whispered. "She's been in shock until now."

Alice had been in shock for years. I wasn't sure she could come out of it all on her own, or if the process wouldn't require long-term and careful monitoring.

Laura came back. Shortest teenage conversation on record, I thought. Her aunt said as much.

"He's not there." There had been a further dwindling of self. She hugged her arms close, as if to protect the little that was left.

"Maybe he's on the way here, then." Alma's voice was unexpectedly comforting and considerate.

Laura shook her head. "He's away. In Pittsburgh, with his grandmother. Until school starts." She looked at Mackenzie. "His mother said the police gave permission."

"And he didn't have the decency to tell you?" Alma was a pretty good all-purpose protector.

"Maybe he couldn't." Laura's eyes glinted too much, and she blinked, hard. "She—his mother—said I tricked him into confessing just because he was once in trouble, that . . . I used him, I was bad, and . . ." She shuddered and stopped, rubbing a hand across her eyes.

"I'm sure he tried to call and that he doesn't agree with his mother for a minute." I couldn't bear the sight of that undersized child holding off a world that offered not one comfortable corner. With Peter gone, what did she have?

"She wouldn't even tell me his grandmother's name."

Before we left, I tried to make it clear to Laura, without insulting either her mother or aunt, that I was ready to do what I could to help. I promised to call, asked her to call whenever she needed me, day or night. I told her that I was leaving for Florida Wednesday morning, but I'd be available until then. I didn't know what else to do or say. I handed her her gift, aware that a book of poetry was a pretty feeble amulet.

OUR ORIGINAL AGENDA HAD CALLED FOR GIFT OPENING ON Christmas Eve. It sounded romantic and adult, gifting and sipping brandy by the fire, spending the long night in search of inspired ways to say thank you.

But we didn't feel festive, so we postponed celebrations until morning. As if a night's sleep would drive the goblins away.

And then there we were, on Merry Christmas itself, surrounded by open packages, and for the twentieth time, Mackenzie asked me if I remembered anything else.

"You mean since the last time you asked? Or the time before that?" I smiled to soften my words, and poured more hot chocolate. It was Christmas, after all. Absolute last chance to get into the spirit of the season.

"Guess Alice's shrink wouldn't like for her to identify a corpse today," he said, ignoring the steaming mug I put in front of him. "It bein' Christmas and all."

"She said she didn't know any Jacob," I reminded him.

"Sure, and that's why somebody dragged the old man all the way out back."

I tried not to hear. I looked around the room, and was pleased by the tableau. Macavity, not interested in his new catnip-stuffed mouse, was nonetheless ecstatic, creeping through the jungle of gift wrap, pouncing on ribbons and shredding tissue paper. The fire crackled, my tiny tree sparkled in the window, and our lavish-but-noncommittal offerings lay about. Mackenzie was wearing the blue-blue sweater. As hoped, it did indeed stoke the flame in his eyes so that looking at him—at least when he wasn't speculating about the frozen man—was potentially hazardous to my health.

I was wearing the zanily striped knee socks he'd given me, although not the matching mittens or scarf. And not the lush sweater. Oh, mine was green, to bring out the copper in my hair, he said. Neither of us grinned, let alone snickered, let alone intimated that we had both gone through the same lengthy and nervous deliberations, or that we completely understood the small print accompanying our gifts.

Instead, Mackenzie said something about great minds going in the same direction and I didn't ask what direction that was.

"Mandy?" he said now.

"Ah, yes. I remember that he was there, that he called Clausen 'Alexander,' which means nothing because everybody who watches old movies on TV knows his name, and he tapped him on the shoulder with the duck-head end of his cane when he didn't respond. And by the way, I was wondering, is it possible that your Christian name is Christian?"

Mackenzie ran his palm, almost unconsciously, over the soft blue covering his chest. If he would just get off the case, shut up, I would be happy to do the same. "It is possible, but not so," he said. "And Clausen looked surprised, but appeared to recognize him?"

I had to stop watching his hands and ask him to repeat himself, and then all I did was sigh, conveying, I hoped, my ennui.

I refilled my own cup with chocolate and popped marshmallows on top with almost no caloric anxiety, which was my only visible sign of holiday spirit.

"Who else d'you think was there?" It was hard to understand him, his mild drawl was muffled as he stood next to the tree, sipping chocolate, facing the quiet street through frost-etched panes. Unintelligible but picturesque, but then, he almost always was.

I kept quiet. With no encouragement, surely he'd stop this gruesome chitchat.

"Because a lame old man didn't kill Clausen, start that fire, then levitate outside."

I joined him at the window, although with the tree and the small size of the room, we had to be very close. Which wasn't much of a problem.

"I have brain fatigue, Mackenzie. I'm on vacation." It was cold and gray outside. We had a fire and each other and no obligations. What were we doing talking his shop? I touched his blue back and thought of the freezing, fog-colored days ahead, of all the hot chocolate we could drink behind frosted windows. And I willed myself into his consciousness, willed him to feel the magnetic pull. Lifted my hand to his silver-sprinkled curls and let the current of my feelings rush through my fingers, into his skull. And there I implanted specifics. There's no time to waste, I telegraphed into his brain. We have to be together, and since you can't go home again, let's not. Don't go to Florida and I won't go to New Orleans. Mandy, I don't want to leave you.

I pressed gently but firmly.

"Damn, but I don't want to leave," he said. I gasped, dropped my hands and felt dizzy with my powers.

"—just when the Clausen thing gets interestin'."

After I bandaged my psyche, I wondered if Mackenzie and I would last into the new year.

"So," HE SAID OVER LUNCH. "WHAT ARE YOU DOIN' TOmorrow?" Of course, if he cared what filled my social calendar, he could have filled it himself. He was in such a rush to escape, he was leaving the night before I did. Even if he said that was the only available flight. "Countless things," I said. "Have to buy sun block and find an airplane book and water the plants and board Macavity." All of which required, at the outside, one of the day's twenty-four hours. "And other stuff," I added lamely.

"And that lady? Those old people? Your good deed?"

I wanted him to have forgotten about that. I myself was waffling again. "Oh, I don't know. They're all the way out in the Northeast, and it's right in the middle of the day. Really inconvenient."

I stood up to clear the lunch dishes, but Mackenzie, demonstrating one of his many endearing traits, took over. He's the only male I've known who doesn't even leave the pots to soak. "I wonder if my mother really promised her I'd be there with cannoli, or if anybody would even notice if I didn't show up." I put away the place mats.

Mackenzie didn't answer. He washed and whistled. Now that he'd broached the subject, he was leaving me to find my own honorable path. I stood at a moral crossroads, debating between "I forgot, Ma," and "Sorry, I couldn't make it, Jenny," and my favorite, the path marked "Least Resistance."

He used the water spray on a pot and muttered. "Damn, I'm gettin' this all wet." He stopped the water, wiped his hands and pushed away the wicker basket that usually sat next to the sink. "Don't you ever read or get rid of your mail?" The basket overflowed with envelopes, the large one from Silverwood on top.

"I read the good stuff, but that's full of junk and messages from the Beatrice Pepper Sexual Clipping Society."

"Sounds like something I'd rip right open."

"You'd be disappointed. The last article was called, 'Do We Need Bodily Secretions to Have Fun?' "

But I went through the old mail anyway. The form letters went into the trash as I pondered my need to open them before discarding them. And finally I reopened the manila envelope from the Tuesday people and contemplated *Mining Silver*, all fifteen duplicated and stapled pages of type and awkward illustrations. If indeed I went to the creative writing class's celebration, it would be nice to read their work first.

"This month's theme" the cover announced, was "I Can Never Forget," and despite myself, as soon as I opened it up, I was hooked.

The first memoir was a man's account of the Depression, of losing his business and home, yet hanging on and riding it through. I skipped around, looking for my former pupils, and I found one by Victor, a brief and humorous memory of playing hookey to go fishing sixty-five years ago. The next two were heartbreaking, one about living in Germany before World War II, and one, by sweet and cheerful Jenny of all people, about losing her child.

I read out loud as I went along. "You see why I liked teaching there?" I said. "There's so much vigor and enthusiasm." I wondered, not for the first time, how I could transfer some of this delight into my Philly Prep students, and realized, not for the first time, that I couldn't. It was both too late and too soon for them to have any real sense of the wonder of ordinary life.

Another one, by Sarah, one of my Christmas cookie bakers, began, "All I ever knew how to do just right was cook and eat, and I'll tell you about the best meal of my life." And she did. And it was delicious reading.

And then I saw Minna White's. I half expected it to be about cannoli remembered, but it wasn't. "Want me to keep reading to you?" Mackenzie had finished at the sink and was settled in the suede chair with a fresh cup of coffee. "By all means," he said.

"It's called 'Virtue Rewarded: An Un-Fairy Tale.' Doesn't seem to be the assigned topic, but there's one rebel in every class, I guess." I cleared my throat.

Once upon a time there lived a man who worked at the Royal Stables, tending the finest horses in the land. He and his wife and son were good, hardworking people and they were happy.

But sometimes, when she read her boy a fairy tale, his wife wished that something not so ordinary would happen. That there were a special test her family could pass, like heroes did. Her husband shared the wish.

One day the King became ill and needed someone to oversee his stables. The man thought it would be him, that that would be his special challenge, but a newcomer was chosen and rewarded with extra gold and praise. In fact, the King called him "my son" and it became his name.

After a while, the horses did not look well, or they disappeared altogether, and the stable hands—except for "Myson"—were not paid for many weeks. The man was told the horses were grazing in new fields. He didn't believe it and said so to his fellow-worker and friend, Etienne. Etienne said not to worry. But then, Etienne never worried. He cared for little beyond his own finery, especially a richly embroidered cloak he wore to and from the stable.

One day, the man found Etienne's cloak in a field. Myson said he had run away, ashamed because he had killed the horses and starved others and now, the sta-

bles were ruined and had to be sold. It was all Etienne's
fault, he said.

But the man knew Myson lied. Etienne never let his
cloak out of his sight. The man's wife said he must tell
the King, that it was hard to say that his adopted son
was a liar and probably a thief, but this was their true
test at long last. They would soon be heroes.

Instead, when the man told the King, the King became angry and called him a jealous liar and told him
to leave the kingdom.

Myson opened his own stables. The man was forbidden to come near it. Impoverished and broken, rep-
utation ruined, he died.

The widow and her child huddled together and lived
like the squirrels and birds. And one day, when deep
snow buried all hope of food and they were starving,
they ate the book of fairy tales, heroes and heroines,
happy endings, virtues rewarded and all.

And that is what I will never forget.

                                        Minna White

"What do you suppose that means?" he asked me.

"I don't know. But it feels as if I were just tattooed with
it. It feels permanent. As the lady says, 'that is what I will
never forget.' " I read it all the way through again. It still
didn't make sense, and it still clung to me.

Ten

NEXT MORNING, WE SAID AMAZINGLY AMICABLE FARE-wells, all things considered, including how early it was. Mackenzie was going to leave immediately after his shift, so there was no other time.

"You'll be back the first?" he asked at the door.

I nodded.

"New Year's Eve in Florida," he said. "Your last night in the tropics. Moon over Miami or wherever. Be careful."

I envisioned the condominium complex's social room, a drink with a fluorescent pink umbrella sticking out of it, the stuttering podiatrist and me wearing fool hats and blowing noisemakers, reassuring Beatrice Pepper and friends that we were having fun.

"I thought to come back earlier," Mackenzie said, "but standby's good as I could get, so I didn't bother you to hurry home. Amazin' how many people are rushing to and from New Orleans."

It was something. More than he'd been willing to say until now.

"So we'll celebrate the New Year on New Year's Night instead of its Eve." He kissed me. "You're not hung up on dates that way, are you?" He kissed me again. "Course not."

He didn't notice that this was not a two-way conversation. Yes, I should have said, owning up to yet another neurosis.

Yes, yes. I believe that certain dates are heavy with meaning
and magical portents and New Year's Eve is the biggie. The
feel of midnight is the feel of the year, according to my
irrational but powerful mental set. Which meant I could an-
ticipate an interminably long, romantically dismal twelve
months ahead, thanks or no thanks to Mackenzie.

"Certainly would prefer spending the time with you, 'stead
of my cousins and all. 'Course with you wanting to see your
folks, I didn't want to push on you." He shrugged. Until this
moment, neither of us, obviously, had even once said what
we really wanted of these holidays. It hadn't been allowed in
the rules of our game, so we were both losing. High time to
change the game. My first New Year's resolution.

"See you in six days. I'll bring champagne." Moments
later, he was gone.

"Fine," I said to myself, tidying the room at long last.
"Fine. *Fahn!*" I had things to do, sun block to buy, people
to see. Maybe Minna White would actually have something
interesting to say about why she was not sad about Alexander
Clausen's death. If, indeed, she was not. My mother had a
habit of holding old acquaintains in suspended animation,
treating whatever whim they entertained when last seen as a
lifelong obsession. The likelihood was that Minna had forgotten whatever it was, or outgrown it, or outlived it while
my mother clung to the memory.

I felt abruptly depressed about how efficiently I had messed
up my Christmas vacation. I dialed Sasha. She had changed
her message, but I knew she could do that by remote. "Sasha
Berg, Photographer. Sorry," her recorded voice said, "but
I'm on assignment and can't come to the phone right now. If
you'll leave your . . ." She sounded on the verge of hysterical laughter and not one bit contrite at missing her callers.

"You're making him sound like a chore," I told her machine. "I know you've picked up your messages, so you
know I need those shots you took at the party, but maybe I
didn't make it sound urgent enough. Even if you're permanently stuck to your assignment, could you drop the film off,
or something? I need those pictures. Desperately. It's your

garden-variety life-and-death situation." I hung up, hoping that Mr. Assignment proved a short-term dud.

Sasha and I spent a lot of time recuperating from the men who visited our lives. The difference was, she had one hell of a good time until the end, while I too often dithered and quibbled my way through the good parts.

This variety of self-analysis sounded even more boring than boarding the cat and visiting a convalescent home, so I dressed in my hundred layers and, with apologies, put Macavity in his cardboard carrier and countered his plaintive protests with a frank explanation of how things stood.

"Listen, little guy," I said, "it's going to be cold and lonely around here. Not homey, and no food, either. You love the vet, remember?" I had to keep talking, nonstop, to prevent a feline psychotic break. Even with my babble, when faced with a car ride, Macavity began jet-propelled shedding. A long enough ride, and he'd be bald. "Remember your pals at Dr. Chang's?" I said. "Think of this as your Christmas vacation. A change of scenery is—"

We were halfway out the door when the phone rang. Perhaps Sasha was back. Or all flights today and tomorrow had been canceled. Or my mother was warning me to stay at home because of hurricane warnings. Or—

But the voice that finally spoke was tentative and small. "Well," it said, sounding discouraged. "I'll call back later, I guess. I, um—"

I galumphed across the room, still carrying the cat and hampered by about twenty pounds of outerwear, and lifted the receiver. "Laura?" I said. "I'm here. What's up?"

"Oh, I thought you were . . . Well, it's not anything, really. Just that my mother . . ."

It was no longer Christmas and we were back to business as usual. Undoubtedly the police had asked Alice to identify the body in the storage shed. "Is she very upset?" I asked.

Macavity mewled nonstop.

"Well, yes, actually." Her breath caught.

"I'm sorry. Did she know who he was?"

"Who?"

"Your mother." I put the cat carrier down, and Macavity grew silent and meditative.

"What about my mother?"

I pulled off my hat. Perhaps it was cutting off brain circulation, interfering with my comprehension. "Could she identify the body?"

"What body?"

"The man! The man we found in the . . . we aren't talking about the same thing, are we?"

"I don't know. What are *you* talking about?"

"About the—never mind. What are you talking about?"

"My mother."

"Yes. What about her?"

I could hear Laura take a deep breath and slowly exhale. "She's away. In . . . at a . . . residential treatment center. A . . . place to rest. She's very upset."

Which was a pretty fair description of how Laura herself sounded. "Oh. Oh my. Oh, I'm sorry, Laura. This just happen?"

"Yes." In a tiny, defeated voice. "A few minutes ago."

"Do you know for how long?"

"No."

"Had she gotten—what happened?"

There was such a long silence, I apologized for having created it. "I'm sorry. I don't know why I asked. Listen, I—"

"Since Christmas Eve. She couldn't stop. All the time. About it, about him. Apologizing. Crying. About her crimes, she said. About wanting to be dead. I think being with my aunt's family, with all of them together, the holiday might have . . . I don't know. I thought when they left this morning, maybe she'd feel better, but she didn't, because even then she kept begging me to . . . to forgive her. The doctor tried a shot first, and she was already on some kind of tranquilizer, but she was drinking a lot, too, so they were afraid, and . . . the police called, too, this morning, about coming to the morgue, but that only—she couldn't, she . . . well . . . So I called the doctor again, and . . . Well, I thought you'd want to know." The tidal wave of information was over.

"I'm so sorry. So sorry." I couldn't think of anything else, or anything truer to say.

Then silence filled our receivers. I pictured her sitting by the hall phone in that hard-surfaced apartment, all gleam and loneliness.

Nobody else was in the picture.

She'd said something about Alma and family leaving. I remembered. A trip to Antigua, wasn't it? And Laura had been left with an increasingly despondent, or hysterical, mother.

Now she was all alone, and that was the real message. She would probably be placed in a group home or foster care as soon as somebody noticed. Except she had let me notice first. She was no better at communicating what she needed this holiday season than Mackenzie and I had been, but she had youth as her excuse, and at least she was trying.

"Laura," I asked, "are you alone?"

"It's okay. There's food, and, um, tapes and books."

"I know you're competent, but I don't like the whole idea of your being alone, so to put my mind at ease, please stay here until we figure out something else. I have a spare room with a roll-away on the top floor."

"Oh, no. I couldn't do that. It's your vacation. You're going away."

"No . . . that was just a . . . possibility. Anyway, it'll be a treat. In fact, for starters, I have to go to the Italian market. Ever been there?"

"No," she said. "But still, I can't . . ."

"Fine. It's done. Pack your bags. I'll be by in thirty minutes. That enough time?"

"Yes, sure, but—"

"Done."

I immediately began reassuring my conscience. My offer had nothing to do with getting out of my Florida obligation or escaping from the podiatrist. It had to do with Laura, with decency and priorities. Didn't it?

My conscience began to look more and more like my mother, a more formidable and skeptical antagonist. I decided on the manatee defense. Could the chairperson of

HLH, Hava Little Hu-Manatee, not take pity on another endangered species? Laura was as gentle and without defenses as those sweet doomed sea cows, only it wasn't motorboat propellers and pollution destroying her. Neither creature had any idea of how to fight, even when it meant saving their lives. My mother would have to understand.

Besides, I'd visit in January.

THE ITALIAN MARKET BUSTLED. CORRUGATED TIN ROOFS rattled in the cold wind over sidewalk tables full of life. Laura and I crossed the street, kicking aside cut-up and discarded produce cartons. We walked past tables of winter fruit—cornucopias of crisp apples, dusty gold pears, deep purple grapes, and oversized navel oranges that reminded me of the need to call Florida and give an update. Past the vegetable displays—hard-shelled squash, potatoes, onions, things with roots and tenacity holding on through the chill; and delicate imports, tomatoes and artichokes and red, green and yellow bell peppers.

This bustling, noisy, confusing market, unlike antiseptic indoor food stores, activated my often-dormant domestic streak. I wanted to devote my life to orchestrating rich and colorful soups, salads, and fruit bowls, to covering my arms with flour as I kneaded bread. Here, foraging seemed a sensual adventure. It was, for example, necessary to compare several vendors' peppers for price and beauty before rushing to judgment. Nothing was uniform, homogenized, prepackaged or predictable.

We weighed eggplants in our palms, compared cucumbers, ducked into tiny shops for a blast of warm air and fresh pasta in one, herbs in another and cheese in a third, planning a feast for the evening. Laura, despite the heavy bags of trouble she was carrying, seemed lighter and more animated that I had ever seen her.

"How could I have forgotten garlic?" I said just as we approached the cannoli shop. Inside, customers filled every inch of floor space.

"I saw some down the street," Laura seemed invigorated by every part of the process, excited by this infinitesimal bit of control over her life—deciding what she'd eat and choosing it. She glanced into the packed store. "I'll get it and meet you back here."

I pressed my way into the crowd and waited my turn, embroiled this time in a caloric argument with my conscience. The filled crepes looked irresistible, but I would resist. I decided to buy Minna four cannoli, one of each flavor of sweet ricotta filling. And reassured myself that I would not touch a single pastry.

However, Laura deserved an after-dinner treat, and offering only one seemed Scrooge-like, so I'd buy one of each again, having them on hand—not for my hands, of course, but . . .

"If I had known you loved the food of my ancestors, I'd never have suggested a WASP minimalist restaurant like Lissabeth's."

Nick Riley successfully terminated my grapples with conscience. "I didn't know cannoli were an Irish dish," I said, oddly glad to see him again.

"I am an Irish dish. But also an Italian dish, thank you," he said. "What are you doing on my stomping grounds?"

I remembered he'd said he lived nearby.

"I thought you'd be at your parents by now." I found it flattering that he remembered such minor data about me. "If I'd known you were in town, I would have called," he added, flattering me even more.

"I had to cancel the trip. Last-minute change of plans. How's your article going?"

"Every time I nearly finish, the story changes. Now that it's officially a murder, I need a handle on what really happened so I don't wind up with egg on my face."

"Would you look at that," I said. Amongst the various Italian delights, there was a square tray of three-cornered pastries, each with a dollop of filling. I scanned the row of labels, unable to tell which identified the tray. "Zuccotto," one said. "Il Diplomatico." "Chiacchiere della nonna." "Torta Sbricciolona."

"What?" Nick said. "Look at what?"

"Those pastries. They look exactly like my great-aunt

Rachel's hamantaschen. Haman's hats, for the Purim holiday. But here they are in an Italian bakery—isn't that intrigu-
ing? A great example of cross-cultural borrowing. I wonder
if they're the Zeppole di San Giuseppe. Do you think that
means St. Joseph's hat? Instead of Haman's?''

Nick didn't even pretend to be interested in my speculations. He was still determined to write the definitive Clausen
article. ''You hear anything more about the case from your
friend on the force?''

''Not really. Like what?'' I tried to concentrate on Nick,
not the pastries.

''Like if they've found the weapon, or arrested anybody,
or have a theory of what happened. For my article. So it
makes sense.''

''Couldn't you write it as a mystery, instead?''

I heard clicking and turned. A woman who looked like a
cannoli herself—white fluffy fillinglike hair topping a brown-
wrapped solid cylinder—tapped impatiently on the display
case, waiting for me to order and be gone. ''One of each
flavor, please,'' I said. ''But twice.'' She frowned. ''Two
boxes, each with one of each flavor,'' I said.

''Wait—'' Why not bring cannoli for the Tuesday group,
too? Something to add to their dessert table. ''Make it three
boxes,'' I told the woman. ''Two boxes, like I said, and a
third with a dozen assorted in it.''

Nick raised his eyebrows. ''I'm impressed. Fear of cannoli
hips would deter most women.''

''They aren't for me!''

''That's what they all say. For a friend, right?''

''Not even that, really. A former student of mine, a friend
of my mother's, it turns out, a poor woman who's pretty
lonely, and blind and crippled. And a cannoli lover. And for
some other old people, up where she lives. My one gesture
of seasonal goodwill—or is it already too late for that?''

''Eight dollars even,'' the woman behind the counter said.
She looked like her feet hurt and she was trying not to notice
it. I counted out the exact change.

''Where?'' Nick asked me.

''Excuse me,'' I said to the cannoli woman. I pointed at

the triangular pastries, tingling with the pleasure of making an anthropological breakthrough. This was how Margaret Mead felt before comprehending whole societies. "What do you call these pastries?" I tilted my head, ready to catch hold of the unfamiliar Italian. "Listen to this, Nick," I said.

"Hamantaschen," the woman answered.

I darted a sideways look, but Nick hadn't listened to her or to me, so he wasn't snickering. He seemed distant, in a scowling and isolated place. "You ordering?" I asked him, since the woman was tapping again.

He looked startled. "One, with chips," he said. Once she handed it to him, he turned to me. "You don't sound happy about your cannoli run," he said. "How far 'up' is the 'up' you have to go to?"

"All the way. A place called Silverwood. The Northeast."

He nodded. "Way out there. But I'm going to be near that area today. I could drop the boxes off for you. Save you a trip."

"Thanks," I said. "But the visit, not the pastries, is the point."

"And this is a friend of your mother's?"

"Yes. From years ago." We worked our way toward the door.

"Your mother lays lots of these things on you?"

I shook my head. "But not for lack of trying," I added.

"Why go now?" he asked. I remembered how he'd pestered the guests at the Christmas party, and how he'd finally given up when they didn't answer, so I chose the same tactic.

My mind hovered around the party still, back to Sasha's photos, into Nick's notepad.

"Nick, when you did your interviews at the party, did you write down the people's names? The guests?"

"Only their first names. I'm not using much of them directly. It's really about Clausen. Why? They can't find out who was there?"

I nodded. Little questions, scraps floating around the case blew into sight. "Did you take a taxi to the party?" I asked,

"I drove my car. Why? What are you getting at?"

"Somebody came in a taxi. Odd, isn't it, for homeless people? Do you know who it was?"

"Why would I?"

"Your research?"

"Mandy, I wasn't asking those kind of questions."

"Sorry." I felt stupid. But Nick didn't seem stuck on the topic. In fact, he returned to my trip to the old-age home. This time he suggested that I skip it and spend the afternoon with him instead.

We stood outside the little shop, stamping our feet and puffing clouds into the air. And then I saw Laura, smiling triumphantly and waving a tiny brown paper bag. She had gone out into the jungle and captured a garlic, and she was so visibly proud I suspected that it was one of the few un-complicated and absolute triumphs adults had allowed her so far. I would try and think of other do-able tests of compe-tence while she was with me.

Nick registered her presence with open surprise. Back and forth he looked from Laura to me as if we were the least likely pair imaginable.

Surely now that the papers called Alexander Clausen's death murder, and spoke of a head wound, Nick couldn't still think this frail child was responsible, could he?

As for Laura, the nearer she came, the more her smile dwindled, as if Nick were some sort of drizzle, dampening her flame. She knit her brows and looked at him with puz-zlement. Then she looked at me, unconsciously copycatting Nick's emotions.

"You've met before, I believe," I said, as all three of us winced in the stinging chill outdoors. "Laura Clausen, Nick Riley. Laura's staying with me a while." I stamped my feet and tried to huddle further inside my coat.

Laura's breath came in rapid, shallow gasps, each punc-tuated with a little steam cloud. "When?" she asked, anx-iously. "Where did we meet?"

"The night your . . . the night of the Christmas party at your house," Nick said. "I was writing a story about your father. But you were probably too busy to notice me."

"No. I remember you. But I'm confused." She sighed deeply, then shook her head, as if to clear it.

"That turned out to be a pretty confusing night," I said. "It's a wonder anybody can remember anything. Listen, Nick, we have to get moving. It was great seeing you again."

"You choose cannoli instead of me, right? What will you talk about with a blind old woman?"

"Whatever she likes. Probably about my mother and the old days. Or she's gotten into creative writing, so we can talk about that. Who knows? We'll wing it."

"Taking Laura?"

I nodded. "Good seeing you." My nose was freezing into a brittle red point.

Before I had gone more than a few feet, he called out. "Mandy!" he said, waving. "One minute." He came up to me. Laura was near the car. "Since you canceled your vacation, your trip, could I—could we see each other?"

"Laura's with me for a while. I don't feel really good about leaving her just now."

"Then all three of us. I promised I'd cook you dinner, didn't I? I'll cook for you both."

"Well, that sounds . . ."

"How about tonight?"

"I don't know, I . . ."

"Or have you already been booked by your friend, the constable?"

I shook my head. "He'll be way down yonder in New Orleans."

Nick rightly took that as a go-ahead.

"Except—you won't bother Laura, will you?" I asked him.

He looked startled, and offended, and I realized how awful I'd made it seem. "I mean, ask her questions for your article. Things like that."

He shook his head. "All I'll do is keep matches away from her."

"This isn't a good idea, if you're going to be like that."

"It was a joke."

"It stunk."

"Listen, everybody knows she started the fire."

"Let's forget dinner, okay? It'd be too awkward."

"Give me a chance. I was only relating public opinion. And anyway, what they think has nothing to do with what you'll think of my cooking. Give me a chance, okay?"

"Give her one, would you?"

He looked abashed and charged full of energy. "I'm sorry," he said. "Truly."

"Now I'll ask her if it's all right." Which I did. She okayed the idea.

"But you seemed upset by him," I said. "Don't feel any obligation."

"No, I was just . . . confused. It's okay. Really."

"Hold on to all those vegetables, though. You and I retain salad-making rights," I said. "And our grand production will reek of garlic." She came close to a grin on that one.

So we were on. Nick would give her a chance and I'd give him one. And he'd see that Laura was not capable of murder, or arson or anything like it.

All the same, I'd keep my fireplace matches under surveillance.

Eleven

"THIS WILL BE UNBELIEVABLY BORING FOR BOTH OF US, BUT I promise I won't be long."

"It's all right. Honest." Laura looked as if she actually meant it. Perhaps any normal domestic activity intrigued her because of its unfamiliarity. Or perhaps she was so used to accommodating adult wishes, no matter how unpleasant, that her smile and earnest enthusiasm were reflex actions.

Silverwood was enormous, a complex into which able-bodied seniors moved and around which they were rotated, as the bodies became less able, until they were in a maximum-care custodial unit.

There were energetic folk off to sales on a bus that said Shopper's Circle on its destination window. There were hearty stay-at-homes braving the cold as they walked the strip of hard December earth encircling the red brick buildings. And somewhere inside, unseen, I knew, were the people who were finished with after-season sales and promenades and who would never, no matter what the sign said, convalesce.

I wasn't sure where the party room was, so Laura and I trotted behind a woman whose silver Volunteer ribbon fluttered on her chest as she led us, giving a tour as we walked. "And this is our dayroom," she said when we'd arrived.

I don't know why they called it that. I would have guessed I was in their twilight room, or their extremely dark plaid room. The floor, the chairs and the love seats were tiled and upholstered in so many subdued tartans it seemed they'd been bought by lot from a Scottish Sofa Outlet. Furthermore, glen plaid drapes were pulled shut, making the atmosphere dusky and the TV picture clearer for antisocial, nonpartying folks. There was no visible day in that room.

Jenny waved at me from the middle of a noisy group, so I thanked the volunteer and walked over with Laura.

We faced a terrifying assortment of temptations, including Sarah and Jenny's irresistible cookies. "A completely unbalanced diet is permitted during the holidays," I told Laura. "Forget the four food groups and have fun." I added our dozen cannoli to the buffet and tried to keep my chomping to a minimum by occupying my mouth with words—compliments for the contributors to *Mining Silver*, and to those sporting new Christmas finery. I inspected and oohed over hammered silver earrings, a soft rose shawl, a necklace of seed pearls, a silk blouse, a tie patterned with tiny fish and a handbag made of wool carpeting. I talked about writing in general with Maggie Towne, the Tuesday teacher, and with those party-goers who didn't have gifts to show off. After half an hour of this, I spied Minna White slowly crossing the room in her wheelchair.

"I brought you a treat," I told her, "but it's really from my mother."

She clapped her hands. "I didn't think you'd do it! No, I didn't think it at all! What a wonderful Christmas gift!"

So my mother had not bamboozled me, at least not by pretending she'd made me a date. I was still peeved with her machinations, but relieved that I'd honored the commitment, especially since I got the sense that Minna hadn't been otherwise showered with presents.

The wheelchair swiveled around and Laura and I were scanned by Minna, a diminutive woman with blue-white hair and spectacles so thick as to make her eyes blurred enlargements. "And who are you?" she said, squinting. "I'm blind, you know. Legally, at least. When there's no party, I come in here to hear the TV and the people. Can't see much at all. What's your name?"

"Laura. I'm with Miss Pepper."

"Well, welcome, both of you. It's so good to have company. Come, let's talk over there." The Tuesday people's party was progressing nicely, and I excused myself. Laura and I sank into a yellow, brown and black tartan love seat facing Minna. "Shall I ask those people to turn off the TV?" she asked. "Nobody pays attention to it, anyway."

"No, please," I said, although it was true that Laura and my ratings were way ahead of whatever soap opera was on. Thirty faces aimed in our direction, and I nodded, feeling vaguely royal. "I hope your taste buds are in good working order," I said, ignoring our audience, "because I brought cannoli."

Minna clapped her hands again. Her tiny size and choice of gestures gave her a childlike quality that contrasted with the wheelchair and thick slabs of spectacles. "Thank you! So kind of you! Your mother said you might, but I didn't let myself count on it. They smell like heaven. Help yourself—eat some—take some!"

"We bought our own," I said. "At that little store at the Italian Market. These are all yours."

She sighed, and looked wistful, and I could almost see through those impenetrable glasses into her mind, where memories ran like home movies of times when she, too, was mobile and could decide to visit the best cannoli baker in Philadelphia. "Is the market the same?" she asked.

"Pretty much. There are some Asian vendors now, and it feels like there're more geegaws—barrettes and ruffly socks—what my Aunt Flo calls 'chotchkes,' but otherwise, it's still noisy and crazy and wonderful."

"Well, I can't wait. It's been years. I'm having one right now," she said, carefully undoing the string and finding one of the crisp cylinders. "Tell me," she said before biting in, "do you ever see anybody from Brooke Street?"

I shook my head, then remembered she could probably not see me. "I was about seven when we moved. I don't really remember a whole lot about it."

"I keep thinking you and Junior are the same age, but I remember now, my Dom, my first husband, died the year you moved and Junior was fifteen, so he's much older than you.''

"And how is Junior?" It wasn't hard making conversation, as long as you didn't mind discussing things or people that held no interest.

Minna took me seriously. She put her cannoli down on the pastry box and considered. "He's . . . taking a long time to—how to they call it now?—find himself. He had a bad marriage, a lot of jobs that didn't work out. Not an easy time of it, you understand? Born with that wine stain on his face, kids making fun of him and all. Then his father dying early, and our losing the house, that was the real thing. And then my second husband, well, the two of them weren't the best combination, maybe. So . . .'' She stared down in silence for a moment.

Junior sounded like an overgrown baby, throwing tantrums because life wasn't fair. I was relieved, and surprised, that Minna didn't try to arrange a date for me with him. Perpetual babies are always being fixed up because they are always in need of repair.

The next former child in the spotlight would be me and the next topic why I hadn't yet married, so I changed tacks. "I read your story," I said. "It's really good."

One of the TV watchers had quietly moved closer for a better view or an invitation or simply as a way of breaking the monotony of her day. "Yes," she said now, "Minna is *quite* a storyteller."

Minna White tilted her head, as if to verify the speaker. Then she smiled. "Don't you listen to Rose Levitt. What does she know? This is a schoolteacher, Rose. So watch yourself. Let me introduce my friends, Amanda and, ah—"

"Laura," I said.

"You can join us, Rose, but you cannot have my cannoli."

Rose accepted the deal. "So, Minna, did you tell them what your storytelling got you?" She turned to me and repeated the question. "Did she tell you about her beau? Scheherazade, we call her. You know, the gal who told the stories and kept the fellas interested?"

"Such talk!" Minna said, shaking her head.

"Am I lying?" Rose eyed the pastry box. I knew what she was looking for—broken off corners, crumbs and crumbles that didn't count as official "eating."

Eventually, Rose dislodged a cannoli corner, and quietly, quickly popped it into her mouth, winking at Laura and me. "So," she said, "you want me to tell them, or will you? Everybody loves a love story, right?"

"Some love story. They aren't going to make a movie out of this one," Minna White said. "Don't tell your mother, Amanda. It's not nice. I've had two husbands, that's enough. And besides, he was so interested, so interested, right? And have you seen him lately, Rose?"

Rose shrugged eloquently. "Do I know everything you do? Do I follow you? Am I in your bedroom? Ignore that remark, young lady," she added for Laura's benefit while Minna gasped.

"Take a cannoli and be quiet, all right?" Minna turned her milky lenses toward me. "You liked my story, then?"

"It was unusual. Not like anything else in the collection. I'm not sure if I understand it completely, though."

"You weren't supposed to understand it. Not exactly. Not all the way. Uh-uh. I know what happens to writers, about being sued. So I didn't use any real names. Except Etienne's, and that didn't matter because Etienne was dead. And I changed everything and made it a fairy tale. The creative-writing teacher suggested that. And everybody says they like it."

"Inmrsfhk—"

"Don't talk with your mouth full, Rose!"

Rose swallowed and smacked her lips. "Including Mr. Wonderful, so tell her about him."

Minna shrugged. "There was this special program last Tuesday during class. We read our things out loud and had cookies and tea. Everybody was invited, and we could bring guests. Even Junior came. And this man. He called himself my secret admirer. He lives somewhere near here, maybe even here at Silverwood. I don't know. I never met him before, even though he said he comes here for book reviews and special events. Good times. He saw my story in *Mining*

Silver and he said he came to the reading to meet its author. Very elegant sounding, I thought. Very gentlemanly. My friends said he was handsome, too. I couldn't tell—he could look like the Phantom of the Opera, for all I'd know. Or care. That's a nice part of being blind, you know. You don't worry about some of the things anymore.''

"Is that all you're going to tell them?" Rose had finished her cannoli and was surveying the box for crumbs.

Minna sighed and shrugged. "Not much of a story. He complimented my writing style and imagination. Said the story haunted him. That's exactly what he said. Then he said he had known an Etienne once, too, so he wondered about mine. Being such an unusual name and all. And we talked. That's all. Mr. Secret Admirer, Junior and me. Actually, the two of them did most of the talking. They really hit it off. So that's the big deal, big story. Satisfied, Rose?"

"What about the flowers?" Rose dipped her forefinger into the filling of both remaining cannoli.

"Mandy, you're thirty years old and you aren't married— your mother told me—so I'm sure you know how men are. Rose is a little bit older than you, like two and a half times, and she still doesn't understand that men are only interested until you're interested back. Then they disappear."

"I heard it was until they had their way with you," Rose said tartly.

Minna waved away the suggestion with disgust.

"What happened to Mr. Wonderful?" I asked.

"He came calling the next day. He brought me flowers, wonderful scents, and acted like he really was interested in me. Not a whole lot of men listen, you know? But I have some good stories. Not just the fairy-tale version. There was lying and cheating and stealing and a murder to cover it up, and my Dom ruined because of it."

"Next time, stick to fairy tales," Rose said. "Men don't like women with sad stories."

Minna shrugged. "He loved the story. He came the next day, too, smelling of extra after-shave, kissed me on the cheek—on the cheek, Rose—and said I should wish him good luck because today was his big test. Like in fairy tales, like in mine, he said, you know? I said, Oh no, that's for young people and fools. That's what I said, I don't know why. Maybe it was too rude. I didn't know what he meant, anyway. I thought maybe another woman. I still think so, because he never came back. Not even today, even though this is another special event, isn't it?''

How had we leaped from Minna's story—the one with lying, cheating, robbery and murder to the overfamiliar ancient one of how men are cads? "About your story," I said, "the real one. Did you say murder?"

"I did indeed. Etienne was murdered. Didn't you get that? They found his letter jacket, you know how boys win one for sports in high school? See, I changed it to a cloak in the story, get it? But it was true. He loved that jacket. It was like it was a piece of him. I don't care if nobody ever finds him, and it was a long time ago. I know he was murdered, and I know why. *And*—I know who did it.''

"You and that story!" Rose said. "No wonder he ran away!''

"It's *my* story. I never told anybody till now. But when that teacher said What do you remember, what will you never forget, out it came, like it had been waiting. Besides, Amanda asked me, so why shouldn't I tell her about that no-good thief! Who am I hurting?''

"Do you realize there's a child here? You'll frighten her!'' Rose winked at us and mocked a yawn, using eloquent sign language to tell us she was bored silly.

"What child? Amanda's a full-grown—"

"I think Rose means my friend, Laura Clausen," I said. "Except that Laura's not a child at all. She's fourteen.''

Minna had slammed back in her chair as if yanked.

"I'm not frightened, Mrs. White," Laura said, "so do go on.'' The Laura I'd known was so webbed in by silence, I was again surprised, although in the last few hours I had noticed that words, few though they still were, were falling out at random, filling up what I kept expecting to be silent crevasses.

"That's an unusual last name," Minna said. "Are you by

chance related to . . . well, I mean, the news stories lately, all I hear . . . is—was he . . . ?"

"Laura is Alexander Clausen's daughter." Even without Laura here, I would not have brought up his name, no matter what my mother had suggested, if Minna herself hadn't touched on it. With Laura here, it seemed nearly impossible to pursue it, however. She'd be glad to see him dead, my mother had said, more or less, and that hardly seemed a topic to explore in front of his daughter. Well, it was ancient history, anyway.

"Your father," Minna said. "Oh, my. He was—well, this is a surprise and . . . My condolences, of course." Her hands were clasped on the top of the pastry box in her lap, and her head swiveled from one to the other of us.

"Mine, too, you poor dear," Rose said. "And we don't have to hear any more sad stories. I tell Minna all the time—there's enough sad things in the news every day. We need to be cheery, to laugh a little instead."

"I hope I didn't say anything to upset you." Minna seemed truly worried. "I didn't realize who you were, or I would never have . . ."

"Of course not." Rose leaned over to pat Minna's shoulder. "Minna is a sweet old thing. *And* a sexpot."

"Rose!"

"You'll see. That man will crawl back to you, to woo you. I know men."

We were again deciphering male behavior, a futile game I had played and lost often enough. A good time to bid farewell.

"Will you come back somebody soon?" Minna seemed to have lost a few vertebrae during the course of our visit. Her voice was low and meditative. "I get lonely. Junior's never here."

"But you said he was here last Tuesday."

"Almost never. And that last time, he talked to my new friend, that man, the whole time. But I don't like to complain."

Why don't people who say that ever mean it? "I'll be back," I promised. "With more cannoli."

She clapped her hands, reinvigorated. "I'll tell you what. I'll let you know what my favorite flavor is. That way, next time, no matter which one Rose steals, the ones left over will still be my favorite."

I said goodbye to the Tuesday group after telling them again how much I'd enjoyed their writing and cooking, and then I returned to tell Minna I was leaving. She grasped my hands and pulled me close. "Thank you, dear," she said. "Thank you for visiting an old lady. And I hope—I sincerely hope I didn't say anything wrong. I had no idea."

I assured her she had been fine, but as Rose walked us to the door, I could still feel her grasp and I wondered at the very real fear that had been in her hands and voice.

"You were a godsend," Rose said as we headed for the lobby. "She's been in the dumps. Holidays do that, y'know. And with that man disappearing and all . . . She liked him, I can tell. I like to joke around, cheer her up, but it doesn't always work. He's broken her heart."

It made me sick to think that even when she was in a wheelchair, even blind, some geriatric lothario could still kiss and run and leave a woman pining away. Wasn't there a statute of limitations?

"He was so elegant," Rose said. "Gallant and old-fashioned. Or maybe it was just the fancy cane that made you think he was like—like Maurice Chevalier, you know? A *boulevardier*. Then it turns out he's just a jerk."

There was this program last Tuesday. He came the next two days. Flowers on Wednesday. The kiss—the big test—on Thursday. No sign of him since.

No. Impossible. Stop forcing connections. "Fancy cane, did you say?"

"Yes. Compared to the walkers we see, anyway."

"I've seen some really gorgeous walking sticks," I said. "Works of art, with silver chasing all through them, or jewels set into the top."

"This was a cane, not a walking stick. The man limped. A flaw, yes, a leg that didn't work, but at our age, you get excited when they can walk at all. Besides, Minna couldn't see it."

"But it was fancy?"

"How could a limp be—oh, you mean the cane. Yes. Ornamented. You know."

"Like what?"

"Why?" Rose Levitt looked at me as if I were bizarre.

"I find cane ornaments fascinating. It's an obsession, frankly. Can't get enough of them, and I love hearing about different sorts."

She gave me a slightly wider berth, but she humored me. "This wasn't much. I've seen nicer, and I don't even think about such things. I can barely remember what it . . . some animal? A duck, that's what it was. Silver-colored, but not silver. Probably chrome, like a toaster oven. Not very fascinating to me, but maybe to you, I don't know."

There's a buzz that starts in the sternum when you're about to fall in love but don't know it yet. It happens sometimes when a passage of prose or poetry is so right that it hurts. And it happens when you finally understand what the picture in the puzzle is, even if you don't have all the pieces right yet.

I was buzzing away. I asked Rose if she knew the man's name or how to find him, but she didn't, not even after she told me how strict her children were about her diet and I promised her her own box of cannoli.

After Laura was back in the car, I said I'd forgotten my scarf, and raced back inside.

"I'm looking for somebody who might live here," I said to the woman behind the reception desk.

She had an enormous, toothy smile. "Minimum care A or B?" She pulled over an oversized Rolodex.

"Which would you be in if you had a limp?"

She scowled and shook her head. "Neither."

"Then he's probably somewhere else in the complex."

"You're talking all of Silverwood?" The toothy mouth no longer smiled. "You'll have to go to the business office for that." She pushed back the Rolodex.

"Where is it?"

"Turn right outside the front door. Up a block, make a left. Can't miss it. It says 'Business Office'."

"Thanks." I waved and turned around.

"But they won't let you see any names. I can tell you that."

"But I really need to—"

She shook her head, slowly, eyes closed. "Against all the rules. Names are private property. No way."

I returned to the counter. "Don't you have some kind of directory right here? This is important. His name is Jacob."

She reached under the counter and pulled out the Philadelphia telephone book. "Jacobs?" She flipped pages with a wet index finger.

"Jacob. First name. And he walks with a cane. He's been in this building recently."

"Give me a break!"

"I know it's hard," I said, "but he's—he's my grandmother's lost love. She's ill—" I am superstitious about making bad things come true by saying them, but both my grandmothers are enjoying eternal rest, so I proceeded to add details. "She can't speak, except to say 'Jacob.' I'm sure you could help me find him."

"If she can tell you he walks with a cane, honey, then ask her to open up and tell you his—"

I straightened up indignantly. "The cane is family lore. Grandma's lost love walked with a cane since childhood. He had *polio*."

She sighed and mimed exaggeratedly wide-eyed interest. "Perhaps the medical director's memory will be sharper. Perhaps he'll remember the combination of Jacob, polio and cane. Perhaps you could request a computer search. Perhaps."

"The other thing is, he's been missing for five days. Couldn't you check it that way?"

"This is the *long lost* Jacob?"

"Five days can seem pretty long when every breath could be your—he was here, in this building last Thursday. Walked out on his own and never came back. I need his name."

"*If* he's not in hospitalization, then he is an autonomous human being who has no reason to inform us of his whereabouts. And, may I remind you that half or more of our residents are away for the holidays, with family or on vacation. This is a retirement community, not a prison. Five thousand people live here. But hey—'' she shoved the phone book toward me—''be my guest. Turn off the lights at 10:00 P.M. and give your grandma my regards.''

I left the directory and its surly guardian. I'll find you, Jacob, I muttered all the way back to my car. Rest assured.

I may have convinced the corpse, but I had real trouble convincing myself.

Twelve

MACKENZIE NEEDED TO KNOW ABOUT THE OLD MAN. THIS was not some crackedbrain theory of mine. This was not the girl-detective antics he made fun of. The city's finest could gain access to Silverwood's business office.

"Hungry?" I asked Laura as I slid in behind the wheel.

She shook her head. "Did you find out who he is?"

"Find who?" Was it possible my sleuthing was less than subtle?

"The man with the cane. The one Mrs. Levitt told you about. You wanted to know because of the man in the toolshed, didn't you? Who was he, then?"

"I don't know. Do you, Laura?"

She shook her head.

"You don't remember ever seeing him before?"

More side-to-sides.

"But your mother knew him, didn't she?"

The child's eyes were enormous and solemn in her small face. She said nothing, just tightened her jaw. "How would I know?"

"I'm only asking. Nobody else can until she's feeling better. But wasn't it when the police called this morning that she really lost control?"

"She's been crying for two days."

It wasn't that Alice Clausen lacked sufficient cause for

tears, it was only their timing that troubled me. "What about?"

"Everything."

Laura looked out her window, and I became distracted, reading signs and negotiating traffic. The streets of the Greater Northeast were clogged with people returning disappointing gifts or seeking bargains, and in any case, I was not overly familiar with this part of the city. In my family it was exotic, unmarked territory known as "The Couldabeen." Whenever, as children, we approached it, Daddy's Dirge began. "This used to be *farmland*," my father said and said again as that section of the city grew explosively. "*Country*. I could have bought it for *nothing*. For a few dollars an acre, and I didn't. Who thought people would want to be way out here? I coulda been rich. We all coulda been rich."

It never mattered when my mother answered, accurately, that he couldn't have bought land back then because he hadn't had the few extra dollars to buy even an acre. We could have been rich and weren't. When I looked out at the condominium complexes and bustling businesses around me, I remembered my father's farmlands and didn't see anything familiar.

I finally reached the expressway and became bogged in a new jam, this one caused by traffic, potholes, and repair work designed to alleviate them both.

"I lied," Laura said in a voice so tiny one could easily have missed it in the rush of tires and brakes over blacktop.

I let her set her own pace. Traffic bucked and crept and stalled even though we were nowhere near commuter hours. I tried to catch her eye, but her profile was set and she was looking at her penny loafers once again. The car, windows up and heater fighting the ice age, filled with silence and overheated secrets.

Laura took a deep breath. She kept her face forward. "She was there," she said. "That night, she was downstairs." She swallowed hard. "She came out of the kitchen. She had a glass—she was getting ice water, that's all." She began to tremble. "But she didn't do anything wrong. I'm sure she didn't do anything wrong. I'm sure all her crying has nothing to do with . . . anything wrong."

I put my hand on hers. "Nobody's saying it does. What are you so afraid of?"

She shook her head and sighed and we sank into silence again.

The traffic loosened, creeping forward and then moving in something like a normal flow. "What is it?" I felt forced to say.

"Why did that old man die? He didn't look sick at the party. Why was he still there? It must have happened after everybody else left, mustn't it? Why didn't anybody call an ambulance instead of putting him . . . where you found him?"

"Those are good questions."

"Could somebody . . . is it true somebody could make you so upset you'd have a stroke or a heart attack? Is that really possible?"

"What makes you ask?"

"I heard noises. Angry noises while I was upstairs. Low voices. Men quarreling. I thought later it was a dream, but Peter heard them, too. Maybe I shouldn't say any of this, but he's away and his mother blames me for everything and he hasn't even called. He could have called once she wasn't around, couldn't he?"

"Maybe not. We don't know." I sifted through her words, but I was really bothered by what she hadn't said. Something logical was missing. "If you heard a quarrel, and Peter heard it, too," I finally said, "why didn't you tell the police?"

"Because at the police station we were talking about my father, about what I did. That's different. I didn't know there was a man in the toolshed then. Neither did Peter. We never mentioned it because I pretty much forgot it, and I guess he did, too."

I didn't buy it. "But didn't the noise wake you? Didn't you say anything to each other about it? Wonder what to do, or just be annoyed? Or frightened? It's hard to understand how you'd forget something like that in the light of what else happened that same night."

She shrugged.

"Why didn't it have more impact? Did you really just go back to sleep—then wake up, later, downstairs?"

She looked at me blankly, all knowledge and emotion erased from her eyes. I had hit something—but what? I kept imagining the two high-school students in the dark, upstairs, tense to begin with, fearful of a dramatic, wrenching confrontation later on, startled by a loud quarrel from below. And then remaining silent about it. Were they so hell-bent on confessing to Clausen's murder that they dismissed evidence that might point elsewhere? It didn't make any sense, and I said so. Laura didn't contradict me. Nor did she deign to respond.

It took at least two more expressway tie-ups before I had it. Something had to be wrong upstairs, too. Something that frightened Laura more than the quarrel downstairs. And what could it be except that her protector and sole ally was in jeopardy, too? "Peter wasn't in your room when you heard the men quarreling, was he?" I asked.

Her eyes widened and fixed on me before they fled to the safety of those scuffed loafers.

"Where was he?"

"I never said he wasn't in my—"

"Come on, Laura, I'm on your side. Where was he?"

"In the bathroom. Down the hall. Near the stairwell."

"You're afraid his was one of the voices."

"I *knew* you'd think that, but you're wrong. Even if he was downstairs—and he wasn't—he couldn't have done anything. He didn't even know that old man and he wouldn't hurt anybody, anyway. But how could I tell that to the police? They'd jump to the wrong conclusion like you did. Because his hair is funny and he looks tough and three years ago he got into trouble."

"He says he murdered your father, Laura."

"He's a good person. Clear all the way through, do you know what I mean? There's nothing secret or messed up inside him. But he remembers how it was to be that way, and he's really kind. No matter what he says, no matter what anybody believes, he wouldn't, he couldn't hurt somebody."

We inched forward a few car lengths, two miles an hour. "All the same," I said in a flat voice, "you're worried that maybe, maybe something happened and he did?"

"He couldn't! But if he did, it was because of me. I'm the guilty one. He was so angry. So angry! I told him about—I told him what you know so that he'd stay in my room. I never told anybody else, never, but I had to tell him, and he was so angry. He didn't sleep at all. Couldn't."

What memories it must have evoked for a boy whose father had been a wife beater. I shook my head, unwilling to fully consider what it might mean.

"He didn't do it," Laura said. "He's a good person."

"I know that. And so are you."

She shook her head. I thought her eyes were moist, but it might have been the light. "Not like Peter," she said. "Not clear all the way through. Not very good. You don't know me."

Damn that father and mother for what they had done. We'd have to talk about therapy soon. Maybe tonight, when things were calm. I wanted to rush her directly into the arms of somebody supportive and wise. I wanted to have a parade, everybody carrying banners that shouted "Laura Is a Good Human Being" in crimson script.

"Because," she said, sounding hypnotized, "I *remember*. I remember how sick seeing him be Santa made me. Santa's about the best thing a kid has and . . . I remembered pushing the Christmas tree onto him. Not feeling sad. I'm not making it up. It flamed, and I didn't feel anything. Not sad. It was like dreaming. Like not being responsible. It was something my hands did for me. Something that had to happen sooner or later. He started to burn—the beard did—right away."

"Did you tell this to the police?"

"I don't remember what I said."

"What did your father say when he saw you push the tree, or when the tree crashed onto him?"

"He didn't say anything. He was napping."

"Napping?"

"On the sofa. Resting." She shuddered. "Resting *up*.

Seeing him that way, dressed like Santa, knowing, it made me . . .''

"Did you tell that to the police?"

"I can still feel the pine needles in my hand. Soft and sharp, all at once.''

"Laura, do the police know your father was asleep?''

She looked confused. "I don't know. They asked me what I did, over and over, not so much what he was doing, I think, and I can't remember a whole lot. Except grabbing at the tree and pushing it. The rest . . .'' she squinted, looked confused and unhappy and shook her head. "So many things I don't know if I really saw.''

"Did he wake up? Struggle?"

"I don't know. I wasn't watching. My nightgown caught fire, and my mother came in from the kitchen and screamed and threw her glass of water on me—''

We were bogged down on an expressway, but I felt as if I were on a roller coaster.

"Had you seen her before then?"

"No.''

"Would you have seen her coming down the stairs? Or in the hall?''

"Maybe.'' She slumped as far down onto her spine as the safety belt allowed. "I know what you're thinking, and you're wrong,'' she said.

Maybe Alice had been in the kitchen for a long time. Maybe she had, indeed, killed her husband before Laura, for whatever reason, out of whichever dream, came downstairs.

Because I was sure the approach of Alice had something to do with the hiding of the old man. I still envisioned Alice at the top of the staircase, calling down, or staggering down and frightening Clausen because she could identify the old man.

"Why did Peter have to leave town?'' It was a soft and timid wail.

"Did he convince you to lie?''

She looked like a frightened forest creature. "I didn't lie. I really didn't remember.''

I sighed and patted her hand. "It's better to remember, if

you can. Better to deal with truth. There've been enough lies and secrets, don't you think?''

It was not a question that needed an answer, so we sat in silence. Again and again, I went back and tried to arrange the players for that night.

Time to think the unthinkable—that someone I felt sorry for or liked a great deal might all the same have murdered Alexander Clausen. Because of course, if he was "asleep" when Laura found him, then someone—Alice? or Peter?—had already killed him. What if nobody was covering for anybody, if nobody was lying and all the confessions were true? What if, one by one, everyone had added to his destruction?

"I can't remember enough," Laura said. "It makes my head hurt, makes me feel as if I'm going crazy, these *almost*-memories.''

We rode along, both lost in confused speculation. I was too distracted to become infuriated with the traffic, barely saw it in fact. I kept trying to focus the swirl of amorphous shapes and shadows I had accumulated. The quarrel. The man with the cane. Minna's story. The murder of one Etienne. Minna's reaction to Laura's last name. My mother's memories of something nasty between Minna and Alexander Clausen. Alice Clausen's being downstairs that night. Peter's being out of the bedroom. The quarrel downstairs. Alexander Clausen "resting" by the time Laura pushed the tree over onto him. These could not be random events, but they were like dust motes now, jumping, floating, each piece disconnected from the whole.

"It makes me feel crazy," Laura said again.

"Me, too." Ah yes, me, too.

"THERE. STRAIGHT FROM THE DARKROOM TO YOU." SASHA had entered my home fourteen minutes after Laura and I did. Now, while Laura established residency, unpacking in the room on the third floor, Sasha spread black-and-white prints over the coffee table. "Not even dry yet—be careful." She leaned back in the chair. "I've been out of circulation. Just looked at my accumulated newspapers and realized what had happened." She shook her head, black gypsy hair swirling, silver-and-jet earrings jingling.

"Atlantic City is sixty miles away, Sasha. Same native tongue, same newspapers for sale. It was the lead story."

"Not in the bridal suite, honey." I looked stunned, and she laughed. "No. I'm not ready for a third husband, but the hoteliers don't check for a marriage license, and it's a nifty room." She put three more pictures out and cocked her head, studying them. "And what's all this life-and-death message business about? Are you playing girl detective again?" Sasha rubbed her palm on the suede of the chair. "Thought you'd sworn off."

"To each her weakness."

She leaned forward. "Confidentially, live bodies are more fun."

"Thanks."

"Not that you'd know that with No-Name the Narc."

Laura walked down, her belongings now stowed in my rackety dresser. Or perhaps she simply needed company. I made the introductions.

"I'm really sorry about your dad," Sasha said. "And for you and your mom and everything you must be going through. That's awful." When Laura remained silent, she didn't press or force a response. Instead, she became very professional, lifting a picture of hands clutched around a water glass, and scowling. "I controlled the urge to trash some of the stinkers until after you give a look-see. I assume aesthetics are not your prime concern."

I always imagine Sasha in a turban, although she avoids all the clichés she's aware of. She nonetheless carried an imaginary crystal ball, or a parrot on her shoulder. She vibrated in a purple, orange and pink sweep of silk blouse over tight black leather pants and high Robin Hood boots. She's a big woman—nearly six feet tall and voluptuous, so the effect was rather overwhelming. Laura sat nearby, more than ever a sparrow by contrast.

"This is a *major* favor," Sasha said. "Without your S.O.S., I'd be in Key West with him. I missed the flight he booked so I could work on these, and when I asked about a flight later today or tomorrow, the woman behind the counter fell off her little stool laughing. There are waiting lists up the ying-yang for anyplace with sun and heat. Don't feel guilty, but this act of friendship has destroyed the entire remainder of my love life. He's *exceptional*, Mandy.'' Long scarlet nails punctuated her words. ''A swashbuckler. A pirate, an adventurer.''

This could translate into his being a gambler and general wastrel. Or, equally probably, a television repairman, computer programmer or insurance broker. Sasha saw through the veneer of reality into the hypothetical and desirable. She had invented herself, transforming nice old Susan Berg into Sasha the Terrible, and she saw no reason not to change whatever she liked about whomever she liked. And she liked great quantities of whomevers.

Sasha had been interested in the eating of food, not the eaters, so there were lots of photos that were useless to me. A tilted coffee cup at an unidentified mouth, gnarled hands cradling pillowy rolls, the back of a student holding piled plates, close-ups of hors d'oeuvres, even the punch bowl, orange slices floating on remembered pink soup.

But there were faces in other pictures. There was Gladys, eating meditatively. You could almost see her preserving the moment, the linens and silver and elegance, and digesting it along with her chicken breast. And the man from 'Nam, his cheek bulging, a half-eaten quiche in his fingertips, his eyes angled sharply to the side, as if wary of a sniper.

And there was Jacob Marley. He sat, his plate full and untouched in front of him, his hands on his lap, his expression intense and concentrated, eyes watching the distance.

I stood up. ''Sasha Berg? Look behind the curtain! Aside from your caustic remarks, you have been incredibly helpful. So just like in the fairy tales, you are going to be magically rewarded for being such a good girl. I happen to have a round-trip ticket to Florida in my possession. It's yours. No down payment. Replace it when I finally go south, okay? It's probably illegal to do this, so are you willing to break some idiot law to be with the buccaneer?''

''Are you kidding?''

"If he lasts into the New Year, then I want a detailed, in-depth description, okay?"

She turned her eyes on Laura. "Not a word of this to that Royal Canadian Mountie she dates."

"Who?" Laura asked.

"Is your mother wildly upset by your change of plans?" Sasha asked. "Should I visit her? I could bring Errol Flynn, which is something you couldn't do."

It needed no comment. Sasha, even while she was still Susan, had been both my best friend and the "bad influence" my mother and teachers had warned me about.

Remembering, I try to be extra tolerant of the oddball combinations I see in my classrooms. Probably, if my old teachers could see me now, working in a school where "originality" is available at a bulk discount, they'd say it was Sasha's fault.

"The return ticket's not till January first," I said. "Make this one of your longer relationships."

"Yegads. Six days!"

"Long enough to have a war."

"Longer, I believe, than one of my marriages. And thank you for asking, but although I am starving from my labors on your behalf, I will not have a late lunch with you guys, even though I need local stoking before I hit culinary waste-land."

As soon as I'd been notified that it was past feeding time, my stomach growled.

"Laura's too pale, too skinny. Must eat junk like sun-flower seeds, or sprouts. The remedy is great take-out. Steak sandwiches. With cheese. And fried onions. Can you not smell it? Feel the oil drip down your arms as you lift it to your mouth? Fries, too. My treat."

Sasha was so gleeful, so charged with energy, it was obvious that her assignment, her pirate, had lots of potential.

"Hey, Laura?" she said. "You ever been on South Street?"

Laura shook her head.

"Come along, deprived suburban child. It's a necessary part of being young in this city. Let me introduce you to city living and walking. And on the way, I'll show you an historical site, the Todd House, where Dolly Todd—later Madison—grew dope.''

"Really?" Laura asked as she pulled a woolly cap over her ears.

"She *said* it was to keep the pigs away from her vegetables, but do you think she would have had to go invent ice cream if it weren't for the munchies?" And they were gone, the Pied Piper and Laura.

I CALLED MACKENZIE AND DISTILLED THE RESULTS OF MY fact-finding mission. He sounded bored. Nonetheless, I kept on going through the list of oddities, through Minna's story and its possible meanings, through Laura's half-revelations, and finally, to the man in the toolshed. I even threw in a word or two about Dolly Madison's dope growing in an attempt to spark interest.

"They know what happened," he said, quietly interrupting me. "A blow to the base of the skull, top of the spine. Brain-stem damage. Didn't even break the skin, and his hair covered it, so you wouldn't have seen an abrasion anyway. There are other bruises, however, like he was knocked around first.''

I was hit by a sudden wave of nausea. I wanted to cry, or shout at somebody. Who was he and why was he killed? Until I knew, I felt as if anybody and anything could be killer or victim.

"Mandy? You were sayin' . . . ? About the old man, Jacob?''

I cleared my throat. "Jacobs, maybe." I cleared my throat again. The nausea receded. I would figure this out, and it would be over, and everybody I cared about would be safe and we'd all live happily ever after, wasn't that so?

"Mandy?''

"He must have lived at Silverwood. Or nearby. Told Minna he went to all the parties there. He visited right before Clausen's party. Except he never said his name. She's blind, but Sasha took his picture at the party, and I have it, so Minna's friends and his neighbors can surely identify him.''

"Okay."

"*Okay*? No more than that? A little praise, a little thanks for my help wouldn't be out of line."

"It was real good work you did, too. Not work you should be doin' . . ." he sighed. ". . . but you will go on doin' it anyway, won't you, so yes, it was fine. You're very bright."

"There's an 'only', isn't there? So say it, Mackenzie."

"Only."

"Only what?"

"Only . . . we knew already."

"About Silverwood? How?"

"Remember how you noticed somebody arrived in a taxi? It's finally been traced. It was one of those special reduced senior rate deals, the kind you have to book two days ahead. The call was put in from Silverwood."

"But you didn't know that that specific man with the cane was the one who rode in the cab." I stopped because I sounded as petulant as a miffed second grader. I wanted to—absolutely needed to—feel I'd done something that made a difference.

"Correct. Except by elimination, we would have known soon. The charters are getting lists of their pickups together. Everything's been slow, because—"

"—it's the holidays. I know. I know."

"And because he wasn't on any of them, it stands to reason that the person in the taxi was in some way different, self-selected. Uninvited. Anyway, we owe all that to you, Mandy. You're the one remembered the names of the carriers. You're the one remembered the taxi. So. You've done a lot, been real busy today. Did you have time to get the sun block and board Macavity, too?"

"Didn't need to. I'm not going. Laura's with me, which is a whole other thing we need to discuss. I want to keep it that way, even though I'm not a relative, until her aunt comes back home, and then she can decide. I don't want her in foster care. Please, will you do whatever about it?"

"Will I—I'm leavin' tonight an'—Laura's with you? Servino said something about her mother wigging out, but I didn't think it through. The aunt's gone, is that it? So you're stayin' home?''

"What would you do?"

He was silent, which I interpreted as agreement. "A shame," he said.

"I never wanted to go. And Sasha is using my ticket, so I won't even lose money."

He was silent again. Mackenzie was about as excited to hear about Sasha as she was to hear about him. Once again, it amazed me that I could like them both so much and they could like each other so little. It surprised me, too, because men who aren't frightened away by Sasha's outsized body and personality usually fall in love with her. Mackenzie said he found her boring.

He was silent, and yet it wasn't a contented "I'm finished" sort of silence, so finally I asked him what the problem was.

"I feel real bad about leaving now you're stuck up here. Damn," he muttered. Beautiful words. "I can't even change flights," he said. "They've been booked forever. I was lucky to get this one. Or so I thought."

His words made me feel positively benign, able to live with the fruits of our noncommunication. "Listen," I said. "You're going to have a great time. Go crazy with Cajun or chitlins or creole or whatever it is you guys eat. Reminisce with every brother and sister and aunt and cousin three times removed, then hurry back on the first. I'll be waiting."

"Right," he said with no enthusiasm.

I thoroughly enjoyed the turnabout, but in the spirit of the season, I cut gloating to the minimum and return to practical matters. "Can you help me about Laura?" I asked again. "Tell them I'll follow whatever rules apply."

"You think they'll believe that kind of talk any more than I do?"

"Mackenzie! It's important!"

"I know. And I'll do it. But I'm really not all that comfortable with it. I wish I weren't going off just now."

"That's nice, and I wish you weren't either, but what does that have to do with this?"

"Oh," Mackenzie said. "I don't know . . ." He sounded

weary and wary, and softened his words into a soggy vowel mass, a long, soft Southern mantra. "Be careful," he slurred out. "I just don't know if you're helping a kid in trouble, or getting eyebrow-deep in trouble yourself."

I didn't know either, but it was too late to ponder the question, because what were my alternatives, anyway?

Thirteen

WHILE I REHEARSED, ONCE AGAIN, HOW BEST TO EXPLAIN my change of plans to my mother, the phone rang. For once, I hoped it was she, because with Laura out of the house I could speak freely.

But it was the wrong time of day, the wrong phone rates and the wrong voice. "Hello dear," a thin, uncertain voice said. "Rose was kind enough to dial your number for me. I didn't want to wait any longer. I enjoyed your visit, dear."

"Thank you." What had I wrought? I had not intended my visit to be the first step in an intimate, nonstop tête-à-tête.

"A very special day for me," she continued. "Your visit, of course, so special, and, of all surprises, Junior called, too."

I found her relationship with "Junior" nauseating, and I pictured him wearing a Hell's Angels' jacket and a diaper. I was sure somebody would try to fix me up with him.

"Red letter," she said. "All the way." She cleared her throat. "But of course. I didn't call about that." Her voice lowered to a conspiratorial stage whisper. "I called about the *cannoli*."

"How . . . prompt! You've picked your favorite flavor, then?" I had not understood it to be an emergency decision.

Macavity rubbed my ankle. The joy of not being boarded

163

had begun to pale, and he was back to his mealtime seduction, neck arching against my leg. This cat enjoyed gustatory foreplay.

"Oh, no," Minna White said. "I will, I'm sure—but I didn't eat them all yet. I'd get sick!"

"You just said—"

Her voice was muffled, as if she were covering her mouth for privacy. "The *cannoli* are our *cover*; didn't you guess?"

I hadn't, and I still couldn't.

"Coast is clear." She became more distinct. "Rose is watching TV now."

"That's . . . very . . . well, now!"

"Are you alone?"

"Yes."

"That child—that Clausen girl isn't nearby? She can't hear?"

"She's out of the house."

"She couldn't have come back in and be listening on an extension, could she?"

"For heaven's—" I took a deep breath. "No, she couldn't. But could you tell me what this is about, Mrs. White?" I tried to be patient, un-Scroogey, to remember she was old and crippled and blind and deserved extra consideration.

"What's it about? It's about how I almost had a heart attack when you said her name. My blood curdled."

I pictured curdle-filled veins. Curdles and why, my brain chanted. Curdles and why. "Why?" I finally asked out loud.

"Because of the story—my story. Didn't I tell you I changed all the names except Etienne's, made it a fairy tale to protect the innocent? Well, I'm the innocent! Me! I didn't want to get sued, or worse. I didn't want anybody to know what I really meant. That's why the teacher said make it a fairy tale. Otherwise, I would never have written it. I kept it a secret for seventeen years. Never breathed a word to a living soul, not even my own child."

"Yes, but I still don't—"

"The newcomer in my story? Myson? The one who steals the horses? That was Alexander Clausen. That's who ruined my life."

I looped my foot around the rung of a stool and pulled it over. "How?" I asked her, sitting down. "What did he really do? What did stealing the horses really mean?"

Her sigh whooshed out of the receiver. "Cars," she said, pausing and panting as if the word had been a desperately heavy load she had finally put down. "He got his first dealership by robbing Donnaker, his boss, well, my husband Dom's boss, too. Just like in my story, except of course Donnaker wasn't a king. Donnaker had a stroke, had to stop working for a year, and this nobody, this new salesman, Alexander Clausen, was suddenly supervising, keeping records, bossing. You know, everything Donnaker had done. Running the show."

While she spoke, I rummaged through the wicker basket until I found the mimeographed newsletter with Minna's story. I correlated her telephone narrative with the "Un-Fairy Tale." She was rather literal, parallel for parallel.

"He got twice the commission the other men did, because of his extra work." She sounded as if she could barely control her indignation, all these many years later.

I skimmed her story while she simmered and fumed. The horses had disappeared. "The cars," I prompted, "where did they go?"

"You caught that, did you?" She laughed with no mirth. "Sold," she whispered. "Not on the floor, not legally. Out of the warehouse where they kept extra inventory, where they took the ones being customized—you know, the fancy special work? The cars were sold and shipped overseas. By guess who and guess who else."

"Clausen and Etienne?" I sounded like Peter Lorre, hunched over the receiver, whispering. I cleared my throat and sat up straight, hoping Macavity hadn't caught the act.

"Yes." She sounded heavy and ominous, like every old horror movie. "The inventory and the money disappeared. Salesmen like my husband didn't get paid. It was a terrible time for us."

She paused, but only briefly, and for dramatic reasons, not because she didn't remember every detail and relish the telling. For years, her story had stayed alive in vivid color, always visible to her, even when she became blind to everything else, always pressing against her tongue and her heart, echoing in her ears. Now it was spilling out, and I didn't have to do a thing in the way of prompting. "See, a man mixed up my husband Dom with Etienne and told him things so that Dom realized what was going on, but only about Etienne, nobody else. And it made sense. Etienne was a poor ignorant immigrant, from North Africa, I think. Didn't finish high school. No diploma, just that letter jacket that he maybe stole. And suddenly, he has fancy clothes, lots of cash—and the other men there not even getting paid. So my husband was real suspicious, but before he did anything, he disappeared."

"Who did?"

"Just when Donnaker was getting better, coming back, Etienne was gone—poof!—except he didn't tell his girl, and he left his jacket and his passport behind so you know he wasn't on any trip like they said he was. He was dead and hidden away, even if the police never found him. They even said it was suspicious. And meanwhile, the business was bankrupt, all those cars sold in secret out of the warehouse, while the ones on the floor sold for next to nothing—'See what Santa's giving away' he'd say in his ads. Called himself that even then, even though it was still Donnaker Motors. And even worse, all the cars still on inventory but missing, all those debts and unpaid bills. And my husband told Clausen about the thing with the warehouse, the customizing, Etienne, and Clausen fired Dom and made it sound like Dom had something to do with the mess the business was in, so Donnaker wouldn't even talk to him. But it was Alexander Clausen all the time. He was the one planned it. He was the one killed Etienne."

"How can you know something like that?"

"I *know*. Because Donnaker declared bankruptcy. Because Clausen suddenly had money to buy the franchise. And the old man still thinking of him like a son! So grateful, because Clausen gave him money to tide him over. It was his own money! The murderer, the liar, the cheat comes out a hero—winds up with three dealerships, plus all those buildings—the condos and office buildings and God knows what else so that they talk about maybe he should be the next mayor—and my husband, may he rest in peace, an honest man, had no job and a cloud over his name until the day he died. Is this fair? But I never said a word because I was too afraid—the man had already killed one person who knew the secret of his success."

"You mustn't be afraid," I said. "He's dead. He can't hurt anybody anymore." True, but even I could see how long the already inflicted hurts lasted. And as if on cue, in walked another of his victims.

Laura and Sasha's noses were bright red, and the brown paper bag they carried had greasy spots. But Laura had such an unqualified smile that I began to believe that steak sandwiches, or even their aroma and excess grease, might be panaceas. Then she put down the bag and pulled an envelope out of her pocket.

"We stopped at Aunt Alma's, and look—a letter from Peter!" She tried to open it without taking off her mittens.

Sasha gestured me to get off the phone. "The cheese will congeal," she said, grimacing.

"I hear voices," Minna White said. "Is she back?"

"Yes," I answered. "So I'd better . . ."

"Now don't go saying anything. Not anything, do you understand?"

"Sure," I said. "But I have one question. How come you used—"

"Is she *listening*?" Minna's obsessive concern with Laura made no sense. What did she think Laura would or could do to her? Did she believe there was a family vendetta, now that she had told her story? And who even knew the story? *Mining Silver*'s readership was a little more limited than, say, *People* magazine's. "Where is she?" Minna demanded.

"Upstairs. Washing up." Laura, engrossed in Peter's letter, examining the envelope now, didn't even look my way to figure out what I might be talking, or lying, about. "So can I ask?"

"I don't know. she might . . ."

"This is about your writing style," I said quickly, and I

interpreted Minna's little pop of an "oh!" as acquiescence.
"Why did you use Etienne's name? Only Etienne's."

"Because it's so *fancy*. Like a fairy-tale name. And because he was dead, so he wouldn't mind and he couldn't sue me. I didn't know it was really so unusual until that man said so."

"Who?"

"You know. My secret admirer. He said he'd once known a man named Etienne. Only one. I'm sure there are more, aren't you? It's foreign, so maybe in Philadelphia it's rare, that's all. But what if there's only maybe one more? Could the one sue me?"

I began to suspect that Minna White enjoyed being afraid of something, almost anything. Perhaps, in a constricted life, imagined enemies broadened her horizons. It might be cruel to completely release her from anxiety. "I don't think so," I said, therefore, and then, to give her something to quiver over now that Clausen was dead, I added, very delicately, "but of course, I'm not an attorney."

She sighed with a mix of pleasure and pain, and then, after her promise to give me the results of the cannoli tasting very soon, we hung up.

"Time to eat," Sasha said.

I wanted a breather to evaluate what Minna had said, to see if it was the key to anything or everything. I settled instead for steak sandwiches and joined Sasha at the glass dining table.

"He's running away." Laura floated toward us, holding her letter.

Sasha had set out homespun place mats, beer mugs filled with ice, a bottle of diet soda and a trio of sandwiches swaddled in white butcher paper with transluscent spots where the greasy treasures had begun working their way through.

"Peter?" she asked Laura.

Laura nodded, face deep in private thought. She sat down with us, almost as if unaware of what she was doing.

"You haven't been talking about boys, have you? Okay," I said, "you have—but Laura, please tell me you haven't been listening. Sasha knows about many things, but not men.'' Sasha, a french fry midway to her mouth, glared. "I take that back. Sasha knows about men—but she can never remember what she knows. So she has to learn the same thing, over and over again, and—what was that? Peter ran away?"

"He's really mad at his mother." A triumphant, vindictive expression flared for a moment, surprising me. It was the first time I'd seen an authentic, complicated teenage girl stick her face out from behind the Laura mask.

"Eat!" Sasha said, pushing a paper cocoon toward Laura. Then in as close to a maternal act as I've seen from her, she unwrapped it, unveiling the fragrant, dripping roll. "Eat, skinny!" Sasha demanded again, and this time, Laura obeyed.

As did I, without prompting.

I wished I could be alone with Sasha so that I could talk everything through. Although, she needed so much catching up, maybe it wasn't worth it. I was shocked to realize that she had been away for a long weekend, not the months it felt like.

The three of us had eaten together only five nights ago, but the party had been held in another time and world. Now the Clausen living room was gutted and boarded up. Alexander was no more, nor was Jacob. Somebody had changed into a killer that night. Alice was in an institution and Laura was living with me. The only people in the same situation now as they'd been on that night were the homeless. Their lives were still unbearable. I lost my appetite.

Minna's story made blackmail a definite possibility. Known murderers were seldom elected mayor. Or heaped with civic awards. Or even allowed to build major civic projects. Assuming the story was true, or relevant to what had happened.

But why would it have waited years and years to explode at the party?

I tried to focus on the thin slices of steak, melted cheese and fried onions. But names and possibilities were what I tasted.

Peter had reason to threaten Clausen. He could have done

it. I wanted to believe in him, but he was a troubled adolescent, he was powerfully made and surely, with his history, abusive fathers were a sore point and a trigger for his temper. And he'd been furious that night, righteously, justifiably furious.

And Laura could have done it, alone or with him. It made me sick to think of either one of them as killers, locked up and condemned, but the fact was, they had cause and opportunity and whatever else the entry requirements were. I bit into my sandwich and chewed on it and the theory.

Sasha was into the wise-older-woman mode. She leaned toward Laura. "Listen to your elders. Cholesterol is a public-relations ploy to boost the sales of cheesesteak and hoagies," she explained.

Alice could have done it. God knows, she probably knew about everything, every offense and lie and crime, back to Etienne, or before. If only she were sober and assertive, or either one.

"See, cholesterol terror makes them not only delicious, but sinful. Irresistible. Not only fattening, but dangerous. Almost as bad for your heart as men are. And look how we are with men."

Etienne could have been the one. If he were alive. Boy, could he ever.

"The only thing left to make them perfect, is to make them illegal."

The old king—Donnaker—could, if he were alive and able bodied. I nearly choked. Laura looked terrified. Even Sasha stopped rhapsodizing as I stood up, coughing, found the phone directory, drank some water, found the number I wanted, and dialed.

"Mrs. White, please," I said. "Minna White. She's probably in the dayroom, where the television is."

"Are you all right?" Sasha asked.

I nodded. I was all right and right, too. I was sure I was. The scattered pieces finally locked one into the other and made a picture.

"Mrs. White," I said when she picked up the dayroom

extension. "The old king—Mr. Donnaker—his first name was Jacob, wasn't it?"

FOR A WHILE AFTERWARD, I WAVED OFF SASHA'S QUESTIONS, shaking my head. The steak sandwich sat on the table, uneaten, except for the part inside me that felt like a bowling ball lodged below my breasts.

Jacob Donnaker. The mysterious visitor who'd read Minna's story. Who had known an Etienne who disappeared. Who'd lost his "stables." Who hadn't known what had happened to him, who had trusted Alexander Clausen, accepted his own ruination and Alexander's triumphs as the way of the world until he read that story and searched out Minna White. One week ago. Last Tuesday. Two days before the party—the day somebody at Silverwood ordered a taxi at the senior citizen discount rate.

How convenient that at the same time, Santa had been making sure that his holiday act of charity was in no way anonymous, so that every newspaper in town had photographs and feature stories on the man's benevolence. It must have seemed a gift, making it ridiculously easy to have easy, anonymous access to him.

But the jigsaw puzzle still had gaping holes, because it was a long trip between Jacob Donnaker's getting out of his cab and winding up dead in the Clausen's toolshed.

Fourteen

ASIDE FROM INDIGESTION, THE NEXT FEW HOURS WENT rather well. I never had my conversation with Sasha, because, hunger satisfied, she remembered the need to pack and get ready for her morning flight, and Laura abruptly decided to walk partway with her, even without the promise of viewing historical marijuana patches.

"You'll be right back, won't you?" I asked, unable to define what I feared might happen to her. After all, she had been least safe in her own home, not outside, and not at the hands of strangers, but I felt anxious all the same. I was a little awkward with the instant-mother role. I lacked a sense of timing, a history I could consult for guidance. I had missed fourteen years of getting used to Laura and gauging such traits as street smarts.

"Right back," she assured me.

"It's freezing cold out there."

"Not so bad," she answered, and then they were gone, and I felt like every hovering, clutching, perpetually anxious mother.

"What the hell," I said. I opened the door again. "Be careful!" I called. Sasha turned around and shouted, "No way!" but Laura looked at me with the same confused, bemused expression I had beamed at my own mother.

Magical incantations completed, I tossed away our lunchtime leavings, wrapping up my sandwich. I'd have the rest tonight. No—I kept forgetting that Nick was coming over, cooking dinner for Laura and me. I imagined him in my tiny kitchen, overcharged, banging pots and pans, dirtying everything at once, talking nonstop. A performance artist and, I hoped, a cook. But I would have been just as happy with the leftover steak sandwich.

Time now, however, to face the music, act like a woman. I took a deep breath and dialed long-distance, and almost immediately launched into an impassioned and, I might say, rather eloquent address on the topics of mothers, fathers, children in general, Laura, her father and mother in as much detail as I could stomach and manatees whenever I needed sweeping generalizations about innocent victims needing protectors, and God knows what else. But I was not one-fifth through when I realized that my mother understood. Her world is enviably clear and defined. There is right and there is wrong. B. Pepper's laws are debatable, but she will never be the one to debate them. Even when she's force-feeding me a stuttering podiatrist, she is following her most basic law which is "protect children." It was from that central point that she spread out to protect other species and embrace other causes.

So she understood what I was doing and why and approved. "Poor child," she said. "She's lucky she has you." And that was that. I was glad to share that woman's genes.

"I'm lucky I have you," I answered.

"And that foot man?" she said. "A real nothing. Can you believe, he brought a 'friend' with him. A tramp. A floozie in his mother's house. You can do better than a man who loves bunions."

"I'll be there soon as I can. I promise. Kiss everybody, okay? I do miss you."

"Be careful," she said. Her head wasn't out the front door, calling after me, but I felt an overwhelming kinship.

"Mom, there's nothing to be careful about."

"Amanda, two men were murdered."

"I'm not involved. I'm an interested bystander, a concerned citizen. That is all."

"I don't know . . ." she murmured.

"Hey—the most dangerous thing I've done today was eat too much. Beginning with a cannoli. You should never have told me to buy some for Minna White. They're irresistible."

"So you went. I forgot to ask. That was good of you. You make me proud."

All it took was visiting an old lady and having a child in, even a borrowed one. An entire conversation and she hadn't once referred to my unwedded state.

"One thing."

The muscles in my neck and upper back contracted in anticipation of the next installment of "Hunt for a Husband."

"About your sweater," she said. "Some of the yarn is . . . tired. But there's enough for a vest. A special one. Long. That you don't button or close, you know?"

I knew. Like the ones in style twenty years ago. I could wear it for a road tour of *Hair.* "A short vest would be fine, Mom." It was worth a try.

"I don't stint on my children. Down to your knees. And I was thinking, if I run out of your yarn, I could border it with some nice navy wool I have."

What I had once wanted was a pink and gray short-sleeved pullover, but I was feeling so positively maudlin about how magnificently she'd handled the canceled trip, that I said that sounded fine. Maybe long, long vests would be back in style by the time she finished.

I REACHED MACKENZIE BEFORE HE LEFT FOR THE AIRPORT. "Jacob Donnaker," I said. "Clausen's mentor, employer and victim. Remember, I told you I have his picture if anybody needs it. Sasha had it."

"Thanks for the name. Saves time. But we have a photo of the, uh, victim."

"Yes, but he's alive in Sasha's."

"I'll let you know. But thanks all the same."

Pity. It might have raised Sasha's stock a few points. "It must have been Donnaker and Clausen that Laura heard quarreling, don't you think?" I said.

"And then there was one?" Mackenzie said. "At which time, out of remorse, Clausen beat himself silly and fractured his own skull? That what you're sayin'?"

"Well, no, a third person—"

"—came downstairs?"

"I thought you'd dropped that theory."

"You keep mixin' us up. *You* dropped it. Well, two of them are out of circulation for a while. That's some relief."

I didn't choose to mention Peter's letter to Laura.

"Of course, you've got the third one as a houseguest, just to even the odds. Damn but I'd feel better if you were on your way to Florida. I don't like this. Not at all. How'd you get so involved?"

"I'm not." Hadn't I just said that? Wasn't it true?

"Maybe I can get back sooner. How'd that be?"

"Wonderful. Incredible. Heart's balm."

"How's that?"

"Try to."

"Mandy?" His voice was low and intense. "One thing. Be careful."

"DIGEST QUICKLY," I SAID TO LAURA. "NICK WILL BE HERE soon, and we'll have to eat again and act as if we enjoy it, too. Somehow, dinner sounded a lot better this morning." Nonetheless, I set the round table again, using my favorite— also one and only—good tablecloth and my best floral-patterned napkins.

Laura looked oddly jaunty, as if she had a pleasurable secret, had somehow outwitted the adult world. I amended the impression to read Laura looked odd because she was wearing a normal adolescent expression, slightly off-putting and unnerving. The old I-Know-Something-You-Don't-That-Would-Drive-You-Up-A-Tree. Basic teenager. The mask was fracturing, crumbling off in bits and pieces. Of course it was going to take lots of time and work and help to truly destroy it, to make her feel safe while exposed, but I could see it beginning, so I knew it was possible.

She helped polish my grandmother's silver, and carefully set three places.

I only had two crystal wine glasses. I added a rather squatty glass, one with a bank logo on it.

"Three?" Laura said.

"Think of yourself as European this evening," I said, hoping I wasn't committing yet another crime, letting a fourteen-year-old taste wine. "A sip, that's all. And you cannot drive afterward." I walked over to the fireplace and lit the kindling.

"Tell you what," Laura said. "I'll wait *two years* to sober up. And then will you give me the car keys?"

My heart lurched and expanded, and it wasn't from my bending over the fireplace or the flash of heat as the kindling caught. I had heard a small stab at humor. No doubt about it. Laura Clausen had let a joke burp out of her. Laura Clausen could laugh a little. Laura Clausen was going to survive. I felt as if I might cry, which wouldn't help her one bit. Instead, I scooped up Macavity, who'd been inspecting my fire building, and gave him a celebratory ruffling behind his ears until he looked like he might swoon. Then, back under control, I went to the kitchen, opening and shutting drawers, rummaging through my meager candle supply. Everything I found had seen better times.

"I stopped at Aunt Alma's again," Laura said.

"Which reminds me—do the people where your mom is know where you are?" I asked her.

"I called there this morning. Right before you picked me up." She sounded old and tired whenever either of her parents was the topic. "I'll call again later. Or tomorrow."

I stopped shuffling through the drawers. "Listen, maybe you can't believe this right now, but you're strong. Strong enough to get through all of this. Let us help you, but understand that you can do it."

For a moment, her expression was like a gulp, like someone wolfing down my words as quickly as possible. Then she grew more wary, distancing herself, and shrugged. I returned to my search for a usable candle.

"I left a note," she blurted out after a pause. "On the door. For Peter. So he'll know where I am."

"Aunt Alma's door?"

She nodded.

"That's not the greatest idea." There were no decent candles in the house, and I wondered why I kept these stubs, but under the theory that there must be a reason, because I was doing so, I put them back into the drawer and kept on doing so. "It's like an ad for a thief—nobody's home here, come in." I also felt extremely queasy about the idea of Peter, angrier than ever, coming here. He was fine and dandy while Laura was his special project, the dragon-protector—at least I thought and hoped so—but how would he react if anything in the status quo changed, or if he felt threatened?

And more to the point—where had he been when he wasn't in Laura's room?

Laura settled on the sofa. I looked up, afraid that even keeping most of my reservations to myself, I had nonetheless shattered the shaky little bridge between us. But she looked serene enough. In fact, she made a lovely tableau with her legs curled under her, the firelight adding a flow to her hair and skin and the little Christmas tree behind her twinkling in the street window.

"I did it in code," she said. "It says "P.—L. with M.P.""

"I get the Peter and Laura, but what's M.P.? Military Police?"

"It's Miss Pepper."

I ducked out of sight and pawed through my junk drawer to hide my smile. Miss Pepper! I felt neutered, my first name surgically removed. Miss Pepper was a concept, a role, not a woman. If Peter deciphered the code, would Miss Pepper be impressed or depressed?

The fact was, there were no surviving candles. I opted for a few votive lights, and even they had seen better votives. "You know what I wish I had," I said, making non-Peter conversation, "those squatty candles you had at the Christmas party. They smelled so good and were so solid; you didn't have to worry about them, and . . ." I froze, the votive candles still in my hand.

"What?" Laura asked. "And what?"

I stared at her, seeing not this Christmas tree, firelight and sofa, but that other one. "The candles," I said. "Do you remember them?"

She shrugged. "Maybe."

"Do you remember where they were?"

"Pretty much everywhere."

I walked over and sat across from her, shaking my head. "Not really. I remember thinking how clever somebody had been. They looked like they were all over the place, but they were only in safe places. Mantel, niches, windowsills and parts of tables that nobody would use. And they were so solid, and stuck onto those heavy brass holders."

She smiled halfheartedly, humoring me.

"You don't see, do you?" I leaned closer. "Think, Laura. That little table next to the sofa—I remember there wasn't room for my punch glass on it. I remember thinking somebody had made sure there'd be no water rings on what had to be a valuable piece of furniture. Because it was filled to capacity with an ashtray and an arrangement of poinsettias."

She shrugged. "Okay," she said. "So what?"

"When you came downstairs—when your father was sleeping—was something burning on that table? Like a cigarette? You said you stared at him. Wouldn't it have seemed odd, definitely something you'd notice if he was asleep and a cigarette were still burning? Think—during all that time, can you remember smoke coming up from the ashtray?"

She shook her head.

"Then there wasn't anything burning there. There was never room for a candle. It would have made the poinsettia a fire hazard." I stood up and walked the short distance to the window. I was churning inside, and she was still sitting like a still life. "You don't understand what this means, do you?" I asked. "Laura," I said as calmly as I could, "it means you did not have anything to do with your father's death. Think—think what you remember! Standing over a sleeping man—then the tree in your hands and the flames.

"Where did the flames come from? That tree didn't have a single light or electrical wire on it. It was all old-fashioned ornaments. How did it catch fire?"

"The candle—the . . ." She shook her head.

"What candles? Where? There weren't any candles in the tree's trajectory."

"I don't see what—"

I knelt in front of her. "Listen, this is horrible stuff, but not as horrible as believing you did something you didn't. Your father wasn't asleep—he was dead, or very near to it. And you interrupted whatever was supposed to happen next. And when you stood there, looking at your father, somebody else pushed the tree at you, at him, and lit it. And while you ran around, while you realized you were on fire, while your mother threw the water on your nightgown, that somebody got away."

"How? That wouldn't be possible without our—"

"The window. Hiding behind the drapes in the big bay behind the tree. It's boarded over now, so I don't know if the firemen or the—that person—broke it. But I think that's how."

She looked pale and ill, on the verge of tears, and she pressed her fingers to her temples.

"Are you okay?" I asked.

"I almost—you say something like that, like some man went out the window, or pushed the tree, and then I see it, think I'm remembering it. I can almost see him, could almost draw him—and then it's gone, altogether gone, and I know I made it up because you said it."

"Do you remember anything like that? Or hearing breaking glass?"

She shook her head. "I don't know. It sounded like everything was breaking. I was screaming and my mother was screaming and then Peter was shouting and, yes, there was noise—and the fire made its own noise, but I . . ." Her eyes were bleak and she looked even more as if she might cry.

"You didn't do it, Laura. You did absolutely nothing except come downstairs at the wrong time."

She kept shaking her head, unable or unwilling to assimilate this, unable to deny it, as if she needed to have killed her father. Maybe she thought she'd settled the score, shown some power, violently reclaimed control of her life. I don't know. We'd work on that later. For now, it was important to make it clear that she was not a killer.

"Would you mind—my head hurts—I'm going to lie down," she said.

"Of course. One question though—you said Peter was out of your room, that you talked later about hearing a quarrel."

She nodded.

"Laura—was he back in your room when you went down-stairs?"

She stared at me, mouth agape.

"Isn't it foolhardy not to even consider—please, Laura—was he in your room when you went downstairs? Or was it only afterward, after the fire, that you compared the sounds and the events?"

Her face flushed, she winced with pain, put her hand to her forehead and started up the stairs. "I need aspirin," was what she said, but her eyes had flashed the message that now I, too, had joined the enemy camp.

"NICE PLACE," NICK SAID. HE PUT TWO SHOPPING BAGS ON the kitchen counter, tossed his coat onto a stool and paced the downstairs room. He was wearing a light blue shirt and an argyle vest and he looked rather jaunty. "Nice," he repeated, "nice sense of color, nice feeling."

"Pretty," he said of the little Christmas tree. "Ummm," of the suede chair. "Uh-huh," of my mother's slipcovered old sofa. The dining table and setting got a nod; a whimsical Klee print, a cocked head and wrinkled brow; the photos in little Victorian frames a long examination; the bookcase a more cursory one; a Dorothea Lange Depression print of a woman, a child's face pressed into each of her shoulders and her own angular face looking for everything, finding nothing, generated a "hmmm." He was interested, but decidely non-verbal. It was a good thing he wasn't writing architectural or design criticism.

His living-area survey completed, he moved into my min-iscule cooking area, and inspected the cupboards. Open, peer, close. "Making pasta with"—open, peer, close—

"crab, shrimp and scallops in tomato, mushrooms, basil and garlic. My own recipe."

"Sounds marvelous."

"Think the kid will eat it? She's around, isn't she? I saw three place settings, but where is she?" Open, peer, shut.

"Upstairs, not feeling too—"

"Good," he said, slamming a door. "A big enough pot."

I wasn't sure I could be close to his energy level for too long without getting radiation burns.

He opened my junk drawer.

"Hey—I don't let just anybody see that, you know," I said "I am not that kind of girl."

"Taking inventory," he answered. "But maybe you'd prefer I ask you for what I need and you hand it over? Kind of kitchen doctor and nurse? Want some wine?"

"Yes, to both."

"So," he said, settling on the suede chair, "how was your visit with the blind lady and her pals?"

"You have a good memory."

"Correct. So how was it?" He was never completely still. His left foot tapped on the floor, as if it had its own motor.

"Fine. Uneventful. She liked the cannoli. A friend of hers joined us and told me that she—the blind old lady—was a sexpot, or a siren. A Scheherazade, with stories that attract lovers, more or less. Perked things up a bit from what I'd anticipated."

"What kind of stories?"

"Oh, you know. Stuff from her past. Memories. Old-lady stories. Speaking of which, how is yours going?"

"My old-lady story?"

"Your story. About Alexander Clausen." The wine was delicious, far beyond the standards and budget of this household. I toasted him with my glass.

"Coming. Coming. Nearly done. Laura going to be much longer? You hungry?"

"I'll check on her in a minute." The pacing of the evening was way off. Maybe he was a restaurant kind of date, needing slow service, delays mandated by management. On his own, he chugged much too quickly. I tried slowing things down.

"Remember how you asked me about Clausen's beginnings, about how he got his start? Did you ever find out?" What if nothing Minna had said was true?

"Why would you care about that?"

"Because *Seventeen* magazine always said to ask your date about his interests." He took the time to smile. "Because putting together an article like yours sounds interesting. Sleuthing around for clues."

"That's an unusual way of describing it." He stood up and stretched. "Makes research sound like detective work."

"Isn't it?"

He shot me a glance I couldn't interpret. Maybe he thought I was making fun of him.

"Come across somebody named Donnaker in your research?" I asked.

"Why?"

"This old woman today . . ." I suddenly felt guilty, thinking of Minna. I couldn't be free and easy with her story, not when she was, irrationally or not, terrified of its misuse. The ethical thing to do would be to first ask her permission, or see if she'd talk to Nick herself. "Nothing," I said.

He waited, as if hoping I'd change my mind, and then he walked to the front of the house and opened the closet door. "Whoops," he said. "Sorry. Listen, is there someplace to wash up before I start things going?"

"Upstairs. Can't miss it."

He took the stairs two at a time. Weird man. Too frenetic. If Mackenzie and Nick could be boiled up together, then melted down and reshaped, you'd get twins with about normal metabolisms. But since they couldn't, I'd cast my vote on the side of the more relaxed tempo.

I pulled myself out of the chair and turned on more lights. It was dark as only the final edge of the year can be. The closet door was still ajar, a reminder that Nick's coat was not yet in it, and my hostessing skills were not passing muster. I picked up the coat and was impressed by its softness. Not the coat of a man who writes for *Oxlips*, not the coat of a late bloomer. This must be one of the fruits of his short-lived real-estate deals. The wine was probably bought and stored during the same flush time.

I glanced at the staircase, and, the coast clear, I checked the label. It was indeed cashmere, hand tailored. Even the label was hand tailored. "Made by Alfred Boyer," it said, "expressly for Dominick Riley."

I hung it up carefully, smoothing the shoulders, carefully putting the white silk scarf over it.

Lots and lots of people were named Dominick. Nothing unusual about it.

Nonetheless, with heart pounding and a quick look up the stairs, I ran to the phone and dialed the Southland. It would take too long, require too much explaining to reach my other option, Minna White.

My mother barely got out her hello.

"Quick," I said, "we never—Mom—what was Minna White's first husband's name?"

"Oh, dear," she said. "Let me think."

The toilet flushed upstairs.

"Don, I think. Yes, Donald sounds . . ."

"Dom, Dominick," I said. "I know that part. His name was Dominick."

"Of course—Dominick. She called him Dom, not Don—"

"Can you remember the rest?" Water banged through the pipes.

"Of course. It was the Dominick part that had me stymied because I knew Minna a lot better than I knew—"

"Mom!"

"What?"

"Minna's last name." I was whispering. The water had stopped. There weren't a whole lot more things the man was about to do in my bathroom.

"What?"

"Her last name."

"Riley. You knew that. Of course. You were so tiny and you thought Minna Riley was soup. You meant minestrone, but it was so cute, nobody corrected you, so you'd say, 'I want Minna Riley for lunch,' and we'd—"

I couldn't hear much because I had suddenly developed the flu, jolting between hot flashes and chills, guessing what the odds were, whether Minna Riley's son, Junior, he of the birthmark now hidden by a beard, the very same person who had learned his family history the day Jacob Donnaker found out the story of his betrayal, the same person who had pretended, probably, to be a free-lance writer profiling Clausen—the Junior who had called his mother today, after I had told him my destination—whether that son Junior's presence in my house could be only an ironic, interesting, almost humorous coincidence.

I figured the odds at roughly a trillion to one.

And then they escalated as I watched four legs come down the staircase. First Laura's, spindly and hesitant, and behind them, Nick's, or Dominick's or Junior's. Well tailored and much more confident. As well he might be, since he, unlike his hostesses, carried a gun.

"One time in the market you shouted, 'Minna Riley with crackers!' Minna—"

"Hang up," Nick-Junior said. His gun was aimed at Laura's head.

"Mom, I have to—"

"Hang it up," he said again.

"What?" my mother said.

"Hang it up or I'll shoot it out of your hand," he said. "After I shoot her." He was inches away from me.

"There's no reason for this!" I hissed.

He shook his head in disgust, and without waiting for the amenities, pressed the disconnect button. Then he removed the receiver from my hand and clicked it onto the telephone.

"What is this?" I said. "What does this mean?"

He didn't answer.

I was pretty sure it meant we weren't going to eat seafood pasta tonight.

Fifteen

"I DON'T GET IT." I HOPED I WAS TELLING THE TRUTH.

"Nothing mysterious about it." Nick seemed both grim and exhilarated.

"Why—why are you pointing a gun at us?"

"Saves time. More efficient. Laura wouldn't come down-stairs otherwise." With his free hand, he directed both of us down onto the sofa.

It was not comforting to have a fidget aim a lethal weapon at me. I wanted to be sure he didn't nervously tap his index finger. He had unbuttoned his shirt sleeves and rolled them up, the better to do his work, and I saw the edge of a large bandage. I remembered his awkward eating at the restaurant that night, the tennis-elbow story. I guess that made better table talk than calling it an "escape" elbow, or explaining how he'd gotten it, pushing his way through a window after murdering someone.

I squeezed Laura's hand, trying to make the squeeze trans-late into "I never ever wanted to put you in jeopardy. Forgive me. Be brave. Help me be brave."

"I'm sorry this has to happen," Nick said. "But damn, it's your own fault. Both of you. You, kid—if you hadn't come downstairs that night . . ." He shook his head, still annoyed by Laura's intrusion.

Laura's eyes welled over, and she pulled her hand out of

185

mine and wiped at them, almost angrily. "I do remember
you," she said with a shudder. "I thought it was just my
imagination. A dream-memory. Something mixed up, but it
wasn't." She was speaking to Nick, but she kept her head
bent. She was almost doubled over, as if her stomach hurt.
As if everything hurt. "This morning, outside the bakery, I
thought—I got so scared when I saw you. It was like it cut
my brain, it was so clear for a second. Then I was sure I was
making it up. Imagining. But I saw you. I saw you standing
where the tree had been. Just for a second, but I saw."

"I know," he said flatly. "I wish you hadn't."

"You would still have set a fire, wouldn't you, though?"
she asked, head still bowed. "So I'd be blamed."

"Probably." He tapped his right foot and scowled. I tried
to scan his skull, read the brain paths, see his plan. His head
went right to left, to the window, back to us, back to the
window. He seemed ambivalent for a man who obviously
had already reached some hard decisions.

"And you—" He meant me, this time. "All that crap
about visiting this blind old lady-friend of your mother's. All
that cat and mouse."

"But she was my mother's friend! And that is why I went!"
I realized, with a thudding fall that my reasons for visiting
Silverwood might be innocent or guilty, but they were also
irrelevant. I had gone and now I knew what I knew. And
Nick knew what I knew. I fought off a powerful urge to
abdicate, to curl into a fetal position and go to sleep, waking
up someday, or not. I blinked hard, insisting on alertness. I
was not going to spend my Christmas vacation getting killed.

There was reason for optimism, I told myself. For in fact,
the living room lights were on, the curtains open, the street
window at eye level. So if, for example, somebody decided
to take an invigorating stroll in the cold and wet winter night
air, and they chose my otherwise barely traveled street, and
then they acted on a sudden urge to twist and contort so as
to see around the Christmas tree boughs, we'd be completely
visible. And surely, the passerby would then immediately
run for help.

Maybe one of those "Little Streets of Philadelphia" walking tours was scheduled for tonight. Just because it was freezing and dark and the day after Christmas didn't mean . . .

The fact was, I'd better think of a plan of my own that didn't involve passersby.

"Right," Nick was saying. "You didn't know she was my mother. And sure, that wasn't a game at the bakery this morning when you asked me who could have arrived at Clausen's party in a taxi."

"I never connected you with anything except that article you were supposedly writing. I didn't even know your first name until five minutes ago when I hung up your coat."

"I don't believe you."

"Buy off the rack next time, Dominick."

"And Laura's being with you, that's a coincidence, too, right?"

"Wrong. Laura's with me for logical reasons. Her house burned down, and her father was killed. And her mother is not well. And her aunt and uncle are away. And I am her friend. And that's why she's here. The question is—why are *you* here?"

"Also for logical reasons."

"I hope they involve shrimp and spaghetti."

He looked at my Christmas tree. "I told you it was dangerous having a firebug as a houseguest. I warned you."

I closed my eyes in a primitive denial reflex. He was going to burn us up. Repeat performance. "You have no imagination. It's obvious that you're not really a writer." I opened my eyes. "There's no deal with *Philadelphia Magazine* and no such thing as *Oxlips*, is there?"

"Hey," he said, with a hint of the old smile. "We call it what we like. You say you're visiting, I say I'm writing. Writing, visiting—"

"I know that one. The next line is 'Let's call the whole thing off.' Can we?"

I had Sudden Stranger Syndrome with my own self. Who was this woman sitting straight as a cadet, heart in a prolonged aerobic workout, tossing second-rate lady-in-peril repartee around as if she were Myrna Loy with slingbacks and a dry martini? Nick didn't seem overly impressed, but then, he wasn't a Myrna Loy kind of guy. I couldn't find out for sure, because our sophisticated banter was interrupted. Twice. The doorbell and the telephone both rang. "Ignore them," Nick said.

I counted the phone rings. Eight. Nine. The doorbell rang a second and third time. Ten for the phone. A rapid knock at the door. Eleven.

The phone person obviously hadn't read the telephone company's suggested ten-ring maximum. Actually, in my house, three and a half rings is enough travel time from any point to an extension. At a saunter. My mother knows it, but she doesn't care when she also knows I'm there. As when I've hung up on her in midcall.

Another knock at the door.

Go to it, I urged the phone. You've never given up before. Don't start now.

Silence from outside. Nick listened hard, then relaxed. "One down," he said. "One to go." He moved sideways to the kitchen divider and the phone.

And then a form, a shadow, at the front window. Never had a Peeping Tom been more welcome. My random passerby. Our rescuer. Nick didn't notice.

The persistent caller persisted one more time.

Nick lifted the receiver and slammed it back down.

Macavity, who had been sniffing around Nick's grocery bag, jumped off the counter.

The window was a mirror on our side, the form on its dark side unidentifiable, obscured as well by the boughs of the Christmas tree, but I imagined him, pressing close for a better view, unable to believe his eyes.

Yes, it's what you think! Two women at gunpoint. Quickly, run for the police!

"Laura!" The voice came from behind the window.

"No!" I shouted. "No! No heroics—use your brain, not your hormones!"

"Damn!" Nick said, walking to the door.

"Peter!" Laura's voice was low and awed. "You found me. Peter found me, Miss Pepper!"

Big deal. Wonderful. I didn't want to put a blight on young love, and Peter had been eliminated now as archvillain, but there were happier, saner options that he had overlooked.

"Come right in." Nick stood at the front door, a malevolent caricature of the gracious host, his gun pointed toward the street. Peter rushed in, ignoring the gun, ignoring sanity, to kneel in front of Laura and silently inspect her. He seemed satisfied, and stood up. Both she and I shifted to make room on the sofa.

But he didn't sit down. "You sure you're all right?" he asked Laura. She nodded. He forgot to ask about my welfare, but I overlooked the slight along with the fact that he'd correctly identified Laura's "M.P." as Miss Pepper.

He wheeled around. "What do you think you're doing, you son of a bitch!" For a moment, I believed. I thought we had gotten to the end of the reel, that by gum, Tom Trueheart had arrived, and Laura and I would be cut free of the train tracks and the villain roundly punished.

Except that Nick advanced on Peter with the gun and said, "What the hell do you think I'm doing? I'm going to kill them, and now you, too, punk. Sit down."

I thought of Mackenzie boarding a plane even as we sat here about to die. How sad would he be? Would he blame this on Laura?

The phone started up again. "It won't stop," I said. "I assure you, it won't, until I answer it and have a normal conversation with her."

"How do you know who it is?"

"Trust me."

"Then answer it," he said. "And sound normal. Say anything weird, or give her a warning, and I will shoot Laura through the skull. Guaranteed."

"Amanda!" my mother said. "Thank goodness! I called before and there was no answer."

Mental telepathy with Peter had failed. Now I could use words, but only if they were coded. Except, my mind was a complete blank.

I looked around the room. Nick watched me warily. Laura and Peter stared. Her eyes were the size of satellite dishes.

"We were cut off!" My mother sounded agitated, worried still. "I thought something bad had happened."

"How *clever* of you!" I said. "How *true!*" Get it, Mom? Something bad did happen, is happening. Call the police. Tell them to get here immediately!

"Don't make fun of me. I was worried about you!"

"As well you should. You have every reason to feel that way." Come on, you're a bright woman. You've worried without cause your whole life. Now there's cause. Help!

"You're upsetting me."

"Yes. I mean to," I said.

Nick walked to the front window, waving his gun at the three of us with each step, and pulled the draperies closed. No more Peeping Toms tonight.

"Fine," my mother said in the suffering-wounded-resigned voice that, along with the child, arrives on the delivery table. "You want to upset me, upset me. Whatever you say. I won't take up any more of your time." She sighed and then decided to do a dollop more of guilt mongering. "I just want you to know that I've planned out the vest. Looks like it'll be very nice with the navy trim. About thirty inches long."

"Eighty-six." I didn't know if she'd recognize that expression for killing something, but it seemed worth a try.

Nick flashed a glance. "A great year," I muttered.

"What? What year?"

"Sorry. Measurement."

"Eighty-six?" my mother said. "For heaven's sake—that's seven feet—a bridal gown with train! Are you crazy?" She sighed. "Look, what I was going ask is if you'd like patch pockets from the navy wool. I think they'd look nice."

"Terrific idea. Navy's very nice."

"Big."

"Very big. How does nine by eleven sound?" She had to get that, didn't she? I couldn't say nine-one-one. I couldn't say dial emergency. She had to understand what I could say. Didn't she?

Nick turned off all the lamps. Only the kitchen was still illuminated.

"Have you been drinking? Many, pockets that size would reach from your neck to—"

"Mom, I want you to do what I said."

"Speed it up," Nick said. "I don't care how long your mother likes to talk. End it."

I nodded. "I wish you'd listen to me, Mom."

"I have been—and I hear somebody who's had too much eggnog," she said. "And with that little girl in your house, too! Eighty-six! Nine by eleven! We'll talk tomorrow. I'm glad everything's fine. Want some advice? Get a good night's sleep."

And that was that.

"I don't know how many other family members think they need a chatting up tonight," Nick said, "but I don't care. Turn on your answering machine." He stood in the shadowy living room, glowering over his revolver.

I leaned over the counter to the little black box, and reached out my forefinger. My last act on earth, activating an answering machine.

I turned the machine on. Then, inspired, or at least hopeful, I pressed another button, one on top, before I turned around.

"Okay," Nick said. "I'm sorry, but this is how it has to be."

"What's going on?" Peter asked. "Who are you?"

"He killed my father." Laura was sobbing. Softly, intently, as regularly as breathing. If we lived, I needed to think about that more, later. Think about how much grief she contained now, for so many, many reasons. "And an old man," she said to Peter.

Nick fanned his gun back and forth across the three of us as he moved to the back of the house. "Wrong," he said.

I stayed where I was, as near the kitchen light, as far from the sofa and the other two as possible, thinking to at least make target practice harder. Maybe we could coordinate ourselves, rush him from separate angles.

"I didn't kill Donnaker," Nick said to Laura. "Your old man did. And that wasn't the first person he killed."

Laura slowly absorbed this, physically, as if she were being pumped with it. Her puffed face swelled still more. There was a slick of tears on her cheeks.

"You didn't do anything. Is that what you're saying?" Peter's voice was deep and menacing. I could almost feel his muscles ache to do something, anything. Despite his hair and black shirt, he was a kid. Blustering and unsure, using a belligerent voice as a weapon against a gun. "You had some kind of *accident*, I guess."

Nick worked his way behind the counter and stuck his free hand into the brown paper bag. Out came a plastic bag of shrimp. Then a cellophane package of fresh pasta.

Were we going to eat first? Some kind of last meal?

"All the old guy wanted was an explanation," he said. "It was like his heart was broken. You should have seen him when he realized what my mother's story meant. Well, hell, you should have seen me when I realized what she was saying. I never had heard about it before. Anyway, all he wanted was for Clausen to make it right. Pay him back. Apologize. Anything. And Clausen killed him. It probably didn't take much." Out of the bag came a mushroom basket and green onions, then tomatoes and fresh basil.

"And what were you doing?" I asked. "Watching?"

Nick shrugged. "I wasn't there. Donnaker was *embarrassed*, like it was all his fault, because Clausen had been his protégé, his son, can you believe it? I didn't care. He had his angle, his reasons to be there, and I had mine. He wanted to make peace. I wanted to make a civilized business arrangement. Clausen had contracts to rebuild half the city. There was room to give me some of it. But when the old guy said could they be alone to talk it out, I figured what the hell—there was time to let them settle their score. I went outside for maybe fifteen minutes. Looked around. Nice neighborhood. House next door has this gigantic greenhouse out back.

"Except, when I came in, the old guy's limp and broken, and Clausen's standing over him with the cane. I had nothing to do with it. Nothing." He put a small container of cream next to the vegetables and seafood.

Laura leaned forward. "I don't understand. Who was he? Who are you?"

"Your father ruined my father. I could have been a rich kid like you. Fair is fair." Nick reached into the bag again, but no more food emerged. Instead, he took out a small can of lighter fluid. I hadn't seen one of those in a while. Not since refillable lighters during the golden age of smoking.

"Your mother came downstairs. She heard noises. Called down. Then clump, clump, she wasn't walking all that steadily, you know. That's when your father started dragging the old guy. Hiding him. Scared, because she must know him from way back. He was her husband's boss. Practically his father."

He pulled out rope—not a great seafaring coil, but twine, to wrap newspapers or packages. Out came matches. The man was prepared.

"Excuse me," I said. "This is irrelevant but—what was all the food about?"

"If Laura hadn't been here, I'd have had to wait for another time. We'd have eaten."

"Listen," I said, "if Alice Clausen saw you that night, she'll remember. If you . . . hurt us, she'll be able to figure it out."

"Don't make me laugh. She'll be lucky if she remembers her name when she dries out." He pulled rags out of the bag. "I went there to make a deal. Clausen wanted things, and I wanted part of them. He was to own the whole damned city—why shouldn't I get my share? Call it my father's long-withheld commissions. With interest. We had a lot to talk about."

"Isn't it usually called blackmail?" I asked.

He flashed a dark flare of resentment. "I call it the truth. We could have made a deal, but he was crazy, threatening me, waving Donnaker's cane, which I wasn't about to have used on me. He forgot. He wasn't dealing with an old man this time. I'm stronger and quicker than he was. So I'm sorry—but not for him. For me! What good is he to me dead? I'm back to square one."

"Grow up, Junior!" I snapped. "Stop looking for the deal of the century."

"I'm not into career counseling just now," he said.

"I don't understand anything!" Laura clutched the sofa cushions and looked close to hysteria.

I watched Nick carefully unwrap the twine. "Don't do this," I said. "Clausen was an accident—a scuffle, self-defense. This is on purpose. They'll figure it out."

"How? If the kid hadn't come downstairs that night, nobody on God's earth could connect me with what happened."

"Well *I'm* not waiting for anybody to find anything out! You're dead meat now!" Peter shouted as he leaped up, looming, black hair wild and eyes on fire. The suede chair tumbling backward as he propelled himself toward the counter.

"No!" Laura screamed, standing and rushing toward him.

Macavity smelled big trouble. His hair prickled and, unwilling to risk even one of his lives, he abandoned us, racing up the staircase. Which made me realize why you don't hear too much about Famous Cat Heroes.

Then I forgot Macavity and feline cowardice, because Nick lifted the gun and pointed—he didn't aim, he didn't seem to think.

"Stop!" I screamed, but he pointed.

And shot.

Peter seemed to rise up, float, then arch and buckle backward onto the floor.

The noise, the sight, exploded inside me. I was filled with screams and blackness and had to grab the counter to prevent myself from falling.

When I opened my eyes, Laura was bent over Peter, crying, repeating his name. She lifted her hand off his sweatshirt. It was covered with blood.

I had seen a million gunshots in movies and television, read about them casually in mysteries, and they were nothing, absolutely nothing, like this thing that had happened here and now in my living room in real life, to a real human being.

Peter groaned.

"He's alive," I whispered with gratitude.

Nick's face was impassive, no more than vaguely interested as he squirted lighter fluid onto his rags.

I took a deep breath, inhaled, and bent over to inspect, to help, to acknowledge what had just happened to Peter. His eyes were open, constricted with pain.

There was blood on his chest, on his side. I didn't want to see what it meant, to track it to the wound. If the truth be known, I wanted to cry. But I looked. I pulled up his sweat shirt, took another deep breath and saw. "It's your arm," I said with enormous relief. "Your arm. The inner part, so it bled onto your chest." I grabbed one of my oversized napkins off the table and made him a flower-spattered tourniquet.

Nick watched, shaking his head. I knew why my actions amused him. I was trying to stop Peter from bleeding to death so that Nick could then burn him—all of us—to death. Great irony.

Because even if Laura could stop crying and Peter could stop bleeding, how could we possibly stop Nick? My escapist flights of fancy had all been blown away by the shot. Please, I thought, grabbing straws. Let somebody have heard that deafening blast. Somebody who won't later have to say she didn't want to interfere.

My prayer was answered. Inaccurately. "Turn it down!" somebody shouted from the adjoining house.

Nick moved around my living room methodically, the gun always pointed in the direction of the three of us. With his free hand, he draped one rag on the Christmas tree, then surveyed the room. "You know, none of this had to happen." He sounded weary. "It's your fault, Mandy. The police were sure it was Laura. Why didn't you let well enough alone? Her *mother* was sure it was Laura. I heard her say it that night, when she came in. 'What did you do?' she said." He pointed the gun at Peter, lying on the floor. "*He* was sure she did it, weren't you kid?"

Peter moaned. "Leave him alone!" Laura said, her voice

just this side of hysteria. "You've nearly killed him—leave him alone!"

"Well, I'm right. I know it. I saw the three of you in there, nobody sure what the hell was happening, what had happened." He placed another soaked rag on the arm of the sofa, standing back to evaluate it like a demented interior decorator. Then, having satisfied himself, he looked directly at me. "Now here's something weird. None of them were upset about Clausen being dead." He went back to the counter for yet another rag. My house would be an inferno within seconds of his lighting a match.

My brain felt frozen in place, petrified, but I had to think. I looked at Peter, barely conscious and probably in shock, on the floor. How to get him out? How to get any of us out? What would he do—toss a match and bolt? Could I get water to the fire fast enough? There was the vase on the coffee table and the crystal decanter on the table.

Ridiculous. Might as well spit on the flames.

And then that line of thinking became irrelevant. He walked over, pushed me onto one of the ladder-back chairs at the table and began tying me up.

"Come on," I said. "Why this?"

He just shook his head. "I'm tired of playing guard. Nobody'll notice twine burns afterward." He wound it around my upper arms, then around my calves. "It'll be chalked up as Laura's last fire. Case closed."

And when Laura reacted with an angry gasp, and stood up to stop him, to help me, he looked her directly in the eye and aimed his gun at Peter again, until she crumpled back to the floor.

My head hurt. My arms and legs hurt where he'd tied them to the chair, and most of all, my pride hurt. To go out like this—like the Perils of Pauline, humiliated, tied to a ladder-back chair!

"So," Nick said, "I'm sorry. But here goes. Laura's turn."

Laura looked up from where she sat on the floor. I thought she was going to say something, or try to run, but that wasn't it. She looked at the door, and then I heard it, too. A knock. Another caller.

"Stay where you are," Nick whispered. "All of you." The warning was a little ridiculous as far as Peter and I were concerned. "Keep quiet till they leave."

There was another knock. Laura opened her mouth, readying a scream. Nick, in the dusky light reflected out of the kitchen, stood right where he was, but even though his back was half to me, I could see him point the gun directly at Peter's face. "Don't," I whispered hoarsely. We were quiet.

The blood was beating so loudly in my skull, and my energy and concentration were so thoroughly on that gun, that I nearly missed it. Except that Nick's head swiveled to the door and Laura's eyes grew round again.

The little "scritch" sounded enormous; heavy, dark and solid.

The scritch of the less than fully committed lovers. Our song. Knock, then try the lock and come in if the door wasn't chained. But that was impossible. He was on a plane. Had been airborne for a half hour.

Within the course of the turn of the key, I ran a half-gamut of emotions. Excitement—saved in the nick of time. Enormous relief. Then terror. Mackenzie wasn't the cavalry come to the rescue. He was a man walking into a trap, opening a door onto the wrong end of a gun. Nick would kill him before he was halfway across the room.

The door opened.

I screamed.

Nick raised the gun, pointed it straight at Mackenzie, who was illuminated—a clear target standing in the light of the doorway, bulky and off balance, an overnight bag in his right hand and a garment bag hanging from his shoulder. He squinted into the gloom, his mouth half-open, figuring out what questions he had to ask to make sense of this.

"Sorry," Nick said. I had heard that before. Also the click, the gun at the ready.

Something had to be done immediately. Opportunity popped open, like a gigantic, startled "Oh!"

The train was barreling down the tracks, the villain twirling his mustache, but the times had changed. Both Pauline and Tom Trueheart were tied to the tracks. No time for even one "Eek!"

Time only to hoist my own rear off those tracks, be my own hero, save the detective in distress.

I pulled at my arms, pushed with my legs, and all it did was give me rope burns. I had one choice of weapons. Me. Us. Mandy and her magic chair.

I looked at where Nick stood, hoped I remembered enough geometry to be right about angles and estimates, and pushed with all my might, thigh muscles knotting until I was up, onto my toes—and then forward, one great wood-and-woman mass in one swift fall. As hard as I could. As fast as I could. That was it, my only chance. Blam.

"Now!" I screamed as I plummeted, fast and hard. My forehead banged into the back of his neck, and he tumbled as the chair and my weight continued our unstoppable downward arc. Pieces of us hit the floor, hard—my knees and toes and one elbow where I bounced off something. His head, from what I thought I heard. His face mashed into the carpet under mine, from the muffled sound below me.

I also heard the thuds of Mackenzie's luggage, and Laura, shouting, "I have his gun!" And Mackenzie, not making a sound, but moving faster than I'd known he could.

Untying me from the yellow ladder-back, freeing me from my humiliating, rear-end skyward, sore knees buckled, head-down position, Nick squashed below me.

I thought Mackenzie said "My heroine," but I had hit the floor pretty hard and I was a little dizzy, so I could be wrong.

He tied Nick up while Laura called for an ambulance and a patrol car.

"Boy," I said when I had my breath back. "Boy oh boy!" I started to laugh, with relief or confused craziness. I think with the sheer delight of being alive, a condition I had strongly doubted was in my future.

"How come you're—you're supposed to be—" I started laughing again.

Mackenzie waited till I was nearly coherent, although little hiccups of laughs kept striking. "I was bumped," he said.

And that was definitely the funniest thing I'd ever heard. "So was I," I said, rubbing my forehead and doubling over. "All over! What a coincidence!"

He looked wary. I tried to subdue my act. In fact, I suddenly couldn't remember what was so funny at all, and I felt as if I were hung over. All over, including my knees.

"Well, they kind of ask for volunteers," he said, "and I didn't get there real early like you should, you know, but with you stuck here, I thought . . ." His expression darkened. "It's obvious you weren't expectin' me." He shook his head. "You sure found yourself a date fast. Although I can't say much for quality control around here."

I raised my hand to protest or explain, but it was too much effort. I sat very, very still to stop the throbbing in my head. My forehead, with no slack to do so, was nonetheless expanding painfully.

"He . . . killed my father," Laura said in a strained voice. She stood at the front window, waiting for the ambulance.

"Liar," Nick said, breaking his silence. "Everybody knows the kid did it."

"But—"

"Hearsay isn't evidence," he spat out. "You have no proof. Not one shred." His mouth curled as smugly as it could, given that his lips were swelling from the impact of his fall.

"There is so a shred." I'd nearly forgotten. I hobbled over to the kitchen counter, fingers crossed. Please, *please* let me have gotten it right. I pressed on the lid of the answering machine and it flipped up.

The tape inside was still spinning. Victory.

I heard sirens in the distance. Several. Ambulances and police cars.

"I pushed Memo," I said to Mackenzie. "The way you showed me. Everything is recorded. He even stood close to the machine most of the time. We can turn it off now."

This time, I was positive Mackenzie said, "My heroine."

The sirens came closer until they stopped abruptly. Doors slammed. The cavalry, twentieth-century style, had arrived.

"Don't know quite how, but you've wrapped this one up neatly," Mackenzie said.

Nick, in handcuffs, glowered at the police. Peter was gently lifted onto a gurney. It didn't seem neat. It just seemed possible.

We helped Laura into the ambulance so she could ride with Peter, assured her we'd join her at the hospital in minutes, and walked to where Mackenzie had parked. I clutched his hand more tightly than my wobbly knees warranted.

Mackenzie helped me into his car as if I were damaged porcelain. Once he was behind the wheel, he leaned over and kissed me, avoiding all the sore spots and making at least my lips and heart feel just fine. We pulled apart and stared at each other, confirming that we were indeed still alive and miming relief, incredulity, and joy. We shook our heads, blinked, sighed, twisted our mouths, and shrugged our shoulders—although I did the last action very, very gently and only once, because it hurt like hell.

We needed, but lacked words to get us unstuck and on with our lives. Luckily, English teachers always carry an emergency kit bulging with other people's words. I pulled a few out of mine.

"Like the lad said, God bless us, every one!"

I thought for a second. "Even Charles Dickens," I added.

"Amen." Mackenzie turned the ignition key and we moved on.

About the Author

GILLIAN ROBERTS is mainstream novelist Judith Greber's *nom de mystère*. Winner of the Anthony Award for Best First Novel for her mystery *Caught Dead in Philadelphia*, she is the author of such successful novels as *Mendocino*, *The Silent Partner*, and *Easy Answers*. A former Philadelphia English teacher, she now lives in Tiburon, California.